Mrs. Meredith

The lacemakers:

Sketches of Irish character

Mrs. Meredith

The lacemakers:
Sketches of Irish character

ISBN/EAN: 9783742843562

Manufactured in Europe, USA, Canada, Australia, Japa

Cover: Foto ©Andreas Hilbeck / pixelio.de

Manufactured and distributed by brebook publishing software
(www.brebook.com)

Mrs. Meredith

The lacemakers:

THE LACEMAKERS:

Sketches of Irish Character,

WITH SOME ACCOUNT OF THE

EFFORT TO ESTABLISH LACEMAKING IN IRELAND.

BY

MRS. MEREDITH.

" Work, work, work,
  In the dull December light,
  And work, work, work,
  When the weather is warm and bright,
  While underneath the eaves
  The brooding swallows cling,
  As if to show their sunny backs,
  And twit me with their spring."
                          THOMAS HOOD.

LONDON:

JACKSON, WALFORD, AND HODDER,

27, PATERNOSTER ROW.

1865.

London :
Printed by GEORGE WATSON, 5, Kirby Street,
Hatton Garden. E.C.

THIS ATTEMPT TO

RECORD THE EFFORTS OF IRISHWOMEN TO HELP THEMSELVES

IS DEDICATED (BY PERMISSION) TO

MISS BURDETT COUTTS,

WHOSE NOBLE AID IN

THE TIME OF THEIR CALAMITY IS NOT FORGOTTEN,

AND

TO WHOSE JUDGMENT THE WRITER SUBMITS HER

SUGGESTIONS ON

THE SUBJECT OF PROVIDING INDUSTRIAL INSTRUCTION FOR THE

FEMALE POOR OF IRELAND.

PREFACE.

To know the Irish poor is to know Ireland. Poverty
is the national characteristic. It is the poor that
constitute the distinguishing element of the country;
their spirit rules in its agitations, and dictates all its
claims. They are the seething mass in its economy;
they work, and they achieve, too, not fortune, but
fame! Make an Irishman rich, and you denationa-
lize him at once, and for ever; you take the heart
out of him: he is no longer the unadulterated representative of old Erin. To be rich in Ireland, places
a man outside all Irish sympathy, and above all
Irish emotion. I cannot make a bull, and say it
turns him into an Englishman, but it is the next
thing to it; he becomes Anglo-Irish—a person ex-
communicated by the real "sons of the soil."

I am satisfied that this is thoroughly inexplicable to the English mind, and I will not attempt to unriddle it on philosophical principles. Nothing but that acquaintanceship with the social circumstances of Ireland, which the present effort is intended to promote, can do it. Now, I do not attempt to describe, in plain terms, the parties nor the systems of which society there consists; neither do I try to exhibit their representatives in ordinary detail. This would but accumulate difficulties, and render the subject even less capable of comprehension. Even to matter-of-fact, prosaic Englishmen, I prefer presenting pictorial sketches of the progress of such affairs in that land as I venture to discuss.

It is quite obvious that dry statistical statements do not inform anybody about Ireland, from the House of Commons down to the readers of the penny papers. The "Reports" lie before them definitely set forth, but beyond that point they do not go—never passing into the mind, and being there assimilated, and turned to "useful knowledge." There is some curious want of faculty in the Saxon constitution to digest this crude mass. England is sick of the subject in this form;

but rather likes it in another—takes it *en bon bon*—to crack a joke upon, and sensitize its comic humour. It is not desirable to see Ireland treated in the latter fashion. In truth, there is a melan-choly note in its gayest chord : the mirth and the fun that seem to superficial observers to preponde-rate in its people, are but wild and unreal excite-ment gone as quickly as effervescence, and leaving a dull remainder of sadness. Their tears are all their own, their smiles are forced from them.

It seems absurd to say that there is still popular ignorance in England about a place so close to it, the facilities for communication with which tend to draw it into the most intimate union; but it is the case, and this is only an additionl anomaly. The Irish cross over the bridge that unites the two countries; but their visit is not returned. Now, one would have thought, that after this step of theirs—this showing of themselves—misconception would end ; but it does not. In fact, we do not see how it is to end, since the means of increasing information are so limited.

There are peculiar bounds set to a knowledge of Ireland, and when any one surmounts them and gets inside the enclosure, and looks intelligently at the interior, instead of spreading abroad the news of his discovery, he immediately closes his mouth, or he calls others to come and see for themselves. All the initiated concur in this; when they get hold of the secret, the impracticability of revelation is their strongest impression; so they leave discussion and speculation to the uninformed, and only in exceptional cases venture upon any description. At best, few offer to exhibit anything more than hieroglyphics, and these are about as informing as Zadkiel's.

Fiction, decidedly, has done more than anything else to make known this *terra incognita*.

The case of the Irish is not one for logical language. That which can be declared by it should be on the platform, where reason explains all phenomena; but to this the social history of Ireland has not attained: it is still at the stage of Puck and the fairies. The mythological era has not yet expired there, nor the heroic age passed away from that island. While British manners have stiffened into solid consistency, Irish nature is lava still, and is bursting over, and boiling round the volcanic centre of its community. The story-telling style of the vernacular is that which is adopted in the present compilation, my object being to exhibit the scenes detailed in as concrete a form as possible.

In publishing these tales of " The Lacemakers," every effort is made to deliver conceptions faithfully. It may seem, perhaps, an attempt on my part to evade criticism, when I impugn the existing degree of popular information on the subject of which I treat ; but I do so in the most inviting spirit, being anxious to induce inquiry into the circumstances mentioned ; and feeling certain that if this be done, my assertions will be fully borne out. " Seeing is believing," and only *seeing* is of any value in such matters as those that are recorded in the following pages. Those who have had similar insight to mine will, I am persuaded, concur in the views put forth, and will acknowledge ·that the sketches are " after the life." This is all that I claim for them ; they are nothing more. The events they narrate are facts, but the plots are fictitious. Names of persons and places are suppressed; and the tales are not all supplied from my own personal experience, but were obtained from various sources.

As I withdraw from the closeness of my connection with the affairs in which I was so long absorbed, my interest in my countrywomen deepens. While in actual contact with them, I could see little but their minute qualities, and that one which I found most singularly interesting, was their handicraft. This feature is very distinctly marked in some of the races in Ireland, and in the hope of bringing one particular manifestation of it to perfection, I laboured with my whole powers for ten long years. At the end of that time I had come to the end of those powers, and I surrendered—not because my theory was baseless and my scheme a failure, for they were not; but because my undertaking was vanquished for lack of that which no individual can supply. Enterprise was not wanting—capital was not wanting—labour was not wanting—demand was not wanting. They were all there; but artistic cultivation was, and this the State alone could give. Hitherto, the hope of

obtaining this has been deluded by a series of legislative blunders, and as yet, the prospect of carrying
out that which experiment has proved to be feasible
and advantageous, is only in the future.

I have written about "The Lacemakers" because they will soon exist only on paper. Their
occupation is gone. The girls of Ireland have no
longer this wholesome, genial work to do. They are
deprived of it by the natural course of events—that
relative deterioration which is the result of the advance of competitors. Nations not greater but wiser
than our United Kingdom have beaten us in this field,
and the ignorance and neglect which have caused this
defeat injure not only Ireland, but the whole realm.
There is a world-market calling for articles which
England is not providing, and morally and pecu-
niarily she and her dependencies are losers by this
supineness.

To any who become sufficiently interested in these
tales of the Lacemakers to give any attention to
the information they endeavour to convey, I would
recommend that they should not close the volume
without reading the two chapters (reprinted from the

Englishwoman's Journal) which contain an account of the needlework movement to which the Irish famine gave rise. I have no doubt that those who do so will join in the wish that, even in such minute details as the industrial instruction of girls, Ireland should have more enlightened consideration from the legislature, than she has hitherto enjoyed.

CONTENTS.

LACE-MAKING IN IRELAND.

Page

Chapter I.—Experiments...Community of interest...Born to trouble
...Use of adversity...Thrift...Educated minority...Women's
energy...Clamour for employment...Ladies' skill in needlework
...Commercial abilities...Schools begun...Pupils and "workers"...Union...Unsectarian spirit...National exhibition at
Cork...Dublin...Results...Sewed muslin...Cheap labour...
Novel lace...Competition..."Guipure"..."Point"...The manner of lace...Benevolent merchants...Transactions...Royal
garments...Little patterns...Gratuitous tradeswomen...Small
employers...Adelaide School...Reduced ladies...Prejudices...
Social grades..."Hotbed" of crochet...Decline of trade...Pat-
terns and stitches...Workers disadvantaged...Suggestive occupation...Artistic training...Widow's cruse...Money a snare...
Domestic service despised..Clones...Perpetuity...The Queen's
advice...Foreign embroidery...Limerick lace...Pillow laces
attempted...Normal School...Branch schools...Centralizations   1

NEEDLEWORK V. DOMESTIC SERVICE.

Chapter II.—Small matters...instincts and idiosyncrasies...Pauper
women ... Industrial culture ... Exotic qualities ... Working
classes of England and Ireland not parallel..."Family
system"...Supervision ... Personal influence...Can a Board
choose ?...Differences not inferiorities..."Don't feel it in their
bones"...Ill-paid labour...Bad servants...Want of resources...
Durability of demand...Machinery extending slowly...Associa-
tion of head and hand...Monetary value...Influence on emigration...Provincial characteristics...Letter from America...The
crochet harvest and the grain crop...Rescued family...Subdi-
vision of labour..."Gingleman's" daughters...Workhouse industry ... National school incompetence ... Resemblances...
Jealousy...Government Schools of Design useless to lacemakers
..Want of inspection..Want of education..*Asile Ouvroir*...
Gift of embroidery and all needlework..Milesian ancestry..
Foreign example   -   -   -   -   -   -   -   -   27

ELLEN HARRINGTON.

Page

Chapter I. - - - - - - - - - - - 55
   ,, II. - - - - - - - - - - 66
   ,, III. - - - - - - - - - - 78
   ,, IV. - - - - - - - - - - 93
   ,, V - - - - - - - - - - 106

THE REDEEMED ESTATE.

Chapter I. - - - - - - - - - - - 117
   ,, II. - - - - - - - - - - - 156
   ,, III. - - - - - - - - - - - 188

MARY DESMOND.

Chapter I. - - - - - - - - - - 205
   ,, II. - - - - - - - - - - 213
   ,, III. - - - - - - - - - - 234
   ,, IV. - - - - - - - - - - 249
   ,, V. - - - - - - - - - - 270
   ,, VI. - - - - - - - - - - 285
   ,, VII. - - - - - - - - - - 297
   ,, VIII. - - - - - - - - - - 318
   ,, IX. - - - - - - - - - - 340
   ,, X. - - - - - - - - - - 354

APPENDIX - - - - - - - - - - - 369

THE LACEMAKERS,

ETC.

Lace-making in Ireland.

CHAPTER I.

Experiments...Community of interest...Born to trouble...Use of adversity...Thrift...Educated minority...Women's energy...Clamour for employment...Ladies' skill in needlework...Commercial abilities...Schools begun...Pupils and "workers"...Union...Unsectarian spirit ...National exhibition at Cork...Dublin...Results...Sewed muslin...Cheap labour...Novel lace...Competition..."Guipure"..."Point"...The manner of lace...Benevolent merchants...Transactions...Royal garments...Little patterns...Gratuitous tradeswomen...Small employers...Adelaide School...Reduced ladies...Prejudices...Social grades..."Hotbed" of crochet...Decline of trade...Patterns and stitches...Workers disadvantaged...Suggestive occupation...Artistic training...Widow's cruse...Money a snare...Domestic service despised...Clones...Perpetuity...The Queen's advice...Foreign embroidery...Limerick lace ...Pillow laces attempted...Normal school...Branch schools...Centralizations.

DURING the last twenty years, a great many experiments have been undertaken, having for their object the relief of poverty in Ireland; and the women of that country have made an amount of exertion on their own account, which should not be suffered to sink into

obscurity as a fact, nor be overlooked as evidence, when
the national conduct and prospects are called in question. The story of this action is as touching and beautiful as anything that the history of nations presents.
It is one long tale of struggle—a war against misery,
in which every woman's hand in the land was engaged
—the delicate touch of the peeress assisting the rough
fingers of the peasant.   Irishwomen of all ranks and
degrees made common cause of the sufferings that
arose in consequence of the potato blight.   The visitation, to a certain extent, affected them all, and
brought them together in a manner that nothing
else could have done.   Intercourse and communication of a nature so intimate ensued, that they awoke
the tenderest sympathies, and numerous movements
were undertaken to lighten the general burden. These
had diverse effects : some were utter failures, and
others but partially successful, but, on the whole, the
social alterations that were achieved have had a good
and abiding influence. The principles demonstrated
by them can never again be controverted, nor
can the proofs that they elicited be set aside by any
theories.   In the connection to which we allude, it
was not the rich and poor who met ; the parties that

were brought into contact were, for the time, alike in pecuniary matters, all classes being more or less involved ; property was temporarily unavailable, and, therefore, interest and kindly feeling were not chiefly testified by gifts of silver or gold. Of these, the upper ranks had, in many.cases, literally, none ; but this did not prevent them from putting their resources at the command of the needy, and "of such as they had" they gave bountifully. That which they imparted was instruction. The intelligent and the ignorant came face to face, and made an acquaintance-ship, by which the most important results were pro-duced. In this season of universal distress, charac-teristics came out without reserve, and a record of the events of the period cannot be without value and in-terest, not only to those immediately concerned, but to all who give any attention to the subject of Ire-land's difficulties.

There are some remarkable features in Irish society which are very little known outside its boundaries, and which, when known, are generally too little taken into account. Among those are details which seem to indicate that the women of Ireland are indeed born to trouble and to hardship, and that they have made

exertions to surmount them, for which they have
never yet had due profit nor credit.

Some sections of the Irish community manifest
decidedly beneficial effects from the discipline they
have undergone; the upper very much more than the
lower classes. These degrees of improvement are
in strict accordance with the right laws of progres-
sion, which give the first place to superior intelligence;
and the precedence is, in this case, very strongly
marked. What the industrial impulse did for intellectual female circles in Ireland was more than a
restoration to fortune. It assured them of a resource
for their needs far above the accidents of transitory
things, for it drew out their powers, and enabled
them to test the value of their cultivation. Sweet
were the uses of this adversity.

Acquaintance with the circles in which this occurred
could alone convey an idea of the extent to which the
problems of domestic economy were daily solved by
their members. Irishwomen lay no claim to the
quality called " thrift"—they freely yield the palm
for it to their neighbouring relatives; but for discre-
tion of expense, the educated among them may chal-
lenge any country. Unhappily, they form a very

small body, in comparison with those that represent, to superficial observers, the feminine capabilities of the nation. But they are a weighty and an important minority. Ireland has a well-developed female power which, without the accessory of wealth, is able to maintain status, and to occupy position with effect. Its expression is audible, and its strength apparent. It is leading the van of modern concern for its sex, and seeking to be permitted to assist in its elevation. Individually, the members of this body have made numerous efforts to promote this object, and it is to be regretted that they do not associate and systematize their schemes. In order to induce them to do so, it will be well to look back at some of their actions, and endeavour to form an idea of their bearing on the country.

When famine ravaged Ireland in 1847, women were found inspired with an energy to work that was truly surprising. Wherever there was a female hand, it was set in motion, and, generally, it seized a needle, and wielded it vigorously for bread. The eagerness to obtain means of support was so pressing, that a perfect clamour for employment arose. To satisfy this, a most remarkable movement took place. Women of the upper ranks developed an extraordinary skill in needlework, and, also, a great commercial aptitude to turn it to a profitable account. The repose of aristocratic society, and the leisure of the cloister were disturbed. Ladies burst the bonds of conventionalisms, and went regularly into business, to procure remunerative occupation for the destitute of their own sex. The female children of the poor, all over the land, became the subjects of instruction in the making up of various sorts of articles for sale. At first, this was done with a very indefinite purpose; but the productions were kindly welcomed, and a great demand promoted the industrial effort. Then there came systematic attempts to consolidate it: schools for embroidery, crochet, knitting, netting, tatting, &c., were established. The Census of 1851 returned 902 pupils in these; but these figures did not represent the extent of the exertion to diffuse the knowledge of needlework. The rapidity with which it spread was almost electric; successive multitudes of girls passed through the initiatory process, and were soon reckoned as "workers," under some of the anxiously active employers. About this time, every feminine handicraft was endeavouring to assert itself, and the women of Ireland united in a grand bond against a common foe. "Nor did the slightest taint of sectarian jealousy sully the sublime charity of the hour,—the voice of nature crying out in her misery was alone heard and responded to ; and in the desire to do good, and to succour a common humanity, people were brought together, felt together, and acted together, who had been estranged all their lives." Thus writes J. F. Maguire, M.P., in his *Irish Industrial Movement* (p. 184) ; and he adds (p. 225) : "These ladies were all of a different religious persuasion from those whom they have assisted to elevate in a moral as well as material sense ; and yet they have never in the slightest degree attempted or desired to take advantage of the singular influence of such a position as theirs, to interfere with the religious belief of their pupils,—a fact which I deem too much to the credit of the purity of their motives not to record."

At the National Exhibition held in Cork, in 1852, a large number of samples of work done by the female poor appeared. Thirty-four of the exhibitors were ladies, patronesses of schools, and a few were men of business who were beginning, about this time, to deal with them for their productions. The following year, in Dublin, forty-six schools exhibited, and an increased number of tradesmen. The goods offered were sewed muslin and crochet lace ; the first was an old acquaintance in the market, the other an entirely new creation. The origin of this latter fabric was peculiar, and the course of its development interesting. The phenomena connected with it, as an experiment in industry, are well worth recalling, and the consideration of them may be useful in promoting other schemes for the social improvement of Ireland. The operations carried on during the period to which we refer, affected the Irish community so considerably, that their results are now easily discernible ; but there is no definite idea popularly entertained, as to how much of the evil or the good of its present condition is referable to them. Some account of that which was really evolved by the action of this crisis will assist in making the matter clear, and it is now imperatively called for by the fact, that the most marked feature of our day is the discussion of the wants of the very class that was then subject to the treatment of the agencies to which we refer.

After the Exhibitions, vast numbers of girls

found employment in the two trades prominently exposed. Manufacturers of sewed muslin took extensive advantage of the cheap labour offered by Irishwomen, and speculated largely in that sort of work. But the novel lace entered into competition with it, and sensibly raised the standard of wages ; it resisted an effort to introduce the manufacture of foreign pillow laces. The weekly earnings at crochet ranged from 6s. to 10s. and 15s.; they kept up steadily for about three years, and attained their highest scale of remuneration in 1857. The early specimens of this lace were beautiful pieces of workwomanship, comparable to the mediæval " guipures," and "old points," of continental celebrity ; they were, in fact, imitations of them. The attempts to resuscitate their styles, and to rival their reputation, were by no means contemptible. Great aptitude for this revival was displayed. The art was easily acquired, the materials were inexpensive, and the market was ready. The employment freely propagated itself, and, after the manner of lace, showed adherence to habitat, and tenacity of type. It settled into several centres, Cork and Clones becoming the most important of them, and these maintained their distinctive characteristics most determinedly. The recognition of the products of the different districts is well established in the trade.

The foundresses of the schools were the first merchants of this commodity. Some of them did large wholesale business, and others confined themselves to private sale. The transactions of the former were from £100 to £500 a month, with warehouses and shops; and the latter sent away weekly £20 or £30 worth of work, to friends in more favoured lands to dispose of for them. In this way, England, France, America, and the colonies received a quantity of the production. Crochet lace was, at one period, everywhere " the fashion." Sympathy poured in heartily, and lightened the labours of the charitable. Consumers increased and multiplied, and no' effort was spared to secure their approbation, and to merit their favour; and with such success, that even royalty did not disdain to adorn its garments with " Irish point." The simple agency by which the wide-spread trade was carried on, was the sending out of little patterns by post, accompanied by requests for orders. The reply to the humble messages was most cordial; men of business especially came forward to help the enterprise to maturity. By these early customers,

the matter was wisely and kindly taken into consideration. Every facility was offered to ladies to
enter into correspondence with them, and commercial
arrangements were made easy to their inexperience.
In this commencement of the trade, before mere
speculators entered the field, there were men found
to deal in it with a truer human interest than pecuniary proceedings usually engage. The position
of the unprepared, disinterested, gratuitous tradeswomen was well understood by these men : and they
assisted them to maintain their difficult undertakings
in a manner which claims a very grateful acknowledgment.   .

The women who made this exertion did a good
deed for their sex; they dealt practically with the
subject of commercial employment for females;
they tested its difficulties by personal experience,
and under circumstances which should render
their example very useful to those who, without early
training, contemplate similar work This latter class
was to some extent brought under the influence
of the lace movement. Many members of it were
engaged as assistant teachers in the schools, and not
a few worked side by side with their humbler fellow-

sufferers from the common misfortune. A system was introduced on purpose to encourage them
to become employers on a small scale, and to deal
directly with the market for their own benefit,
and a society was established in Cork for the purpose of enabling such persons to avail themselves of
the lace trade.

Mr. Maguire took notice of this circumstance
(*Irish Industrial Movement*, p. 222), and says:
"Of the many schools which have been brought
under my observation, I do not know any one
which presents more interesting features than
the Adelaide School. At its first commencement
it differed in no way from the ordinary industrial school, in which young persons are employed
during the day; but since then its whole character
has changed, and it may now be described as a central dépôt for the reception of work and the transaction of business. It employs young persons of
limited means, or reduced circumstances, who are
now but too happy to apply their talents to a useful
and practical purpose, and in most instances with the
purest of human motives,—the wish to confer even
modest comforts on relations who have fallen victims

to the great calamity of this country, which has brought down to the dust so many lofty heads and proud names. The number engaged in connexion with the Adelaide School amounts to 120. . . . The weekly payments are now about £14 a week, with prospect of considerable increase."

This undertaking rapidly extended. No gratuitous assistance was offered, and the number of ladies applying for admission to it was very great. Every variety of capacity and qualification was presented by the candidates, but the abilities requisite for the attainment of the proposed object were rare. The educational condition of the class was found peculiarly deficient. Superficial " accomplishments" were un-available in the case, and they were plenty enough ; but the knowledge of accounts—the power of expression in writing,—together with that cultivation of intelligence which can alone be accepted as proof of right to the title " educated," were so remarkably absent, as to impede the successful introduction of artistic information amongst them.

As the Adelaide School progressed, the failure of its pupils from this cause was one of the principal features in its business. The difficulty of inducing persons to submit to the disciplino and training necessary for the undertaking was extreme. Prejudice against business life, and the distinctions of social grades, stood mightily in their way. Even want did not always conquer these obstacles; and the numbers who succeeded in securing any advantage from it were in great disproportion to those who applied for help during its course; at a rough estimate, they were as one to ten, and that at a time when the School had business for a far greater number of hands than it could obtain.

In 1857, when the trade began to decline, about twenty-two ladies were engaged in connexion with the School, and the average wages which they paid for labour amounted to more than £100 a week. While they held their ground, the character of Cork crochet was tolerably well sustained in the market. This lace never was of the highest class, although Cork was said to be the "hot-bed" of the work; but before the competition for the article became so strong, it was approaching something respectable.

A great many benevolent ladies in the city and surrounding districts were promoters of the art. To

Lady Deane's School, and to those of the Blackrock, Youghal, and Kinsale convents, as well as to Mrs. Meredith's (the Adelaide School), it was indebted for a well-kept-up supply of new patterns and .stitches; and these continued to be provided, as long as the establishments were maintained. Local speculators, however, contended for the trade, and it had to be surrendered to them.

The Adelaide School was the latest to give up, but in 1859 it succumbed to the pressure. Some of its pupils continued to produce small quantities of very fine goods, and many are still working, but under very adverse circumstances. Almost all the hands in the whole neighbourhood turned, all at once, to the inferior sorts of the lace, and the production of any of the better kinds is now attended with an expense that absorbs the profits. Even at a premium, it is difficult to induce lace makers to take the necessary trouble—the habit of working carelessly is so confirmed. This ignorant line of conduct has, of course, wrought its own injury. The material rapidly deteriorated, and the position of the worker has become increasingly disadvantageous. It is to be feared that, in this generation, the error

into which the lace-makers have been betrayed will
not be retrieved. The grotesque-looking coarseness of
the fabric with which the fluctuating demand has
been supplied, bids fair soon to terminate its own
existence ; and for want of being properly treated,
the Irish lace trade threatens to come to an end.

"Irish point," the highest development of crochet
lace, was a very suggestive production, and there existed no reason why it should have been as evanescent
as the crisis that gave it birth. It was the index
of a power created to endure, and to become an agent
in preventing similar piteous catastrophes. The
difficulties of its culture were not internal, but external. It is peculiarly controllable, and that which
opposed its management, and rendered it a disorderly,
troublesome manufacture, was not a quality of the
work, but of the workers. The first teachers of the
art were educated ladies, and they had powers which
could not be imparted by them to their pupils. Acquaintance with the principles of beauty and grace-
fulness, familiarity with antique laces, and works of
fine art, do not come with the use of the hooked
needle ; and it is much to be regretted, that, at an
early stage, no training in these essentials was pro-

curable. It was not then recognised, and it is not now practically acknowledged, that all such offspring of the parent stock of industry demands the fostering care of the State, that it may arrive at a healthy maturity, and increase and strengthen the resources of the nation.

The large number of women that engaged in the needlework effort form an important item in the population of the kingdom : 300,000 are said to have been employed in sewed-muslin-work, and 20,000 in the indigenous lace. These constitute a grand force, available for the benefit of the Irish community ; and in the hour of necessity it effected a good service, the memory of which is still warmly cherished. When men's hands were useless, little girls' fingers, by means of this lace-work, provided for families ; and like the widow's cruse, the provision failed not while the famine lasted.

But all earthly blessings are liable to the taint of our mortal natures, and this was no exception. Money became a snare to the ill-trained female multitude. An injurious expenditure of it occurred ; and the results were apparent in the deteriorated morals of the lower classes. This fact is cited

by some people as an evil attributable to crochet
work; and many condemn the industrial movement
altogether, in consequence of the social inconveniences they erroneously ascribe to it.   One of these
was the withdrawal of women from domestic occupations. Increased rates of wages failed to induce them
to become servants, as long as they could procure
any sort of a living by needlework; and a strong
tendency to neglect the useful application of the art
of sewing, in the desire to pursue the ornamental,
prevailed very extensively. It must be confessed
that these circumstances have produced a very
marked effect on society. The national characteristics came out in full force under them, and betrayed a deplorable condition of educational destitution. The Cork districts especially presented the
distressing spectacle of increased means without corresponding social elevation; and many evils continue to exist there, which may be fairly regarded
as, indirectly, the result of the industrial movement.

In some parts of Ireland, this lace trade met with
exceptional circumstances.

In the county of Monaghan, there is a district into

which it has settled with better and more permanent effect than anywhere else.

The wife of the rector of the parish of Clones taught crochet-making to some little girls, and it soon spread over the whole neighbourhood. After a time, the number employed in it became so great that it assumed the formidable proportions of a large mercantile concern. At this stage, Mrs. Hand, the foundress of the business, did not desert it, though, overwhelmed by the extent of the undertaking, she was about to do so in 1854. But her lacemakers made a brave struggle to retain the direction under which they had commenced to work; and they addressed Mrs. Hand on the subject, in an interesting letter, which tells the history of the school so completely, that we must give it place in our summary of the movement.

ADDRESS TO MRS. HAND.   *Rectory, Clones.*

" MADAM,

" We, the undersigned, beg your acceptance of the accompanying Piece of Plate as a small token of the very sincere respect and gratitude we feel towards you for your unremitting kindness. On

your coming to Clones, you found us in a state of
the deepest distress, utterly destitute of any employment, unskilled in any art. By your unaided personal exertions you introduced, and had us instructed in, the manufacture of crochet lace—a work
before then unheard of in this neighbourhood. You
patiently bore with our ignorance, kindly encouraged our efforts, liberally rewarded us for our labour,
and now you have the satisfaction of knowing that
you have been the means, under God, of enabling
1500 individuals (at least) in this parish to earn a
respectable living. Dear madam, we are not skilled
in writing addresses, but we beg you will accept this
effort on our part, to evidence in some manner that
we are conscious of your goodness. We entreat
you not to retire from the work you have so successfully carried on, though others are engaging in it,
when all the difficulties attending its establishment
are overcome. We feel assured that we will be
the losers if you do so. Praying that He who will
not overlook 'even a drop of cold water' given
in His name may abundantly reward you,

    " We remain, your obliged and grateful
        workers,

"Signed on behalf of the rest of the workers by a good many of the girls."

REPLY.

"MY DEAR FRIENDS,

"I have received your kind address with the greatest pleasure and satisfaction, conveying me your grateful sense of the exertions which God has enabled me, successfully, to make in your behalf since I came to reside among you. ' To Him be all the glory and all the praise.' To have received such an expression of your esteem and gratitude would have amply repaid me for all the trouble and anxiety which I have had, and I cannot help feeling sorry that you should have thought it necessary to accompany those expressions with so handsome a proof of their sincerity. But believe me, I gladly accept it as a token of the warmth of the Irish heart, which, unless misdirected, always beats in concert with kindly feelings; and your beautiful and costly flower-stand will be a happy emblem, I trust, of our continued regard and mutual love to Him who is the 'Rose of Sharon and the Lily of the Valley.' I need scarcely add that I shall bequeath it to my children as a memento of my residence among you, when I and their father shall have run our course. Too true it is, that I found you in deep distress, and am only thankful that God devised means in some measure to remove it in this parish, and made me the happy instrument in that removal. Indeed, had it not been for the sewed muslin work, which my and your kind friend Lady Lennard introduced some years ago, and the employment I have been able to afford, the fearful visitation of famine would have been still more severe and more disastrous.

"Permit me to add, in answer to your requisition, that I shall continue, if health and strength be given me, to carry on the work, and I trust that you, by increased diligence and attention, will feel no difficulty in keeping up the credit of the Clones lace, and preventing its falling into disrepute among the higher classes, in consequence of competition and the production of an inferior style of work.

"Praying that the Lord will prosper your handiwork, and enable you to derive all the good, and as little of the evil which is incident to every human undertaking, I remain, your sincere Friend,

"C. HAND."

In compliance with this request, Mrs. Hand retained her position, although it entailed much tiresome exertion of mind and body, and no little worry of spirit. Some four or five years after this, she was compelled to withdraw, but she induced an accomplished lady, who had been trained in the best schools of art, to settle in Clones, and to undertake the business for her own benefit. The effect of this was admirable. Good designs and correctness of finish continued to characterize Clones lace long after others had lost their celebrity. The district is still leavened by the skilled instructions of this lady, and a standard of merit is kept up. Even at its reduced price, the work provides a respectable livelihood for many women in the locality, and the fruits of the steadiness of their trade is seen in their improved domestic condition.* Mrs. Roberts of Kilcullen, and Mrs. Tottenham of New Ross, and many other ladies, made goods of a very superior sort, which were known in the London market by their names. Their skill, and that exhibited at Clones, was the result of peculiar culture; and it is only to be deplored that it had not the element of perpetuity, since with

* Appendix A.

the individuals disappeared the principles of guidance
that would have prolonged the trade.

The sewed muslin manufacture, which was also
more the subject of a great commercial speculation, than of a diligent elaboration, is now likewise suffering a severe depression. An address was
presented to Her Majesty, praying her to aid in
the restoration of this article to public favour by
according to it her royal patronage. Like a good
tradeswoman, the Queen suggested, in her reply, that
the commodity should be better cultivated; and
directed that the best instructions, and the newest
patterns, should be sent for to France for the purpose. This is an impressive admission of a national
deficiency, and on it is chargeable many of our
industrial disasters. Foreign embroidery takes the
lead of all that Irish labour can do, for the same
reason that her lace is beaten from the field. These
two employments, so peculiarly suited to the genius
of Irishwomen, are both now involved in the same
predicament. Neither are keeping pace with commercial progress, although they abundantly possess the elements of power. Of the capabilities of
the crochet lace manufacture to bear consider-

able extension, no doubt is entertained by those who understand the nature of the fabric and its possibilities. The highest authority, that of the originators of it, goes to affirm that it is revivable and revisable, submissive to culture, and that its fertility of resource is far greater than that of the pillow laces, or of Limerick lace, a species of work which had almost run its course before crochet had begun.

This latter article never attained any high degree of cultivation; and none of it now is as good as similar lace produced elsewhere. It is closely akin to embroidery, consisting of "running," "tambouring," and "appliqué," on a woven foundation. Like all such things, the loom rapidly follows up its efforts, supersedes it easily, and not unfrequently passes it by, leaving its best pretensions in the shade. When the needlework effort began, some enterprising tradesmen made a vigorous attempt to re-establish and revive the credit of Limerick lace. Messrs. Forest of Dublin opened schools, in which some very respectable goods were manufactured; but they failed to produce anything of intrinsic value or staple character.

The introduction of pillow laces into Ireland was a movement of considerable importance, and deserves special notice. The success that attended the crochet experiment induced the belief that these would be likely to be equally successful, and some ladies, aided by a London merchant (Mr. Goblet of Milk-street), tried to procure it a fair share of the popular favour. They established a normal school in Dublin, and branch schools in various parts of the country, but the employment was insufficiently remunerative, owing to quite different causes from those that suppressed the crochet industry.

These three sorts of lace work, together with embroidery, and plain sewing, were zealously taught, all through the country, by their several partisans. Various degrees of success attended their labours, and one curious phenomenon occurred uniformly, in connection with their exertions. The manufactures did not always thrive, but they invariably settled down into localities, no two selecting the same neighbourhood as an abode; and, in every case, they fixed so firmly into their elected districts that they still continue to characterize them.*

---

* Appendix B.

CHAPTER II.

.

Needlework v. *Domestic Service.*

Small matters...Instincts and idiosyncrasies...Pauper women...Industrial culture...Exotic qualities...Working classes of England and Ireland not parallel..." Family system"...Supervision...Personal influence... Can a Board choose ?...Differences not inferiorities..." Don't feel it in their bones "...Ill-paid labour...Bad servants...Want of resources... Durability of demand...Machinery extending slowly...Association of head and hand...Monetary value...Influence on emigration...Provincial characteristics...Letter from America...The crochet harvest and the grain crop...Rescued family...Subdivision of labour..." Gingleman's" daughters...Workhouse industry...National school incompetence... Resemblances...Jealousy...Government Schools of Design useless to lacemakers...Want of inspection...Want of education...*Asile Ouvroir* ...Gift of embroidery and all needlework...Milesian aucestry...Foreign example.

THOUGH the employments of women are but small matters compared to the great subjects with which legislators have to do, they afford some clue to information derivable from no census calculations, and which no statistics can supply.

In the State provision for the education of females, and in much of the philanthropical application of remedies to our social disorders, the want of recognition of instincts and idiosyncrasies is distinctly visible.

Most of the popular efforts for the benefit of
the poor women of Ireland are attempted in complete ignorance of the resources and dispositions
they are developing. While schemes are being
matured, and theories discussed, of which they form
the subject, they are growing up in the midst of
influences, which they assimilate after their kind.
These act, and react, and if we would promote any
of their good effects, and repress their evil, it must
be by knowledge of the action set up, as the result
of the operations.

The wretchedness of pauper women, in and out
of Irish workhouses, is abundantly published; and
not one word too much has been said on the painful theme. The section of this class under Poor-
law care is not showing any improvement, and that
which is endeavouring to support itself by labour
is falling short of its aim. Notwithstanding the
prosperity of some of our classes, there remains a
permanent mass of pauperism, acting as a counter-
poise to the progress of the whole country.

The female poor form a heavy weight in this
balance. They encumber the attempts at adjust-
ment with innumerable difficulties. All proceedings

to alleviate the case are frustrated by their inca-
pacity. They are a body of crude material, and
the tone of the whole system is impaired by this
portion of it not performing its proper function.
Wisdom would dictate that the efforts which the
suffering members make to help themselves should
be considered, and that where remedial effects are
discernible, assistance should be administered. Industrial culture should be undertaken according
to this rule in order to achieve success. Institutions
and projects not so regulated must be utterly abor-
tive, and, while they attest good intentions, make
the ignorance of those remarkable who attempt
them. The production of exotic qualities should
be the last object of our schemes, the development
of those that exist the very first. Most of the plans
proposed for the cultivation of Irishwomen's powers
seek solely to induce them to become domestic, and
suggest nothing but training them to foreign household habits, without regard to their faculties for
such employments, or their facilities for carrying
them out.

" I will not pretend to speak concerning Irish
poorhouse girls, of whose condition such contra-

dictory evidence has been lately given before the Parliamentary Committee," says Miss Cobbe, in one of her pamphlets;* but those whose observation has been considerably exercised on them may undertake to speak of them and also of their next of kin, the women of the working classes. Now we must state, that much that relates to both these is not fairly brought before the public mind, because of the habit of mixing up their case with that of others, whose circumstances are widely different, and because few social reformers are as forbearing as Miss Cobbe. There is no parallel whatever between the females of England and Ireland in these two ranks. The race predominating in the latter country requires an entirely different course of treatment from that which suits the people of the former. Hence the benevolent and wise plans of Mrs. Way, Mrs. Archer, Miss Twining and others, which befriend the poor women of one country, could only be available for those of the other with many modifications.

The advocates of the "Family System" of rearing girls who come under the guardianship of the State, are worthy of all support. This is the only

* *Friendless Girls and How to Help Them.* (Victoria Press.)

principle that respects the design of Him "who setteth the solitary in families," and accords with the divine and human object of all law, the promotion of the spiritual and material interests of the being legislated for. The societies working out this idea afford abundant evidence of the beneficial nature of its results; but though they tend to physical and moral health, and secure a great improvement in women's circumstances in England, in Ireland the benefits arising from it would be limited.

The Irish girl's domestic experience would be necessarily confined to the condition of the household in which she might be placed; and this probably would be so low in the scale of civilized life that, while her feelings and affections are gaining the home roots, whereby woman's nature can alone be nourished, she would be running the risk of forming habits, that may bar her progress, and cause her to swell the ranks of the helpless among whom she lives.

There is something more than the "Family System" wanted for pauper girls in Ireland; intelligent female supervision is an indispensable agency in the administration of the plan. This should be in the form of official visitors, authorized to report to the guardians on the state of the children, for whose maintenance and training they are responsible.

The advantage of permission to receive these inmates could be made an encouragement to domestic improvement, and the efficient performance of the work of inspection, would contribute to the welfare of more than one class of the community. This duty is done for charitable societies practising the "Family System," by ladies; and it is to their work that any success which attends the arrangement is mainly due. We venture to assert that it is in the manner in which this action is carried on, that the potency for good of the whole proceeding lies. The plan of the Protestant Orphan Society is said to "contain all that need be sought for to guard and protect the orphan client of the State,"* and the life of this is its close and accurate supervision. The families accepting the care of these

---

* *On the Workhouse System,* a paper read before the Statistical and Social Inquiry Society of Ireland. February, 1862, by M. S. O'Shaughnessy, Esq.

children come under a directing influence of the highest order. Godliness, cleanliness, and industry are encouraged by individual · personal address, which, depending on the assurance that "faith cometh by hearing," goes forth to do this labour of love.

Dr. Handcock, in one of his papers on "The Family System," asks a very important question, which applies with greater force to female than male children under Poor-law guardianship. "How can a board composed of persons in one rank of life, choose the proper trade for orphans in a totally different rank (*and of a different sex*), of whom they know nothing, personally, as to their tastes, opportunities, connexions, or abilities?"

Obviously it does not attempt these, not super-human but eminently super-*board* exertions. But put these bodies *en rapport* with the spirit so power-fully working through woman's agency; let them suffer her to do her acts of charity, with the force of legislative permission, and then the connexion will be made, which shall convey the vital current of humanizing, civilizing, Christianizing instruction, not only to the pauper classes of our society, but

D

into the heart of the domestic circle of the working poor.

The faculties of the Irish female population never produce spontaneously, the same sort of household conveniences and comforts as those indispensable to English family life. This condition cannot be got rid of. It is an idiosyncrasy. There are people in Ireland, as well as in France and Italy, who cannot conform to the habits and manners of their Saxon neighbours; but who, nevertheless, attain a civilization and refinement of their own. Differences are not necessarily inferiorities. Our girls "don't feel it in their bones" to wash, cook, and polish; and they do not readily yield to the popular urgency to employ them in this species of servitude. For them the work in demand has no ascertained value. It gives no promise of social elevation. No labour is worse paid for in Ireland than this, nor has any other done so little for those depending upon it. The *Edinburgh Review* (April, 1862, page 421), gives a picture, which we regret to say is but too life-like. After describing the usual morning routine of Irish housekeeping, the writer says : "When we have once seen the open way in which they are treated as suspected persons, we can no longer wonder at any complaints of bad servants in Ireland. The wonder is that any self-respecting man or woman should ever go to service." The fact is, they have not this self-respect. Their want of educational training, and the absence of any choice of modes of gaining livelihoods, drive them unwillingly to this work.

A scarcity of this household labour would be a benefit, not only to the servant, but to the mistress; and every industrial resource should be encouraged that would increase the number of means of earning bread. Under their operation, domestic circumstances would have a fair chance of improving. Competition with other sorts of employment would compel advantages to be accorded to this; and the probability is, that in an independent class pushing up from lower ranks, will be found better women to supply domestic wants, able to comprehend modern requirements, and willing to engage in household service on terms of mutual profit.

Ladies who are visiting workhouses, and selecting girls to train to household duties, are doing a great good; but they cannot do all that is required.

They must leave behind a large body of non-elect; and what is to become of these? The State provision for their instruction ought to afford some teaching to enable them to fall into the ranks of the workers of any manufacture within their reach; and these manufactures would increase if skilled hands were more readily procurable by employers.

Commercial men who avail themselves of Irish-women's labour are unanimous in complaining of its quality, and their grievance is as worthy to be entertained as that of housewives. Nothing but cheapness could compensate tradesmen for dealing with such unprepared hands, and the low rates of payments are not an evidence of their illiberality, but the fault of the system of education, *which gives no special information* on the subject of those indus-trial employments, that are likely to be useful to those who have to work for their daily bread.

There is great ground for complaint of the way in which the needlework manufactures of Ireland have been slighted. While they have been doing more than any other agency to elevate its depressed female population, and have formed a passage from pauperism to independent life which has been largely useful, the notice taken of their efforts has not been such as to make them firm, and increase their extent. Of one branch of these alone, the advantages are manifest. The durability of the demand for these manufactures will last as long as the "fashions" of the world ; and it is certain, that on one branch of them machinery entrenches but slowly. They have a living force among their elements, with which no cogs, wheels, nor steam-engine can compete. The association of the designing human head with the elaborating hand, forms a combination of power, that no other contrivance can approach ; and, in order to render these invincible, we have but to enable the former to multiply its conceptions *ad infinitum*, and the latter to increase its capability of giving them expression. But even should fingers extend into joints of iron and steel, we shall not be astray in encouraging women to seek subsistence in ministering to a taste for ornament, which commerce is making world-wide.

The monetary value of these manufactures was equal, at one time, to one-fourth of the linen trade ;

sewed muslin exports rating at £1,400,000 per annum, and lace at £144,000.

There can be no question of the benefit of such
resources to a country, and of the good of their
competition with each other, with plain sewing, and
with domestic service.

Plain-sewing is now almost entirely under the control of the machine, and the calculation that semps-
tresses would be injured thereby is no longer relied on.
So far from its depressing the value of their art, it is
now known that it promotes it. Skill in needlework alone enables persons to use the new sewing
process profitably, and the stimulant to excellence
is greater than under the old system. Wages in
factories are higher than those paid for finger labour, and there is no decrease in the numbers employed in the making of useful commodities. These
are being produced cheaper than heretofore, and
their consumption made possible by classes formerly
below the reach of such refining matters. Perhaps
we may hail this effect of machinery as a blessing
singularly providing for Irish people's need, and
hope for well-clad people, when they shall be enabled

to purchase ready made that which they cannot be induced to make.

The large sum that embroidery and crochet brought into the country, tells very distinctly on the social condition of Ireland. From it came chiefly the means whereby the emigration of women from that country was enabled to keep pace with that of men for the ten years between 1849 and '59. It is no exaggeration of facts that leads to the conclusion that the number of female emigrants in that period, 569,036, may be multiplied by ten, to give the amount in sovereigns provided for the purpose of emigration by this instrumentality alone. Thus, more than £5,000,000 went out of the country, but a balance of nearly £9,000,000 remained to fructify at home, and has done so to a very important extent.*

The older and greater of these two needlework manufactures was not the principal agent in this proceeding. Sewed muslin, though in action since

---

* Ten years' income from needlework manufac-
    tures £15,440,000
Sum used for emigration   .   . 5,690,360
Balance spent at home .   .   . £9,749,640

1822, had not taken this effect on the community, until the industrial impetus of 1850 began its fermentation in the community; and even then, it was not in the ranks of its workers that the migratory spirit manifested itself in the greatest degree. Ulster became the seat of the embroidery trade, and the section of the population least under the influence of the tendency to emigrate engaged in it the most extensively. In this province, the preponderance of the Scotch Saxons, or Presbyterians, over the Celts, subdued the propensity a good deal. Notwithstanding its larger number of people and greater wealth, the proportion of emigration was only 16·71 per cent. in it, while in Munster, where the mass of inhabitants is more unmixedly Celtic, it was 23·17. The districts in which this movement was strongest were those in which the lace trade was most active. Whether these facts have any connexion or not, they are co-incidental, and worthy of being taken into account in the consideration of Irish character.

From Cork, the greatest field of this employment, a large number of crochet-workers emigrated, their own earnings supplying them with the means.

In the schools, the girls, though suffering extreme privations, frequently hoarded their money for this object, and, while saving it in too small sums to be received in banks, they entrusted it to the ladies who had provided them with this trade. A letter was lately received by one of these from America, telling of the easy circumstances of the writer, who had been eight years ago a pupil in the Adelaide School, and stating, by way of illustration, that she is "rich enough now to dress better than her former patronesses."

Mrs. Hand, of Clones, greatly encouraged the saving habit, and much of the money so accumulated was used for emigration.

The hindrances of ignorance and poverty are much greater in the south than in the north of Ireland, and any success in the south is worth more than in the north in testifying what Irishwomen can do. Besides emigrating, by this means, they have done other and more wonderful acts. There is evidence to show that, although struggling with every disadvantage many have attained a good step up in the world through its help.

Several places such as Carrigaline, Coachford,

and Cloyne, purely agricultural localities, derived some valuable assistance from this employment, though it cannot be said of any of
them, as it may of Clones, that " the crochet
harvest was only second in importance to the grain
crop." Of the 12,000 workers at this lace in the
area including Cork city, suburbs, dependencies,
and neighbouring towns, at least one-half were of
the class which lives ordinarily upon provision
contributed either by law, or by private charity. Of
these people several can now be found earning
comfortable livings. A few of the best hands now
at this business in Cork are from these ranks, and
so are many who are now respectably and profitably
engaged in other commercial occupations, while many
became domestic servants, and others married. One
of the number, in reply to inquiries on the subject,
said : "A good lot of girls never looked back since
the day they got their first crochet hook."

Many ladies who interested themselves in this
employment could give details which prove this
point. The writer's experience furnishes some,
that are not unimportant.

A small bundle of dark cloth, dripping wet, sat

on the end of a form, on a miserable winter's day, fifteen years ago, in the crochet-school of the Cork " Poor Relief Society." The humanity of the object was scarcely discernible through the dirty encumbrance of its dishevelled hair, and the involution of an old cloak that composed its only garment. But this was a person, and had a mind of its own, though as untutored in the conventionalisms of civilized life as the gorilla of M. du Chaillu.

When the teacher entered the room, it found a voice, and proposed a most business-like bargain :—

" Give me a needle and a reel, till I make some of this," pointing to a girl's work, " and here's a penny to lay down for them."

" Where did you get the penny ? "

" I begged it."

This conversation was of so ordinary a nature that it made no impression at the time, but the transaction it established brought about results worth recording. It was recently recalled by the pupil and her instructor, when they met, and, in the course of conversation, referred to their introduction to each other.

This same child, through her exertions, enabled her mother and sisters to come out of the workhouse, where they were when she entered the crochet school ; and they all became workers at this trade; the mother a "washer," one daughter a "pinner and tacker," and the other two made "bits" and "barred." In a short time they had a little home, and have since managed to keep it. In explanation of these technical words it must be told, that the fabric is made in a peculiar manner in Cork. The method was invented for the purpose of bringing the manipulation within the compass of females of various ages and degrees of skill, and it was a perfect success; for old women and little children are able to produce of the article jointly, and by uniting with one accomplished hand, several can avail themselves of it, who are shut out from other sorts of needlework.

This division of labour makes this manufacture very beneficial to poor families of the south of Ireland. In the north and midland counties, the work is done on a different plan. The whole piece is finished by each hand in Clones, New Ross, and Kildare. The pressure of need was never so expediting in these places as in the more southern counties; and better opportunities were afforded, for elaborating and cultivating the character of the goods. In these cases the bulk of the production was more condensed, and the payments less diffused; hence the consequent results are more apparent. When the difficulties of the trade are considered, and the competition in each separate portion of the article allowed for, the individual instances of workers in Cork making money by it deserve peculiar notice, as demonstrating cleverness in construction, and developing qualities of a high order.

The four little daughters of a "gingleman" (cabman), who had taken shelter in the poorhouse there, with his wife and six children, came out one by one, and, by means of this employment, freed the rest of their family. The writer has been offered a complimentary drive by the reinstated father of these girls, and feels bound to state that ingratitude is not the common result of this system of "out-door relief." The schools in which this power was acquired were perfectly independent of the State provision for the training of the young.

It is remarkable, that while no stimulus seemed provocative of industry *in* the workhouse, outside of it the progress was extraordinary. Materials and teaching supplied to *habituées* in residence there, were waste—lost labour. The National School education did not develop this industry to which female intelligence, by an inspectorship, minute and particular, which perceived the capabilities of its poor countrywomen, directed the course of their genius.

Now, this action naturally set up deserved to be supported.

The industry burst up in several places like water-springs, and it should have been looked to and preserved. It is not too late to do something for them; and any interference that may be attempted should be strictly local. No vague legislation will answer the case, it must be investigated, and made a distinct point of application.

The resemblance between the Irish and their continental relatives is, in some respects, so strong as to favour the adoption of measures in Ireland, similar to those that have been successful abroad. In the needlework industries many features in common with their foreign cousins may be traced;

but,—alas for the disadvantage under which poor Ireland struggles !—no governmental care fosters the development of its tastes, and therefore they remain undefined and ineffective, while rudiments abound for the formation of trades, as profitable and beautiful as those from which the French, Belgians, and women of other countries derive support.

It is hard for Irishwomen to suppress the rising of jealousy, when they view the lovely productions which foreign women contribute to the International Exhibitions, while they feel that for such occupations they have peculiar talents, but *no means whatever of cultivating them.*

By a recent arrangement, access to the government Schools of Design is provided for girls from National Schools; but some idea may be formed of the futility of this offer, when it is stated that *in the principal seat of the lace manufacture, the instruction afforded conveys no information applicable to the introduction of the artistic element into that work!* There is no system of inspection connected with this department which reaches the case of these pupils. They are left to their own devices, and with an education insufficient to enable these devices to subserve their proper interest, as may be expected, they gain little by their application to the Art Schools.

Children for whom the public purse is chargeable should be individualized and personally superintended, and their progress recorded and directed. Not only for their own sakes, but for the benefit of the trades of the country, there should be an object for study set before them.

Frenchwomen have an immense advantage in the *Asile Ouvroir*. This institution is annexed to the ordinary literary schools, and is always closed when they are open. It is free to girls of all classes, whether attending the other schools or not, and the law compels them to cultivate the description of work which the employers of labour in the district demand; and it provides every facility for improvement in arts connected with it.

Such help as this would be a great benefit to Irish girls. The National System of Education does not afford it to them efficiently, although it has a special industrial department included in its organization, expressly intended for this purpose. The difficulty of making this useful is greatly to be regretted; for, besides supplying the want of instruction in needle-work, it might be made influential in moral training, without interfering with religious teaching, and without exciting sectarian feeling. If properly ap-plied, this institution is capable of advancing the interests of Irish needlewomen materially; and there is but one hindrance to its utilization, but that one is fundamental. It cannot be done unless *female inspection* be employed in carrying out its scheme. Under the superintendence of nuns, the best efforts are made to render the government grant available; but even in the earnest, patient hands of these ladies, it fails to accomplish what is required; and where schools are under the control of clergymen, or of lay patrons, there is no security whatever that female industrial training will be rightly attended to. The models and tests adopted by the Commissioners of Education are not such as would be approved of by competent judges of needlework, and hence the cer-tificate of merit adjudged under their Board in this department is of no recognized value. This state of things is most undesirable, and might easily be ob-viated; and we have some hope that it will be so,

E

because the association of women with men, in the management of such affairs, is now an established principle—established by the admission of Florence Nightingale to the sanitary councils of the nation, and by the approbation of Miss Burdett Coutts' scheme for extending educational benefits.

The wants of poor Irishwomen are now well known to women of the higher classes; and among these ladies there is surely some one who would, if allowed, come forward and assist in permanently relieving the distressed of her own sex, by investigating the condition of the industrial schools, and arranging a systematic inspection of them, with a view to the classification and cultivation of the peculiar talents and abilities of her countrywomen.

The old race of Ireland wants something from its legislators. Its women beg for a boon that could be easily granted; nay, they deserve it, by the sacred right which entitles those to help who help themselves! So far forth as they were able, they have tried to exercise their talents. They have not neglected* the gift of embroidery and all

---

* Lectures on the MS. Materials of Ancient Irish History, by Eugene O'Curry. Dublin: Duffy, 1861.

needlework, which was in them since the far
back age, in which the beautiful Eimer was courted
by the Ulster champion Cuchulainn. This noble
lady was found by her suitor engaged in giving
instruction in such arts; and if any learned Irishian
will translate and publish the minute description
of a lady's dress, contained in the story of the
"Courtship of the Woman of Little Dowry," who
was sought in marriage by a monarch of Erinn
in the sixth century, it will be seen that, in those
days, no small amount of cultivation was bestowed on
the manufactures, to which our countrywomen are
still addicted. It is far from uninteresting, to know
that we have such an instance to show of the per-
sistence of tastes and pursuits among the various
races of people in this island. In the case of
crochet lace this is to be particularly remarked.
Quite distinct from the pillow laces, the common
property of many mixed families, crochet is not
imitative in its manipulation, it has had no formula
or models to copy from, no foreign forerunners to
take pattern by, and yet it took its place in the land;
avoiding the small portions of the country where
the other sorts of lace prevail, and maintaining

its distance from sewed muslin and from other kinds
of needlework it stands the representative of an
inherent power in an old stock.   The Spaniards
used it for some of their ornamental work, and
this favours the report of its Milesian ancestry; but,
with or without a pedigree, and in conjunction with
all other manufactures in which the female population of Ireland have employed themselves, we com-
mend it to the consideration of the guardians of
pauper girls, and the educators of the working classes
in that country.   Give Irishwomen special training
for their peculiar faculties, and there can be no reason
why Ireland should not be, in the British dominions,
what Vosges, Ypres, Malines, and Valence,   are
in their respective countries.

Ellen Harrington.

Ellen Harrington.

CHAPTER I.

On a glorious morning in June, 1848, H.M.S. *Breeze* steamed into a small harbour on the west coast of Ireland. Ships develop dispositions with peculiar distinctness; and this one, in every motion, expressed eagerness to accomplish its mission.

The *Breeze* had, on many occasions, proved strong to bear Britannia's sword, but this was the first time she was sent to do her deeds of charity. She was laden with food for the relief of the famine-stricken inhabitants of the district; and, forward in love as in war, before she came to an anchor, preparations for the delivery of her cargo were rapidly progressing. There were groups of people on the shore anxiously watching the approach of the ship's boats. The

moment the meal-casks and flour-bags were landed,
hunger broke through the stone-wall of order, and a
rush was made on the provisions. It was a savage
scene; all hands seized on what they could get;
many ate the uncooked substances with ravenous-
ness, and the imperiousness of empty stomachs superseded all official arrangements. The sailors, awed by
the presence of an unknown foe, offered no resistance,
and men, that had never yielded to an enemy, suffered Want to carry off their freight unmolested.
The officer in command found his sense of duty
strangely subverted on this occasion; impelled to
regard suffering more than the "circumlocution
office," and starvation as stronger than "red-tape,"
he did not attempt to restore order in man-of-war
fashion, but let Nature have its way on both sides.
Very soon the rough tar was seen helping the weak
peasant, and testifying brotherly interest in his
miserable condition. Many, with little Gospel
knowledge, performed Gospel acts, and "he that
had two coats freely imparted to him that had
none."

Mr. Hartley, the lieutenant in charge of the steamer,
inquired for the clergyman, to whom he should have

delivered the stores; and who must now certify for him, that, though irregularly, they had reached the proper quarter. The parsonage was pointed out to him; it was at a little distance, and, as he walked towards it, the painful impression produced by the occurrence he had just witnessed, made him very thoughtful about the means of permanent relief, for a state of things that he could not have believed in, unless he had seen. When he reached the indicated house, it was some time before his knock for admittance was replied to, so he had leisure to remark the exterior of the premises. Originally they had been handsome and extensive, but they were now sadly dilapidated and neglected. The lawn had felt no tiller's hand for many a day, and no sign of animal life broke the monotony of the grounds. The house itself, with its many closed windows, looked like a sick man composing himself to sleep through his decay. Even a bold outline of cliffs, a background of quiet verdant hills, a winding valley, permitting a gentle stream to steal into the bay, failed to give the idea of a pleasant residence, so oppressive seemed the poverty that had laid its hand on the habitation. That potato-blight in Ireland paralyzed everything:

people stopped short in their building, repairing, decorating, even house-cleaning ; civilized life was at a stand.

Mr. Hartley's contemplations were disturbed by the opening of the hall-door. A stout little girl, whom he had seen on the shore, battling for her share of the meal, was the porteress. There was some difficulty in inducing her to admit him ; and more still in persuading her that he must see the Rev. Mr. Longwood. She was bent " on taking in his message," or on his " calling again in an hour or so : " at last, she admitted him, and asked him to be seated.   After some time, Mr. Longwood made his appearance ; evidently he was just out of bed, and was in very delicate health ; he seemed a kind, agreeable sort of man, and was both courteous and conversational : he and his visitor soon made acquaintance with each other, and with the business that introduced them.   In the course of a somewhat prolonged interview, the officer learned enough to make him regard the man that sat opposite him as a hero, whom he could not emulate. Fasting was an enemy that he did not often encounter ; and the stratagems and defences described by the poor clergyman, were to him feats in a campaign which he dared not undertake.

It transpired, in conversation, that Mr. Longwood was recovering from the epidemic fever, and that his wife was lying down in it, and that their only nurse was the little girl that had opened the door. With much kindness and pity, and already feeling quite a friendship for the uncomplaining sufferer, who so simply told such a sad tale, Mr. Hartley took his leave.

When he was going down the avenue, a young man rode past him, and he observed that he dismounted near the house, released his rough horse from bridle and saddle, and let him run loose in the grass, while he himself familiarly entered the dwelling.

Hartley, on reaching the high road, turned in the direction of a village that he perceived at a little distance; and was not many minutes walking along, when he heard a voice calling after him:

"I say, Captain, don't walk so fast. Let me be talking to you."

On looking back, he saw the same individual that had gone into the Parsonage, a few minutes before, so he stood and waited until he came up.

"Tom Neligan, M.D., at your service, sir," said the pursuer, lifting his hat, bowing, and waving his hand towards himself. Hartley returned the salutation and fell into line to walk with the stranger, and submit to the "talking to" for which he had been called back. It ran on in the following manner :—

"So you've brought the food at last! The moment that I heard how you let the people lay hands on it, I made after you to blow you up. Why, it would be as well to let them die for the want of it, as to allow them to burst from the eating of it, as I expect the half of them will now do! Didn't you know we have no boilers? And how is the meal to be cooked? and who is to do it? Why didn't you bring the bread ready-made?—A set of fine boys all of you! If it was ye that were wanting it, what good stuff would be baked for ye; and the dinners laid on plates, and everything to your hand! But you won't set us up with such attendance!"

Hartley could hear the accusing tone of this style of address no longer :—

"Sir, said he, "you are strangely ignorant of the nature of my duties. Your complaints should be addressed to the Commissariat Department."

And, turning on his heel, he was about to part company abruptly with his singular companion, when the doctor exclaimed,

"Holloa, I offended you, did I? Well, I'm sorry for it, but you must not quarrel with a man who wants a new friend to help him to save some of the old ones."

And, putting out his hand, he made a very humble apology, and smiled so pleasantly, that Hartley, though offended by the imputation of mismanagement, did not refuse to accept the proffered *amende.* He also now observed, that the man was as queer in his appearance as in his speech, was dressed in a very nondescript fashion, and was encumbered with three or four game-bags and a fishing-basket, all of which hung about him, as if he were a stand for their especial accommodation; the only possible conclusion was that he was deranged, and must be humoured accordingly. But his conduct in the village which they were just entering, gave proof, that, whatever his mania was, there was method in it; and that it did much in its own way to relieve the miserable destitution which every step revealed.

" Look at that side of the village, captain," said
he, " every house there is shut up, nearly all the
people that belonged to it lie buried in that ditch,
where you see the earth red; and not a day passes
that two or three more don't join them.

" Come into my Dispensary,—but sure it is 'kit-
chen' it ought to be called, and kitchen-stuff is the
physic I ought to have in it—I'm afraid the boiler
won't be up until we are all past wanting it."

Groups began to gather round the gentlemen, and
the hearer discovered, that though but two days had
elapsed since the doctor's last visit, many of his patients had found their rest in the long sleep that
knows no waking; he mourned for them somewhat
in this style :—

" Don't tell me, the Doolans are all gone, and the
Roddys—eight strong men, in all, let alone women
and children! Driscoll, you're all right again.
Here, take this drink of broth."

" Yes, yer honour, I'm on my legs, thank God!
Still I'm sorry to be the one to be going to turn the
sod over Leary and Looney, that are lying on their
backs yonder."

" You! man, you're not able."

"An' sure I'm saisoned for it, doctor, glory be to God!" (crossing himself reverently,) "any way, none of thim that are not, ought to go anear that ditch."

"Dead, or alive, you're all dangerous company, my poor fellow. This gentleman and I will dig you a fresh hole. Captain, this will be a real charity; not a soul here is strong enough to use a spade properly, and they can't bury the bodies deep enough. Will you bear a hand?"

"I'll do better, if you wait a little, for I'll send you men, and get a trench of some depth dug for you; but where is the churchyard?"

"Four miles off, and there's neither money, nor strength, nor time to get at it. To convince you of the necessity for this rude and hasty burial, just come in here."

They entered one of the best looking cabins, and, as soon as they got accustomed to the gloomy light, they saw in one corner of the wretched apartment, a man lying on his back, almost naked, and evidently dying; a woman was sitting upright near him, rigid in despair; two children were dead at her side, and one, in the delirium of fever, lay tossing and moaning on her lap. The doctor produced a bottle from his basket, and administered a cordial to the mother, the only creature able to swallow in this almost tomb. The poor woman rose, laid aside the baby, and staggered over to her husband's side; at that moment he drew his last, long breath, and the miserable wife fell across his body, also giving up her weary life.

Such a sight drove Hartley into the open air, and it was many minutes before he rejoined the doctor, who had no time to give way to his feelings, and who was now found in the midst of a wretched crowd, to whom he administered mingled doses of orders, rebukes, pity, and cordials; while their thanks, prayers, blessings, and complaints, produced a medley of sounds, in which the various tones of the sufferers with the voice of their benefactor made the chords of a beautiful melody, whose key-note of kindness was easily found. With this in his ears, Hartley turned to Neligan, anxiously hastening to discover how he could contribute to his assistance; and now, indeed, he listened to his *clinique* with growing respect, as they continued to walk through roads that seemed to lead, at every step, to some fresh and more distressing case of misery.

" Captain, no pharmacopœia can furnish me with formula to suit the various symptoms of this radical disease. We want ready-made diet, or bring us cooks and kitchen-ranges ! The very whiskey, that used to assist the work of digestion in their half savage stomachs, is also absent; and without stimulant it is of no use to give them nourishment; with the help of it, they used to turn potatoes into humanity quickly enough; but now all the soup and stirabout they swallow, is as much outside them as ever, without ' the drop' that used to excite their functions, and preserve their tissues."

Hartley took the doctor on board with him; and the boat that brought him back to the shore contained a contribution to his Dispensary of the grog for that day of every man on board the *Breeze*.

"Deeds like these," said Neligan, "shall be rewarded when the great Inquest sits on our poor souls."

SOME days after these occurrences, the steamer entered the same bay; and the officer proceeded as before to land his cargo, which was this time better selected, and with improved arrangements. His new acquaintance had occupied much of his mind since his visit, and he had dwelt with great sympathy on the poverty and affliction of the clergyman and his family, and on their evident shrinking from making a claim for the help, which they needed quite as much as the poorest of the parishioners. As Mr. Hartley climbed the cliff, his name was called from a distant point, and, hastening forward, he met the little girl from the parsonage, running towards him in great excitement.

"Mrs Longwood is dead," she sobbed out.

He took her hand, and nearly joined in her tears. With all the frankness of a child, she poured out her

sorrows to him; and on the way to the house, he found
out that she was still the only attendant on the sufferers: that they had exhausted not only their stores,
but their energies and strength, in ministering to the
wants of the neighbouring poor; and that, without
nourishment or comfort, the poor lady had sunk
under the disease from which Mr. Longwood was
rallying, only to return to circumstances of privation
of which it was most touching to hear.

When they entered the house, it seemed truly
as if desolation pervaded it. Walls, floors, and
furniture testified to the presence of domestic disturbance, and calamity appeared to have settled
on the very hearth. Mr. Longwood was sitting
beside his dead wife, and was for some time quite
unconscious of their entrance. The struggle with
which he received even the kindest sympathy, was
very great, and it was not without difficulty that
Hartley induced him to withdraw to another room,
in order to permit the last sad offices to be performed
for the corpse. In an hour or so, the house began
to fill with the poor people that were left in the
neighbourhood; all eagerly pressing in to express
their feelings, and mourn affectionately over the re-

mains of their benevolent friend. Loud and melancholy was the *keen* that burst from the very hearts of the distressed creatures, who assembled at the scene of sorrow! It was very trying to poor Mr. Longwood—very saddening to Hartley, who, from the story they wept out, gathered a long tale of self-denying charity.

While the men and women crowded round Mr. Longwood, with most sincere concern and sympathy, Hartley could not help perceiving that the Doctor was right, in insisting on immediate burial for those who succumbed to the prevalent disease, as it was eminently contagious, and the people were singularly devoid of precaution against it, or of suitable arrangements for checking its progress. He held some conversation on the subject with the little girl, who seemed to be the only person in the household able to do anything. From her he learned that the Longwoods were entirely without money; and that no coffins, nor means of regular burial, were to be had, nearer than a town five miles off; that no horse could be procured; and that not a single person could be found strong enough to walk that distance.

A small enclosure round the little church, never

yet used for interment purposes, offered a fitting
sepulchre for one whose sacrificed life well entitled
her to the honour of a new tomb; and Hartley proposed to bring up his men, and to relieve the family
from a duty which it would have been extremely
difficult for them to perform.

The crew of the *Breeze*, knew what it was to con-
sign the body of a comrade to the deep; but it was
strange work to them to enshroud a lady in naval
canvass, dig her rough grave, and lay her tenderly in
it. Poor Mr. Longwood tried at the grave side, to use
" the form of sound words " in his hand; but the cry
of nature from his heart, responded to by many an
echoing spirit, superseded all other burial service.
When the interment was over, Hartley, on whom
he had leaned through the solemn scene, begged
him to come off with him on board his ship, and
offered the kindest hospitality most pressingly; but
the firm refusal to quit a post now dearer than ever to
him, convinced the good-hearted officer that it was useless to urge the matter farther. The girl's statement
of poverty oppressed him, he longed to open his purse
to his new found friend, as he would have done to
a brother; and he resolved to find a way to serve

him against his will. The time to sail drew nigh ; in
parting he placed a bank-note in the little girl's hand,
using almost the words as well as the action of the
good Samaritan.

Another fortnight, and the *Breeze* again approached.
the creek. This time Lieutenant Hartley was met on
the beach by the parish clerk (himself a resurrection
from the prevalent fever) : and informed that Mr.
Longwood had been laid beside his wife ; and that
his brother, Mr. Frank Longwood, had but just
come in time to close the weary eyes of the martyred
minister, and that immediately after he had set out
for Dublin, leaving "Miss Ellen" to share the
humble home of the clerk, and promising to pay
for her accommodation, on a very low scale of remuneration. Hartley was truly shocked at this
sad event ; and felt it as deeply as if he had had
an older friendship, and a longer intercourse with
the family, whose closing scenes alone had connected
it with him ; and he was not a little disappointed
at the abrupt ending of his connexion with it,
and the absence of any recognition of his services.
The brother, he thought, might have written him
a line ; and even the girl ought not to have

forgotten his interest in the troubles of the household.

The clerk told Hartley that Mr. Longwood had been
about five years curate of C.—, and that the Rector,
an Honourable and Reverend gentleman, lived in
France. It was believed that Mr. Longwood received no payment for his services, besides the produce of the glebe lands; and since the famine came,
this must have been nothing to speak of. The little
girl that lived with them was the orphan child of a
brother of Mrs. Longwood's; her name was Ellen
Harrington, and she had never known any maternal
care but that of Mrs. Longwood, her mother having
died in giving her birth. Her activity and cleverness seemed a pleasant theme to the clerk, who said
that he believed he should not have been alive
that moment, but for her care and attention during
his illness.

The exertions of this young creature were so
amazing to Mr. Hartley, that he resolved at once to
do something to assist her; and, if in his power,
to provide her with some resource for her living.

"I should like to see the poor little thing," he
said; and the clerk, who was also the parish school-

master, conducted him to the school-house, which was
close by.   This structure was just then being availed
of in every possible manner for the benefit of the
neighbourhood.   It was, beside being used for school
purposes, turned into a depôt for relief stores, and an
office for providing Government employment, for any
that could or would take it.   The clerk and his wife
were employed giving out the food and clothing to
crowds of applicants, who came all through the day ;
and it was their duty to inform any able-bodied men
that appeared in the groups, that they could get
work at road-making, in such and such places, the
rate of wages, &c., being stated to them.   A very
few, indeed, of the numbers that applied for help
were of this last class ; inability to labour being well
marked in the majority of cases ; so that their chief
occupation was the distribution of the stores.

The attendance of the children at the school was in
excess of the average in better times; their want, and
the supply of food that was given there, driving
them to it as a means of subsistence.   The regular
work of literary instruction was compelled to be set
aside, and a new feature was introduced into the educational system of Ireland. When Mr. Hartley entered

the room in which the juvenile assembly was usually held, he was for some seconds overpowered by the fetid exhalation from the inmates, which filled the whole apartment, and rendered the atmosphere noxious. It was an effort of peculiar difficulty to overcome the disgust it excited, and to brave the danger it announced. It was fever—perhaps death—to breathe it; and even to a man who had dared cannon-balls, it was an unwelcome risk.

The children were seated round the room in ranks, and the exhibition of rags, held together as if by a spell, so as to form some attempt at clothing, was the first sight that struck the visitor. All sorts of garments were in use, and worn as convenience suggested, wholly regardless of their proper application. Old clothes, that had been sent from all parts of the kingdom, were serving the purpose of covering, in a manner very different from their original design. Necessity had obliterated the distinctions of sex, and boys were wearing petticoats, but betraying their knowledge of their unsuitability by gathering up the extra folds into a grotesque knot on their backs. Old waistcoats and coats were impartially distributed; and skirts and

handkerchiefs were all that some of the girls had on.
The scene would have been comic, if it had not been
miserable ; and if the cause could have been forgotten,
the masquerade would have been amusing to a looker-
on.   At a small table in the centre of the room sat
Ellen Harrington, so busily engaged that Mr. Hartley had full time to observe the whole picture, which
was presented by the room and its curious collection
of children, before she noticed him.   A heap of
cotton-thread was before her, which she was dividing
into skeins, and next it rose a pile of little balls,
and a lot of small calico-bags.   Standing round her
was a group of youngsters, boys and girls, some
winding cotton, some holding the skeins, and some
waiting, anxious for their turn to begin similar
work. Every face in the school beamed with eager
interest and curiosity, and every eye watched the
new occupation, with all the zest of childhood, and
all the peculiar intelligence of the bright vivacious
race to which these little ones belonged.   At length
the girl became aware of the presence of a stranger,
and she rose, and was deeply affected on perceiving
that it was the friend who had been so strangely provided in the hour of her bereavement. With a dignity

and self-control beyond her years, Ellen soon con-
quered the burst of natural emotion that seized her at
the sight of Mr. Hartley; and she was able to give him
an account of all that had occurred since he was last
at C—. To her the events of the past two weeks made
a crisis, which fixed her fate to be one of entire self-de-
pendence for the future. She spoke of it as such,
and, with calm simplicity, announced her determination to accept no help from her late aunt's brother-in-
law. " He has quite enough to do to keep his own
family," she said; "and I am well able to earn my
bread, and shall do so, in some way or other."

She added this, with innocent confidence in her
own powers, and no distrust of the world, nor dread of
the obstacles she would probably find in it :—

" See, I've begun already, and you've helped me;
With some of your five pounds I bought this cotton,
and I'm about to get the children to make it up into
crochet edgings, for which I am to pay them so much
for every dozen yards; and then I am to send the
edgings into Cork, to a lady there, who will sell them
for me in England, charging a little more than I pay
the girls, as a profit for me : so that, if I have a deal
of work, I shall have a large gain, and get quite rich,

and the poor children will be earning a living! Is
not that good? I'm so very glad to have a chance
of supporting myself, and of helping many!"

The prospect that seemed so delightfully hopeful
to this earnest mind, did not at all present that aspect to her listener; but not wishing to damp her
ardour, Mr. Hartley merely replied:—

"I not only wish you success, but I will try to
procure it for you. Here is another five pounds
to help you to pay your workers. You won't
have it! Pray do take it:—let it be, then, as
a loan, if you will. I honour your independent
spirit, but it may become pride if you over-indulge
it, and hurt your undertaking altogether. Give
me the address of the lady in Cork; I am going
there, and will consult with her as to how you can be
best assisted."

In a few days, Mr. Hartley made his appearance
at the relief school in Cork, and told the foregoing
particulars of a case already known there, through
the applications for work, made by the energetic
heroine of the desolated parish of C—. He also
entered warmly into the scheme—then in its in-
fancy—of setting up a regular lace manufacture, for

the employment of the Irish female poor ; and as his
ship had made its last voyage in the relief service,
and was about to go on a foreign station, he undertook to be a correspondent, and an agent for extending the trade of the new establishment.

From time to time, good orders for laces came
from friends, interested through his kind mention of
the effort that was being made ; and he maintained
a regular intercourse, by letter, with the industrious
mistress of the crochet school at C—.

CHAPTER III.

In 1850, the "Ladies' Irish Industrial Society" made the effort referred to in our introduction. They set up a normal lace school in Dublin, for teaching girls to make pillow-laces, Valenciennes, Maltese, and English. A good house was taken by them in the Irish metropolis, and teachers were brought from Belgium, and from England. About four-and-twenty inmates were received, young women from different parts of Ireland, and their expenses of board and instruction were defrayed from their own resources, or by their patrons.*

Ellen Harrington was one of the first applicants for admission to this institution, and through the benevolence of friends, numerously enlisted on her. behalf by the kind naval officer, she obtained the means

---

* Appendix D.

of remaining in it, as long as the Society carried on its operations.

The education provided by this school, went on from lace manipulation to the artistic culture of the branch of the art of designing connected with it. One of the best pupils in this class was Ellen Harrington. Her proficiency was so great, that when the committee decided on abandoning their undertaking, and giving up the "Normal Lace School," it was thought so great a pity to check the promising career of such a genius as the girl developed, that she was sent to the Kensington School of Art, in order to continue her course of study, through the whole curriculum of the Government School of Design.

Ellen Harrington's progress there was highly satisfactory. She became an artist and a lady, in the true sense of both words. Her drawing entitled her to certificates of merit, and allowances of money, which gave her means to pursue her student life.

It was a great pleasure to the friends who had placed her in a position of singular difficulty and trial, that her associations in London were all that could be desired for her ; and that her virtuous life vindicated their confidence in the purity that resides with honourable industry. Her genuine piety was recognised by those with whom she lived ; and her faculty for art, and diligent and laborious exertion to utilize it, were known and respected by her teachers.

About this period of her history there is little to be said.

In the midst of the great city full of homes, the lonely girl lived a stranger's life. It was cheering to hear that she was progressing towards a competent income ; though it was not by the means that her friends intended her to use. Instead of learning to design for the lace which had employed her earliest powers, she became a teacher of drawing. It was very desolate, that dull routine of existence—from the easel at Kensington, to the daily lesson in the rudiments of drawing, given for bread, at the strain of every nerve and muscle, long walks, and long fasts, done to economize money, and cheap lodgings and isolation, submitted to to secure savings for rainy days ! She had few acquaintances in the wide, wide world of London, and no sympathisers. When a familiar face from her native land beamed upon her solitude, it was greeted with showers of tears, which rainbowed her dimmed prospects of pleasure and joy.

It is not a little remarkable, that the warm-hearted Irish girl was over four years in England, and yet was not absorbed into any social circle. There was some of the pride of connection with an upper class of society, in the cause that withheld her from mixing with the people with whom she came into contact; and there was a characteristic reserve, and a delicacy of mind, which refined her above the tone of the community in which she was domesticated. Ellen Harrington's case, though a triumph as regards the scheme by which she was elevated, and though perfectly successful as an undertaking for self-support, did not, as an experiment, realize the important result of securing a competent lace designer for the peculiar manufactures of Ireland; and it furnished a proof that the schools in which she acquired her art education, afforded no facilities for her object. Her Irish friends, knowing that she had the proclivities of her country-women for emigration, were not surprised when she wrote to them to say, that she had a wish to go to the colonies, under Miss Rye's protection; and they prepared to

G

enable her to do so as comfortably as possible. The arrangements for her voyage to New Zealand were nearly completed, and she had written affectionate farewells to all to whom her heart owed them, when an event occurred that changed the whole current of her feelings.

There was great excuse for this apparent fickleness. Only those whose attachments have been often riven from their holdings, can estimate the terrible trials that Ellen Harrington had to endure from time to time. Her early afflictions were followed up by blows and shocks of the severest kind. One by one, her loved ones had gone beyond her reach, and communication with them was cut off, leaving her to mourn, in utter desolation, her friendless position. Some had crossed the Jordan, and were gone the journey from which "no traveller returns;" and among these was Lieutenant Hartley. Of her connections by relationship she knew very little, and the willing, but unavailable friendship of Mr. Frank Longwood was also early terminated by death. The schoolmaster of C—, and his wife and family, had emigrated to America, and no tie bound Ellen to the objects of her earliest affections, save the bond of cherished memories.

After Ellen Harrington went to the Dublin Normal Lace School, the Crochet School at C—— was carried on under the management of the parish schoolmistress. Very good common articles, such as plain collars, and edgings of the simple, regular patterns, were produced there; and it continued tributary to the parent institution for a long time. The connection between this dépôt, and its county branches, was kept up with mutual advantage; the village schools were instructed by the samples sent to be copied, and supported by the orders, forwarded them for supplying specified quantities of goods; and the central establishment derived an income from a discount charged for the service which it rendered under this arrangement.

Communication was maintained by weekly transmission of work from the country, and return of cash from the dépôt to its rural dependants; but occasionally an interview between the corresponding parties was required, for the purpose of having a perfect understanding of the business details; and in this case, an intelligent girl was generally sent into town, and lodging was provided for her in the School-house, where she supported herself during the time that it was found necessary to have her under instruction. By means of such an arrangement as this, the knowledge of the lace-work was extensively spread throughout the south of Ireland; and among the many interesting settlements made, the little school at C—— was not the least important. Its history includes some rare instances of individual exertion, and some facts that strikingly illustrate the peculiarities of the country.

The depopulation of this neighbourhood, which occurred in 1849 and 1850, seemed to sweep away the bulk of the labouring poor, and the inhabitants that survived the calamities of those years, were of the class that had little holdings of land, and who had been capable of more industry, and better situated for carrying it out, than the very lowest orders.

The girls that came from time to time, with their lace from C——, were specimens of those Anglo-Irish families, out of whose ranks spring people that would do credit to any nation. Those workers were mostly daughters of men, whose an-

cestors had been English colonists, of the hated
"Cromwellian" stock. Their names, and the close
resemblance their habits bear to their kindred on the
other side of the channel, leave no doubt as to their
relationship, and such residents often characterize
the districts they inhabit.

On an average, the C—— school was in receipt
of four or five pounds per week, for its edgings,
but none of the highest class of laces appeared to thrive
there. The monotonous row after row of simple
work, executed exactly to pattern, and sent in regularly for sale, was all it ever attained; but this was
well and profitably done. The qualities of the
workers were registered in their productions, which
were of good value and honest measure, but no taste
was displayed for the florid, showy style of work,
that obtained commendation in other localities, and
into which the makers wrought the images suggested
by their vivid imaginations and lively passions.

One of the peculiarities of the crochet production
was, that it seemed to grow under the hands of its
makers, and to be developed according to their
intention; and this intention was truly nature's own,
for there never was a more ungoverned manufacture.

Given the first idea—the impulse—and provided with the implements—the needle and the cotton—they ran along, fabricating with amazing speed, and weaving a web which exhibited a curious picture of their state. Their crude fancies knotted and gnarled the thread into shapes so various and extraordinary, that to examine them became a study—not of lace, but of people. Poor little girls! their notions of beauty were as rudimentary as those of the early races; their efforts were parallel to some that remain on the monuments of Nineveh and Egypt. They seemed, indeed, to begin at the beginning of woman's decorative conceptions, and unconsciously to produce the same forms that suggested themselves to the Babylonians, and to Pharaoh's daughters, ignoring all that subsequent civilizations have done for feminine taste.

This unrestrainedness gave the thing some of its most interesting features. The seed was sown broadcast, and the return indicated the nature of the soil into which it fell; even the degeneration of the growth into a weed, does not militate against the force of its evidence as to the condition and character of the ground wherein it fructified. The art was taught here, and there, and everywhere, and those who took to it, generally, in a short time, did what they liked with it, and then there came up quantities of material—not raw, indeed, but dressed into the most complicated entanglement of designs, according to the degrees of sophistication of the workers. How they wearied themselves, to find that which was never yet seen under the sun, and how they toiled and laboured, to make out a way in which to express their sense of the beautiful, is known only to those to whom their appeal was familiar, in the constant craving for patterns and help.

During this demand for crochet lace, a girl was sent on a message to a lady, who received her in her dining room; the moment she entered the room her eyes wandered all over the walls, and she seemed entirely forgetful of the presence of the lady, and of the errand on which she had come. Her strange manner was at first taken for the mere gaze of rustic wonderment, and was endured for a few minutes, exciting some little amusement; but when it lasted longer than seemed reasonable, and continued in spite of attempts to attract the girl's attention to the business in hand, it produced alarm, lest it

might be an indication of insanity; and its persist-
ence beyond all bounds induced a strong feeling
that it was dangerous.

It was necessary to write a note in reply to the
communication that had been brought, and the lady
proceeded to do so; and, in order to do it without
disturbance, she desired the messenger to wait in
the hall. With an intensity of fervour that amazed
her hearer, the girl preferred a request to be allowed
to stay in the room. The lady, hoping she was
harmless, though by no means comfortable under the
infliction, acquiesced, and went on to indite her
letter. An exclamation which burst from her companion, and which sounded very like the rapture of
an enthusiastic admirer of some scene which gave
special delight and enjoyment, made her look up.

The girl was in an ecstasy; she was engaged in
copying the arabesques off the wall papering!

Utterly unconscious of the attention she was attract-
ing, the artist went on with her work, and before the
note was written, she had manipulated a little scroll
with her needle and thread, and triumphantly produced it, declaring that "there was money to be made
out of *that!*"

No lace but this crochet could have been dealt with in this manner; all others submit to a certain amount of external control, and it is because of its singular qualities that we venture to deduct so many inferences from the vagaries of this species of employment. In the process of its dissemination, it was very observable that only some hands went to it, as it were, *naturally*. The motions it requires from the muscles are the reverse of those used in ordinary sewing; "point" needlework, "bobbin tossing" on the pillows, or other feminine handicrafts; it is, in fact, a movement *from* the body, not towards it, as in most other cases, and this kind of work was not taken up by all temperaments and organizations alike. It seemed to be appropriated exclusively by some members of the Irish family, and to be rejected by the others. Some that took it up among the Anglo-Irish treated it as the girls at C— did, and kept it within rules and restrictions, according to the nature of their orderly habits. With them it was simple matter of imitative necessity, not of genius and spirit; it was to them a stern business effort, not a wild enterprise, and had nothing in it for them but the plain prose of a commonplace work. To the others, it was a poem wrought with passion, and like the climate of the island, "half sunshine half tears," it was a mingled tale of smiles and sorrow.

This tale, with all its incidents, cannot even now be reduced to the level of ordinary narrative; it enters into details of which history generally takes no cognizance, and yet, in that *not* distant day, when the distinctive qualities of different races shall be the subject of investigation, in their closest minuteness, this faculty of Irishwomen will be received in evidence that will classify their capabilities for taking part in the community of labour.

Among the remarkable attributes of this lace were its localization, and the effects of this localization. Stitches settled, pitched, rooted themselves, and they could not be transplanted. The mode of working in one place could not be taught to the girls of another, so as to produce quite the same effect. This was tried with great energy and perseverance by the importation of workers, but it never succeeded. Each place persistently kept its own stitch; in no other neighbourhood could the identical turn of the thread, and the exactly similar loop, with equal tension or laxity, be procured; and this peculiarity is common to other laces.

There are* stitches in use in many continental localities, which remain firmly fixed in districts, and are
not transmissible; and the same sort of adhesiveness
is perceptible also in regard to any designs that are
developed by untutored workers. Organization, no
doubt, determines the action of the hand, and necessarily confines stitches to certain personal conforma-
tions. ' Connections, therefore, easily centralized
stitches in different circles, and when this was done,
there came a further effort, which indicated the influence of localization in an interesting manner.
In combination, the stitches formed a pattern, and
this pattern became a picture, and this picture was
nothing more nor less than the characteristics of the
neighbourhood, as they appeared to the eye of the
maker. Here, in the small matter of crochet lace,
the wondrous feminine idiosyncrasy betrayed its
curious working, and the conception of the mind,
through the vision, was developed in natural order.
Crochet was topographical, and described its birth-
place with a surprising accuracy. That produced in
the boggy districts was full of minute fibrous inter-
lacery, and the specimens from the mountainous,

* Appendix E.

rocky places had a peculiar style, which displayed some notion of cubic proportions, while the pieces fabricated in the soft, damp, watery places of the green, fresh, vegetative south were overrun with flowers and foliage of the most luxuriant variety.

CHAPTER IV.

THE reports from C—— to the parent school, had much interesting matter in them: they told of girls who had realized sums of money sufficient to pay passages to America, for themselves and their parents; and of others, who had made good use of their earnings, in restoring comforts to homes that the famine had miserably impoverished. Even the little orphan relics of the families, that were engulphed in the burial ditch, of which we had heard from Lieutenant Hartley, re-appeared in those accounts; and the names, also, of some of the patients for whom Dr. Neligan worked so hard, were mentioned sometimes in the payment-roll.

The pleasant record of their industry kept the memory of this gentleman quite fresh in the minds of their friends; and when, one morning, he was announced as a visitor at the relief school, he was received as an old acquaintance.

The conception formed of him, from the description given by his naval friend, was amply borne out on personal introduction. Dr. Neligan was no easy-going, quiet practitioner, content to be a medical stipendiary, and willing to stick to the fortunes of his dispensary.

His rapid sketch of the decline of the whole country round about C——, was told in a breath:

"All the beggars and labourers are cleared away, and the decent old farming people, that used to be strong and comfortable, are now the poor on the road-sides. I got enough of being doctor, cook, and undertaker to the lot, and won't stay to bury the second batch. There's nothing for it but to cut and run, while my own shoes are whole. Four parsons, three priests, six magistrates, and a score of policemen have dropped through; and only that I have nine lives, I'd have laid my bones in that same charnel house. As it is, the flesh is worn off of me, and I've scarcely a suit of clothes to my back, or a penny left in my pocket. I'm going to America, and when I tell you where I'm getting

the ways and means, you'll say there are grateful
hearts in some of the living skeletons at C——.
I gave it out awhile ago, that I was sick and tired
of my life, and that if I had the price of my passage,
I'd go to Canada to my brothers, that are there
thriving and driving, while I'm slaving and starving;
but I had no notion that any one would take notice
of my grumbling. Well, about a week after I
had said it, as I was eating my breakfast one
morning, I was told that two little girls wanted
to speak to me, and when I went to the door, I
saw they were some of the crochet workers from
C——.

" 'What do you want, colleens?' said I, and one
of them, with much blushing and stammering,
opened a great package which she was carrying, and
showed me a quantity of lace work, holding out
piece after piece for me to admire.

" 'We've made these for you, sir,' said she, 'and
if you don't take them from us, it will break our
hearts, so it will, yer honour.'

" 'Why, what on earth could I do with those
rags, children? I can't wear them, or eat them,—
what use are they? Dont be foolish,—go sell them,

and buy yourselves some tea, and have a *rookawn* on the profits.'

" ' Oh, don't laugh at us sir, like that; but be reasonable, and simple with us. We don't like to presume even to offer them to your worship; but there's more value in these ' rags ' than you'd think. They're a fortnight's work from us all, all round; and they wor done with all the veins of our hearts; and if you took what's there to Cork you'd get *eight pounds* for them, and that would be a handful towards your passage to America. And 'tisn't that we want yer honour to go, or that we can bear the loss of you, at all, at all; though we'll struggle through that, plaze God; for you done enough, *He knows*, and we're full to the throat when we think of it all. We don't want to take any more of yer life out of you; so, go where you'll have plenty, and your aise to it; and we'll pray that your soul may have everlasting satisfaction, in the other world, out of all the trouble it had here. And, sir, when you're going across the say, we'll give you another week's work to take over with you, for we hear it's worth double the price in America that it is here, and you can sell it there, and it will help you on your road, and keep you from being beholden to strangers, until you get to your own brother's house.'

"Oh, what an offer that was! No hundred pounds of English gold laid in my hand, would have been equal to the 'rags,' that now outshone diamonds to me! I don't know how I answered in words, but I acted like a baby, and found myself hugging the bundle, when the girls left me to myself. I was not long in coming off here, for I'll take the venture, and if these 'rags' turn into a trade for me, those that gave me my first stock, shall be no losers. So, here goes, 'to throw physic to the dogs,' where it threw me; and to take up a pack and travel the world! A pedlar's life is better than a profession that keeps a man on the verge of the grave all his days."

And so, Dr. Neligan became a lace merchant!

His change of occupation was by no means a mistake, nor did it fail as a speculation. He entered on the branch of the lace trade, which Irish female industry had added to the world of commerce, just as it was opening its largest field, and in it he had the ability and opportunity to make a good standing.

H

America was at this time a great market for
crochet, and Dr. Neligan went over there with a very
considerable stock. He had great success in dis-
posing of it, and in making an extensive connection, which finally formed a lucrative business for
him. The export of Irish lace to America became a
very important matter from that time forward.
Some £4000 per annum, was said to have been paid
to different schools by this one dealer and ex-physi-
cian, who embarked impromptu in the trade!

The little girls at C— had no cause to regret their
generosity. Dr. Neligan repaid them, with interest
upon interest; and they and he had a deep mutual
satisfaction in the interchange of beneficial communications. He worked for them, and they worked
for him; and never, probably, was a truer link forged
between fellow-sufferers, than this most humane
commerce made into an elastic chain, binding together inseparably those whom no distance could
detach. Wherever there was a sale for the commodity, Dr. Neligan pushed it. Far and near he
was heard of as the most indefatigable labourer in
the business. He did it *con amore;* "for life and
country," might well be his motto, and if he

do not quarter some such memento of his achievement on the armorial bearings of his family, yet the heraldry of gratitude will tell how honourably he won his spurs, in the cause of the poor Irishwoman's industry.

But not even his great energy, nor the almost superhuman exertions of the anxious workers, could sustain the trade beyond the ordinary length of a fashion. The girls wrought in patient submission, while prices rose, culminated, and fell ; and they continued hoping against hope, as the worth of their labour declined, that the demand for the fabric would return. They, poor, ignorant creatures, had no idea of the odds against which they were working ; and they are, to this moment, as little aware of the cause of the utter cessation of sale for their goods, as they are of the scientific explanation of the potato blight. The conduct that they pursued, with regard to the occupation that had been, for so long a time, a source of profit to them, was very similar to that of their male relatives, with regard to the crop that used to procure them their living. Both parties obstinately clung to the belief, that each returning season would restore their resources as bountifully as formerly. They continued to plant, and to crochet, in faith and confidence; and no disappointments dissuaded them from their fruitless speculations.

Potato gardens sown year by year, in spite of warning of disease, and dug in sorrow and regret, were in mournful harmony with the habits of those who persisted, against all discouragements, in making lace to sell at a price that did not replace the cost of the raw material. It was a kind of natural game of hazard in which they were engaged; and it could only be terminated by the conversion of their foolishness into that wisdom which is derived from experience alone.

For a couple of years nothing was heard of Dr. Neligan; and then news came that he was in Australia, sheep farming. A letter from him, from his distant station, came to an Emigration Society in his native land, giving most interesting information, and valuable advice, concerning the sending out of women to the colonies; and with his help many girls were transferred to the New World, and assisted to make homes in a country where famine is unknown.

To a man who has passed many years in a remote part of Ireland, the hardship of living in the bush must be, in some measure, lessened by the fact of its not being very much more rudimentary than the condition out of which he came. Dr. Neligan's description of pastoral life in Australia formed an amusing parallel to that which he had led at C—. With regard to domestic arrangements, the comparison was greatly in favour of the colonial system of management.

" Out here," wrote he, "money brings all the appliances of civilized housekeeping, and invention fits them to the circumstances of our case. We have here contrivances that procure us every possible comfort. If a man but work for the means, he can have brought to his hand, in this remote region, all the luxuries that modern science has discovered. I often contrast this land of abundance, and of trained, educated labour, with the country— destitute of resources, intelligence, and energy—that I left. Poor C—! its shores unfished, its mines unexplored, its soil untilled! I declare, even money was not of the ordinary use there. I have a painful memory of the difficulty of living like a human being in that outskirt of creation. It is said, that, when the Creator was making the world, he threw his waste materials on the west coast of Ireland; and I believe some such thing must have occurred to account for the condition of the place. But, whatever the formation may be, man has done nothing to make it better for himself. The race inhabiting it in my time, was so far from being domesticated that it was not even a cooking animal, and could neither prepare its own victuals, nor construct its own dwellings, so as to favour its own interest. The aborigines here are no more helpless than the Irish paupers. Saxon powers are doing greater things in this region, in months, than they have been able to accomplish in Ireland in centuries. I protest that no Australian savage would be more puzzled to know how to make a five-pound note supply the unknown necessities of a distressed multitude, than Ellen Harrington and myself were, when the Englishman gave her one, at the time that Mrs. Longwood died. I'm sure I didn't know what to do with it. We had plenty of materials for nourishment and clothing, but the power of converting them into an available state was unattainable.

"It is, to me, one of the inscrutable mysteries of Providence that women should have been endowed

with gifts to make *lace* and not *bread !* Let none of
that sort of people come here. Those so curtailed of
feminine talents had better stay where the exchange
is near enough to change their produce into bread
so quickly as to keep them from hunger."

These considerations were very rational, and syn-
chronised with an instinct that acted in connection
with the emigration tendency. Crochet workers emigrated extensively. Every farthing that they could
spare from the pressing necessity of the passing hour,
was saved for this purpose. The barest modicum of
food, and the smallest possible expenditure in clothing,
sufficed for them. They mortified every present desire for enjoyment in order to hoard for the one object
—to leave the country! It was the old tale; they had
heard that there was bread in America, and, like the
seed of Israel going up from their Canaan—their
Erin, dear as it was, they would forsake for this land
flowing with plenty. They did not select Australia
Felix for their exodus, they stuck to the nearer con-
tinent. It was at hand, they could pay the passage
money more easily, and get there sooner ; but this
was not all ; their "people" were there, and their
drift lay in that direction. However difficult of ex-

planation this peculiarity may be, it was like the lace cause, an independent free agency, and had its special results, unmodified by the interference of any control whatsoever. The attempt to get an answer from any of the intending emigrants, for the hope that was in them, that life in America would be better or happier than in Ireland, was vain. They went across the Atlantic in blind obedience to a vague impulse, and who shall say that it was not a guidance as divine as it has proved felicitous?

Lacemakers, to a woman, made for America; and in America they and their generations will be found, rising probably to wealth and station, but never forming a *domestic* community, nor emulating the distinctive peculiarities of the race with which they have been so long connected, and by which they have been so slightly influenced.

American peculiarities are coming out just now in extraordinary vigour. How much of them are due to the Irish element, tempered by climate and circumstances, it would not be easy to determine; but that, to a very considerable extent, these are working in the United States is an acknowledged fact. And since woman—the mother and the home-ruler—must affect every commonwealth, that of America cannot escape the influence of those who, whether they made lace or not, have in them that nature, to some of the peculiarities of which we may find a clue among the tangled threads of crochet work.

CHAPTER V.

Dr. Neligan's adventures were not ended when he wrote the letter from which we have quoted; and the next we heard of him, was at the International Exhibition of 1862.

People come to and fro, now-a-days, so easily from the antipodes, that one is no more surprised to meet friends from the Cannibal Islands, in London, than to encounter their neighbours on roadside paths near their own homes! Tom Neligan had so strong a sense of this, that he made the voyage from Australia to England with a feeling of pleasurable anticipation at the idea of all the familiar faces that would greet him, and of all the friendly hands that he should clasp in the Great Fair to which he and all the world were gathering! In his glowing imagination, he pictured his Irish relatives and connections enjoying the spectacle he was about to visit, and he revelled in the thought of encountering them, when they were perhaps assembled in parties, or of suddenly meeting them singly in the courts and aisles of the Palace of Industry. How they would exclaim! And how delighted he should be! The very idea was refreshing to his warm heart. Sometimes he speculated on seeing some persons from the old country, whose looks should betray that the famine was not yet quite gone; and in whose system a few lingering symptoms of the recent plague of poverty remained; then, he charmed himself with the thought, that he carried a remedy in his pocket now, which would cure the complaint that he so well understood.

"I'll pay their way out to Australia, and make men of them, and every man shall bring his wife; and that will serve us all every way; and if I can't tempt a nice girl to come back with me, I'm not Tom Neligan."

The metropolis of the mother country was not at all new to Dr. Neligan, and so recently had he been in it, that no very great novelty was presented to him in his walks about its streets. But the familiarity of the scenes and the objects in them, had no attractive influence for him. No affection was connected

with anything he saw; and, alas! all his expecta-
tions of happy re-unions with loved associates were
utterly unfulfilled.

He wandered many days about the Exhibition, and
never once found a face that he recognized among
the multitudes of people that he met. The sensations
of astonishment and admiration that he experienced,
at the first sight, of all the wonders there, kept him, for
awhile, from keenly feeling his disappointment; but
as soon as the novelty of the scene wore off, he felt
the pang of the privation of companionship most
sorely—the blighting of his cherished hopes.

The gorgeous display ceased to dazzle and confound
his emotions; the riches, and treasures of art, the
wonders of mechanism, and the beauty of imagery,
palled on him. He longed more fervently than ever
for a congenial soul to sympathize with him; and in
a paroxysm of genuine grief, he turned his back, one
day, on all the splendour before him, and threatened
himself with going back in the next ship, for a pun-
ishment for being so silly as to think that every-
one was, like him, "making money with one hand
and spending it with the other."

Dickens's connection of the employment of a

toll collector with misanthropical sentiments, had always amused Neligan ; and, with this fancy now in his mind, he wondered much, whether the men who guarded the turnstiles at the entrance of the Exhibition, did not entertain gloomy views of society. With a complete revolution of feeling, he began to imagine that he should like to have a chance of cultivating those exciting sensations—malice and hatred, and of indulging them by getting some post which would enable him to make the duty of paying tolls and taxes as irksome as possible to those whom it might concern.

"'Twould give a man a nice opportunity of being hard on a world that is hard enough to forget him. I wish some way of getting into a row respectably was open to me this minute! The end of a quarrel is always the beginning of the best of good fellowship. The worst of these English people at home is, that they are so slow to say a friendly word; they don't understand the thing, when a man is trailing his coat after him to get up a fight!"

Soliloquizing in this manner, our traveller pursued his course along Piccadilly, and became more and more dangerously irascible as he proceeded.

Every one that brushed past him excited his ill-temper; and, in no very amiable mood, he took his place in an omnibus to return to his hotel in the city. The conveyance was so nearly full when he entered it, that it was with some difficulty he found a seat, and when a lady got in immediately after, he felt impelled to go on the outside, and let her have the space that he had just secured.

The recent endeavour to stifle his good nature had not yet begun to cause him to forget a chivalric regard for women; and it was with true gallantry he rose to offer his place on this occasion to a fellow-creature of this sex.

The lady in question was tall, and closely veiled, her figure was slight, and voluminously draped in sombre garments. He could not observe whether she was young, old, handsome, or ugly, but he had a sudden sensation that it was not the first time he had seen her. Eyes do not alter with time and age, although their setting may become corrugated and discoloured; they betray resemblances that other features lose; and the eyes that now gleamed on our Doctor awoke strange memories that he felt through his tingling nerves while he mounted the 'bus. As he sat on the roof and rode along, he chased the clue of remembrance through a chain of recollections, until he arrived at a certainty as to the identity of the fair one, he had thus, in a manner, captured :—

"She sha'n't escape me," said he to himself. Every time any of the interior passengers were set down, he watched them, and when the object of his special interest alighted at Chancery Lane, he got down, and followed her up that celebrated thoroughfare. He could easily, at any moment, have come up with her, passed her by, and beaten her best paces ; but that indefinable sensation withheld him, which makes the boldest man timid in addressing a woman who always retains the sanctity of her sex. Along Searle Street, and into Portugal Street, he walked after her, step by step; and when, at length, she paused at the office of the " Female Emigration Society," it was with mingled feelings of reluctance and desire to attract her attention, that Neligan put himself in her way, as she was about to enter its door.—" Ellen! — Miss Harrington!"

" Dr. Neligan!"—

The disjointed exclamations that followed these words of recognition may be imagined. The pleasure of the meeting was mutually overwhelming.

The "interesting, educated, lady-like, middle-class" emigrant, did not make her appearance that day at the time directed by Miss Rye. Instead of having an interview with the good ladies who were about to provide her with an introduction to colonial life, Ellen Harrington passed an hour with her hand under Dr. Neligan's arm, wandering about Lincoln's Inn.

"I'm due at —— Square to give Miss — a drawing lesson at three o'clock, she said: "I'm sure you will not ask me to disappoint this kind friend and pupil."

"Well, not if you press it; but I insist that it shall be the last lesson you give in this way. It is hard to part with you, even for a moment, now; but you are as right, and as good as ever. Go; —and to-morrow we shall meet, and every arrangement shall be completed, to prevent anything separating us again."

Whether they were married on the next day, or on the following, is not known, but the ceremony was certainly performed as soon as it possibly could.

The outfit provided for Ellen Harrington's emigration, under the care of the valuable Emigration Society, enabled her to proceed without delay, and in much comfort, with her husband to his distant home.

The Redeemed Estate.

The Redeemed Estate.

CHAPTER I.

FIVE-AND-THIRTY years ago, in the town of Kildine, on the day before the opening of the Spring Assizes, a handsome, family, travelling carriage and four dashed into the narrow streets of the old borough, and drew up at its head inn. This was the equipage of the High Sheriff of the county, and it was bringing him with his wife, and two daughters, to town, to take their places, as leading personages, in their respective positions, in the coming assize-doings.

The High Sheriff had been M.P. for the county some years before, and was a man of influence in society, not from his personal talents, but from his pedigree and possessions. He may well be intro-

duced as a very fair specimen of the Irish gentry of
his day; he was one of a class that included within
its bounds a large proportion of the owners of the
soil, in every county in Ireland. ·

John Fitzwalter, Esq., was no exceptional character, nor did the state of his affairs form an extraordinary case. The style of living he kept up was
common, in the social sphere to which he belonged,
and his circumstances and conduct represented those
of his fellow countrymen in his own rank of life.
The time at which we are looking back was in the days
of travelling by post, the age before railways and
telegraphs—those mighty agents that have altered
the character of the world! The cattle along most
Irish roads were very good, but relays had sometimes to be provided from the private resources of the
travelling party. It was so on the occasion to which
we refer; the Fitzwalters drove their own horses all
through the journey; and, at the last stage, had four
greys waiting for them, in order to enter Kildine
with a splash, and excite some *éclât*. They accomplished their wish, and attracted a considerable
amount of observation; but it is questionable
whether the exhibition had the desired effect on the

public. Even at that period, it was beginning to be popularly known, that the magnificence and display of the aristocracy of Ireland, were in excess of their income. The nature of their wealth was already pretty generally understood, and there remained few on whom the most lavish expenditure could impose, or impress with the idea that solid riches were associated with it.

Mr. and Mrs. Fitzwalter and their daughters, Catherine and Margaret, both the latter being very young girls, neither having attained the maturity of seventeen years, had not any idea that their pretentious arrival at "the Hibernia" gave subject for more speculation than admiration. Their steaming, prancing horses, their men-servants in handsome liveries, and their maid-servants, two of whom were mounted outside, made a "turn-out" which seemed to indicate station and importance, and which was calculated to mislead any person uninitiated into the mysteries of Irish life.

The High Sheriff found the "Sub" waiting to receive him, and anxious to have some conversation with him. As soon as he had conducted his wife and daughters to the apartments prepared for them, he announced his intention of dining at the club, and directed that dinner should be served to Mrs. Fitzwalter and the young ladies immediately.

"It is not too late for shopping, Elizabeth," he said to his wife, "and if you and the girls are not tired you might see after your ball dresses. Don't spare a pound or so to make yourselves look creditable."

This considerate advice set the young ladies in high spirits; and they could not control their desire to begin the pleasing preparations for their first ball. Not so the mother, who pleaded fatigue, and sat silent and thoughtful, listening to the girls' raptures with an ill-concealed *malaise* and distraction :—

"My dear children, mind what I am going to say, if you are not too wild to think of anything but partners and dancing. It is out of the question going out this afternoon, to buy the little things we want for our dresses."

"Little things for our dresses? Why, mamma, we want the dresses themselves! You can't mean us to go in those shabby white frocks?" exclaimed both the girls in a breath.

" I do mean it, dears. I am very sorry indeed,

bitterly sorry—no one knows how keenly I feel it—but it must be so."

"But, papa said—"

"Oh, yes, I know what he said, he is very kind, and wishes to please us; but there is a reason why we should deny ourselves this gratification of our taste. I cannot tell it now to you, my darlings, but some day you will know it; and it will justify my seeming harshness. You will be glad of your forbearance—trust me!"

"Well, mamma, if you speak in that solemn way, you must be obeyed; and we will say no more about it."

"There, I felt sure of my daughters' confidence in my judgment; and now, loves, we shall just try to be contented in our old dresses. Remember they are by no means disrespectable. Those frocks of yours are Indian work, and cost a very large sum. Very few young ladies will be at the ball with such expensive or such becoming garments. Age does not render such dresses less valuable; in fact, it enhances their worth, especially when they are so well preserved as yours are."

"Thanks to the exquisite darning, that you made

us practise on them, mother, dear. At all events, there will not be girls in the room who have put more stitches in their clothes than we have."

" And probably none who know how to do it so well. You have been diligent and industrious, and it will be well for you, perhaps, that you have cultivated your needlework skill. It was the thing I learned best in my early days; I had little talent for anything else; and when I was sent to France to school, the turn I had for work was so remarkable, that the nuns kept me at it constantly. Have you seen my old lace trimming? I've repaired it most beautifully —you could not tell where the rents were, and I've added lovely little scraps of my own manufacture, as good as the real '*point de Venise.*' I am quite proud of it, I assure you. Oh, we shall look very grand ! My lace is fabulously old—of a very rare sort. It is known to have belonged to my grandmother, the Duchess of Beaufield, and will show magnificently on my black velvet dress. After all, no style of dress is so elegant as that which consists in wearing standard articles, of ascertained worth ; none but the very upper classes can have them, and only really educated ladies can appreciate them. You will find, when you mix with many circles of society, that your laces will be marvellously admired, by all whose taste is worth consulting."

While the mother was consoling her pretty daughters, the three pairs of hands were industriously employed, as it was their habit to be.

They were busy at an occupation that cheap hosiery has now almost put out of date. Each had a stocking under repair, and their texture announced an age when women knitted cobwebs. A spider might have spun the silk of which they were made, and the menders, in this case, were as dexterous as the fabricators.

The hours went on towards bed-time; and they had worn the subject of the coming ball thread-bare, as well as finished their "grafting," and were talking of sleep, when Mr. Horace Fitzwalter, the brother of the High Sheriff, was announced.

Catherine and Margaret sprang up to greet "Uncle Horry" with enthusiasm, but the mother received him with greater quietude and decorum. He embraced his nieces warmly, and kissed his sister-in-law's cheek with affection and respect.

"So, Elizabeth, you've come to town to get rid of

your daughters. Girls, don't be too hard to be pleased, or fellows will turn into old bachelors, like me."

"Children, don't mind uncle Horace," said the wary mother, "he'd put all sorts of nonsense into your heads. I'm sorry he came so late, for you really must go to bed, and get rest after your long drive."

"Yes, do, little ones, and keep your roses fresh for to-morrow night; and I'll come in the morning and help to get you ready for the fray. We shall be at work all day—arming at all points for conquest. Well, Katy, who is it to be? First or last partner—which? As to you, Maggy, my opinion is, you're already settled for—a certain dark, tall dragoon has been naming my sweet niece too often to leave me in ignorance of his views— blushing!—come I'll tell no tales."

"Go, girls, pray go! Horace, don't be silly; let them be off, like a good fellow, and sit awhile with me, I want to speak to you."

The door opening, and the "good-night" of the uncle and nieces, were almost a game of romps.

Mrs. Fitzwalter looked on with a calm seriousness that, at length, arrested Mr. Horace's attention.

When the girls were fairly gone, he turned with perfect sobriety of manner, and in a very sympathizing tone said,

" Sister, you are too low, how is this ? Are you ill ? "

" At heart, Horace. How can I be otherwise, knowing all I do of our affairs ? Would you believe it, this very evening, John's last words were to direct us to get new ball-dresses ? as if we dared, or could, under present circumstances."

" Oh, that's his game, is it ? He wants to keep up the sham as long as possible. You could easily have them ; the credit is good for awhile longer, and you and the girls may as well get all you can out of the wreck. It will be time enough for you, women, to suffer, when the pinch really comes. I am the only one in the fire at present, and I'm regularly wound up. *I* have no credit—never had. The nature of my charge on the estate, is as well known, in its length and breadth, as a man's name. Every one knows what it is worth—not a groat, not a stiver !

It never was a real settlement, for my father had no personalty to settle, and no power to put a charge on the estate, so that deed of his is so much waste paper. John, certainly, has not attempted to claim exemption from its payment, he used to honour my draft very punctually; but he has been failing me of late, and I've had to live in a way I don't like. My circumstances are the most critical of any member of the family, for I'm this minute without house, or home, or a penny in my pocket—faith, I don't know how I get along at all! Only for the luck I have at play, I'd be in quod now. What made you let John go to the club, to-night? If he has any loose cash they'll ease him of it. There's a bad lot there."

" I'm sure, I could not help his going," said the sad wife, looking woefully at the dying embers in the fire-grate, " he was off with Mr. Townley the moment we arrived."

" That is a great rascal, and will soak that fool of ours through in an hour, while he, himself, will be as cool as a cucumber, and will bet, and win, with the steadiness of a judge. If he is not in league with the enemy, I'm a fool!"

" But, Horace, is there nothing we can do to meet our difficulties ? "

" Elizabeth, how easily you put the case, for a woman that thoroughly understands it—' difficulties!' that is no word for our circumstances. We are in *the fix* that nothing can ever set right. Our affairs are past extrication. There is no use in cloaking the matter from ourselves. You and I are forced to stare it in the face, and to watch for, and wait, and suffer, a fate we cannot avert. I have done with disguises and fictions with you. It is of no use hiding our feelings from each other. You are not one of those soft geese that a man is afraid to hurt, for fear you'd go off in hysterics. John must come to plain talk with you. He has carried too high a hand, and been far too imperious. I came to say something to you to-night, and it is this—whisper, come very close to me, for these walls are only wainscotted; there is nothing for John and me—for all your sakes,—but—I hope you'll bear it, Elizabeth, like what you are, a true-hearted, brave woman—it is our sole resource; we must do it, and that at once."

Breathless, the poor trembling Mrs. Fitzwalter

hung on his words, with quivering lips, and uttered, " What must it be ?   Oh, tell me, Horace ?"

And her heart beat in terror lest it should be some unheard of horror.

" I hate to break it to you," he said, " but it must be done—flight is our only hope !"

Mrs. Fitzwalter did not seem so very much surprised as might be expected.   She had some knowledge of the expedient.   It was not a very uncommon one; some of her country neighbours had already availed themselves of it, and that her husband's turn might come to require such a proceeding was not distant from her imagination.

" Is there any immediate reason for his absence," she said.

" Judge for yourself," replied her brother-in-law, handing her a letter.

While she read, the face of the strong, resolute woman became almost rigid, and she returned the document, and maintained a silence more expressive of her deep distress than any words could have been.

" He cannot go too soon, now," she groaned at last. " Oh, Horace, where is he ? perhaps taken ?   My children, my children !   Poor girls !   And that ill-reared boy! Oh, Horace, what must they do? What shall I do? I can't leave them, and yet must I not go with John?"

" No, indeed, Elizabeth, nothing of the kind! You must stay and keep possession. You are the first claimant on the property—jointures go before all debts. Whoever seizes, must first settle with you. Don't forego a halfpenny, there's nothing else for you and the children to live on."

"Horace, Horace! there is not even that, it is mortgaged these five years."

" Oh, woman! what do you tell me?"

" Just this—I gave it up when that Sullivan was so clamorous, and John raised as much on it as saved him, hitherto, from that claim."

"Fool! dolt! idiot! blunderer! and worse too, to cut the ground from under his family's feet. What made you consent? How dared you have forgotten your children's interest? This is, indeed, a pretty mess! I never for a moment counted on such a misfortune! It changes the whole colour of my plot. I calculated on your having that provision safe in hand, and thought of your paying my little score, and setting my 'corpus' at liberty,

K

that I might help you to hold out at Knocklash.
Now, that hope is cut off. John and I must go
together; and after hearing of his villany, I don't
care if I never saw his face."

"Stop, Horace, I hear his step!"

And at the moment, Mr. Fitzwalter entered the
room.

Although both his wife and his brother felt deeply
incensed against him, they were relieved to see him,
for both believed that the sub-sheriff had been leading him into a trap.

There was no disguise any longer necessary between
these three.

Mrs. Fitzwalter felt herself and her children out-
rageously injured, and she showed it, like a woman,
for she burst out into a tremendous passion.

Nothing that the two men could say pacified her.
She strode up and down the apartment in anguish of
mind, and vented her bitterness in hot, impassioned
words of wrath at her husband :—

"Begone," she cried, "leave us as you've made us
—beggars. Go, where we may see you no more! My
children and I will hide our heads in the Poor-house,

and your name will end—where it ought—among paupers! Oh!" she groaned, between her teeth, " to think that I, the daughter of a nobleman, should have mated my pride with such a race! It is not the loss of your wealth I am distracted at, it is the loss of your character. I no longer respect you, now that I know your dishonest pretences, and the flash, sham, and humbug in which we have lived. Why did you not tell *me*, your wife, the truth from the first? Why did you woo me with a lie, and use a credit you knew to be false, to deceive my relatives, and thus gain a bride from a rank above your own? Oh, John, my love was no question of money! You won it, and it was given in all honesty and good faith. I became yours, whether rich or poor, but, oh! not to be cheated and made a fool of. I could have begun the world with you as a humble farmer's wife *once*; but you've killed my better self, you've stifled my affections! I can't—I won't take disgrace, though I will take poverty—but it shall be alone. I'll struggle for my children—they are all the world to me!"

"Are they nothing to me, Elizabeth?" cried the

unhappy man. "I shall have to part with them and you, for no one knows how long—God help me! if no human being does."

And Mr. Fitzwalter wept like a child.

The sight of his tears somewhat mollified his wife's anger; and she paused in her vehemence, and seemed disposed to hold a more conciliatory tone.

"Well, what do you propose to do?" she said.

But words would not come from the now deeply affected man. He leaned his head on the table, and gave way completely to his emotions.

Horace Fitzwalter left the room at this crisis of the scene, and we will leave the miserable couple to their sorrowful privacy, while we follow him down stairs in the hotel, to an apartment of it, which was exclusively the domain of its hostess, Mrs. M'Swiney.

He approached this sanctuary through an entrance provided for the accommodation of persons who wanted an interview with their landlady, without going out to the front of the bar, which faced the principal entrance, and which was the usual audience chamber for the public.

A glass partition divided Mrs. M'Swiney's little sitting-room from the external office; but, from the inside snuggery, all the transactions outside were visible. It was near midnight, but being assize time the house was open later than usual. The High Sheriff being there, brought a good many who had business with him into the hall, and the barmaid was not idle, even then, for two men who had waited several hours for Mr. Fitzwalter, were taking drams to sustain their strength, under the inconvenience of his staying out so late.

Mrs. M'Swiney was also waiting impatiently for the same customer, to whom she felt it was due that the house should not be closed until he was in for the night.

She was sitting by her bright little fire, and arranging her head-gear, replacing her grand widow's cap, by a comfortable *bonnet-de-nuit*, when Horace Fitzwalter came in as unceremoniously as if he were one of the household. Mrs. M'Swiney was accustomed to his free and easy ways, and was not at all disturbed by his presence, as he drew a chair, and, placing himself next her, put his feet on the fender.

" Mr. Horace, when is your brother coming in, to let us all go to bed ? I'm glad it's not here he's drinking, for I've been sorry enough lately to see the sign of so much liquor on him, that used to be such a splendid, fine young man. He's very cut up this last year or so; but isn't she beautiful? and those lovely creatures of girls! My heart warmed to them, and they kissed me as if they knew me all along! I remember their mother, as slight and delicate as that eldest one, when she came here with her first baby—that boy that's such a trouble to them now. I'm distressed to think that there will be bother in that family; Master John is an awful wild fellow for his years. Oh, how his poor mamma cried when he was expelled from college that time!"

"Mrs. M'Swiney, I'm glad to hear you talk in this way about my unfortunate brother; you feel kindly towards us; indeed you always were a friend: I knew it since the time you used to box my ears for stealing tarts out of your store-room! Will you be a real friend in need *now?* Can I trust you? Are you able to keep a secret? Can you do a good turn, that will make us all your obliged servants for life?"

"Oh my, Mr. Horace! What can be the matter? How can I help you?"

"Do you know what these men are that are drinking outside at the counter?"

" Well, I think they are some of the Court-house jobbers, that want to secure employment from Mr. Fitzwalter."

" Nothing of the kind ! they are bailiffs, and when they serve him with the writ they have in their pockets, he'll be a prisoner for life."

" Then they never shall do it in this house, as sure as I'm in it," said Mrs. M'Swiney, and she passed quickly out into the bar.

Horace Fitzwalter sat down coolly, and watched her proceedings. A warm partisan was the landlady of "The Hibernia," and she had a strong tie to the Fitzwalter family. Her sympathies were highly excited for the present generation of it, from intimate knowledge of the affairs of the last one.

This arose from a source that she never mentioned, and her discreet silence secured an amount of good-will that might not have been accorded her had she sought it on other grounds. Mrs. M'Swiney's mother was nearly related to old Mr. Fitzwalter. They were brother and sister's children—" cousin Germans" she called the connexion.

John and Horace Fitzwalter knew this to be the case, and it formed a bond between them and the

hotel keeper; and though they did not acknowledge
it by any particular intimacy, they made it evident
that they felt it, and were on confidential terms with
her. On the present occasion, Mrs. M'Swiney was a
most useful ally. She manœuvred the bailiffs so
successfully, that the gentleman inside in her parlour
saw them go away in a state of royal content,—stupid
with drink, and charmed with a likeness of the
Queen, on the face of a new sovereign.

"Well done, old lady!" said her observer, " I
knew you could do it; but there's work upstairs for
your management."

And here Horace gave her an account of the scene
he had just witnessed in the drawing-room.

The practical mind of Mrs. M'Swiney suggested
immediately various modes of action. She and
Horace sat until it was nearly daylight, planning
and arranging the escape of the netted debtors.
Both brothers were in similar predicaments, owing
to the way in which one was dependent on the other,
and it was as necessary for the one to run from his
creditors as for the other. Bailiffs were watching for
both; it was only a question of time as to their incar-
ceration.

"What would stop *your* duns' mouths, Mr. Horace?" inquired Mrs. M'Swiney.

"Indeed, a hundred pounds would do it, for a while, at all events."

"Well, you shan't cut away for the want of that, this time. I'll lend it to you, and do you stay to help the poor woman and children over the mischief."

"Lend it!—why, my good old woman, I'm not fit to borrow twopence! I would not take a loan of sixpence from you, but I feel all the same obliged, and thankful to you, cousin Mac!"

"But you shall,—sure aren't you my own flesh and blood? but no matter about that—I'll get it back somehow, never you fear, and if I don't, why I have neither chick nor child belonging to me. But, come, I must set off this unfortunate creature upstairs; in the morning the dogs will start after him again."

Mrs. M'Swiney rose to the dignity of a great power, in the esteem of her crestfallen relations, that night. She came to the rescue; and her assistance enabled them to get through one of the knots, in which they were entangled. By her arrangement, in a few hours, Mr. Fitzwalter was safe on the high seas, in a ship bound for Lisbon. The vessel was a Portuguese schooner, trading in fruit, and its captain was a friend of the landlady of "The Hibernia." She happened to know that he was in the harbour, and that his ship was outward bound; and she herself conveyed the fugitive on board, and induced Captain Briario to give him a passage. When she was leaving Mr. Fitzwalter, she took a very impressive farewell of him.

"I must be plain with you," said she to him; "you deserve your fate richly, and I am very angry with you; God forgive you, and enable your friends to do so. Here are one hundred sovereigns for you, make them go as far as you can; don't make a beast of yourself with drink; write to me, and I'll manage for you to hear from your family, and that they, in return, shall hear from you."

With a convulsion of grief and penitence, the wretched man wrung her hand, and in a voice broken with sobs, promised to take her advice. At length, mastering his emotion, he gasped out his incoherent and characteristic thanks:

"May my son and my son's son remember my obligation to you, and may they acknowledge that our blood is akin, and that you stood well by your broken down cousin."

Mrs. M'Swiney finished her kind work and intervention that day, by bailing Mr. Horace Fitzwalter before the *locum tenens* of his brother, the absent High Sheriff, whose disappearance was not at all surprising to the "Sub," and who was good-natured enough to keep all suspicion off, by creating a rumour of "a fit in the night."

This intelligence was industriously circulated, and soon spread all over the country. The whole town of Kildine, including the judge, grand jury, and officials of the court-house, and, most important of all, the creditors of Mr. Fitzwalter, were kept in great excitement all day, by the announcement of the sudden and alarming seizure of the High Sheriff by apoplexy.

Dr. Green, a friendly physician, was in and out of "The Hibernia," every hour or so. Horace Fitzwalter went about with an air of unfeigned bewilderment, and his manner convinced the most anxious inquirer of the gravity of the case. The very servants of the hotel were deceived. Not one was allowed into the pretended sick-room. All offices necessary

for the sufferer, were supposed to be rendered by
Mrs. M'Swiney herself, assisted by the afflicted wife,
and her own confidential domestics. These latter
were, happily, trustworthy under such circumstances as their class generally is, in Ireland. The
device was quite after their heart, and they entered
on it *con amore*, and performed their parts to perfection, as they usually do in similar affairs.

The newspapers of the third day following Mr.
Fitzwalter's flight, contained a notice of his death,
in their obituary columns ; and, owing to his having
been a well-known personage, a few more particulars
than usual were furnished, and the statements were
well backed up by the rumours got up by the servants, who were adepts in the business of misleading
the public. There was at first some doubt as to
whether or not there would be a coroner's inquest; and
it was well known that if there were, no twelve men
in Ireland would have extorted a word from one of
these that would have thrown the least light upon
the case. There is a perfect science, known only to
the lower order of Irish, which reduces the process
of parrying legal inquiry to a regular system ; and
skill in it is honoured as something creditable

to the abilities of its possessor. To get off a witness table without having had a word of truth elicited, under the fire of a clever cross-examination, is an achievement which wins no ordinary fame.

There was some little regret expressed that an opportunity of gaining this, was not likely to be afforded on the present occasion. Mr. Fitzwalter's old coachman considered himself defrauded in a cruel manner. He had signalized himself more than once in a court of justice, and had an experience of the difficulties of puzzling counsel and judge, which was envied him by many an aspiring tactician, but he had never yet "sat on a body," and he had a strong desire to do so. There was what he considered a nice piece of manœuvring lost to his faculties, and he could not forego it without complaining.

"Now, Magrath, how can you go on with such talk," said Mrs. M'Swiney, "an inquest would be the ruin of us : 'twas with the height of management that I kept it off, and only that the coroner and I are such friends, and that I made it up to him, he would have had the business done."

"To be sure he would, and why not—dacent man ? Why for should he lose his guinea, and the docthor his guinea? and every one of us would have stood to them, and they'd get their own out of it, and no harm done to any one."

"Well, I'm surprised at you," replied the land-lady, "not to be glad to escape a bundle of lies."

"A bundle of lies is it? an' sure, any way, they'd be only *one bundle*, and I'd be swore to 'em, and I'd stick to 'em to me dying day, by vartue of my oath; but, now, a child might stagger me, any moment. The first time I have a sup in, it will all come out; but if I had the book kissed on it, it would make me as safe as the ground, an' I'd feel honest and respectable in me conscience."

"Oh, I see, you are afraid of yourself, but I am not a bit doubtful of you, nor of any of those that helped a master that never injured them, nor any one belonging to them."

"You may say that, Mrs. M'Swiney: he was no-body's enemy but his own, and I wish him luck all over the world; he'll come to no harm through me. You're sure you have the coroner under your thumb? I'd be onaisy any day these ten years to come. Oh, he's a purty boy that old Mr. Dunne! There was me brother six months in his grave, and he had

him up to look at, and all because the old fool of a
woman that laid him out let it slip how he came by
his death—as if it was any affair of hers, the prating
goose ! "

" What did he die of then, Magrath? was there
any discovery ? "

" He was shot, and we never took the bullet out
of him, and it was lead, and so there it was, my dear,
as large as life ; and him that did it swung for it, and
it was a burning shame, for we had him marked, and
we'd ha' given him what he gave, in our own good
time, with God's blessing."

Mrs. M'Swiney was as well aware as our reader,
that she was listening to sentiments that ought to
have thrilled her with horror, but all she felt about
them was *the ought*—such facts had ceased to do so.
Familiarity with such phases of vice had deadened her
sensibilities with regard to them.   Frequent contact
with the peculiarities of this class of Irish character is
extremely deteriorating in its effects. Though it may
not end in the utter obliteration of the sense of right,
it leads to the toleration of an amount of evil, that
injures the individual and the community at large.
A confused idea is often found to exist in minds

otherwise upright, that there is a rough virtue lying somewhere at the bottom of all this untruthfulness and scheming; and apologists tell us that it is "attachment," "honour," "pride," and other motives to which they think only a modulated degree of guilt can be ascribed; and with these they try to stifle down the reality into a more attractive picture than the naked sin would present. This bewilderment of preception constitutes the great difficulty of dealing with "the finest pisantry in the world," and it is one that seems to be quite as insuperable now, as it was two generations back. The little children of to-day manifest it in the same manner that their parents and ancestors did, and it is not a little remarkable, that it survives the education which was expected to put an end to it.

The conversation about the inquest between Mrs. M'Swiney and the coroner, did not terminate the matter. Mr. Dunne, it would seem, was not satisfied in his legal conscience, and could not rest as easily on his pillow as was desired by his friends.

A few days after all this danger was thought to be passed, this functionary called on Mr. Horace Fitzwalter, and mentioned the necessity for holding a formal enquiry into his brother's death.

"You know, my dear sir, how I am compelled to be strict in my official capacity. The absence of burial laws, or of any thing of that sort, throws an immense onus on me."

"I didn't know you felt it so keenly," replied Horace, "but of course you must do your duty. I don't oppose whatever the law is in the case. However, I thought that *you were fully satisfied* (this with emphasis) *as to the event which has happened*. Mrs. M'Swiney led me to suppose so."

"Oh yes, of course, I am personally, and that is everything. I must take care though to make my impression general, which I cannot do, unless I give it with the weight of my public seal. People will talk—aye are talking—we can't help them, you know, but we can prove them to be wrong, and this I'll do, don't fear me."

Fitzwalter was by no means sure of this, but he dare not betray his fear, and he was quite unable to read the meaning of the coroner's words, which he perceived had a *double entendre;* so he had recourse to the ready-witted landlady, who again came to his aid, in his new difficulty.

"I did not think, Mr. Dunne, that you would disrespect me and my house so much as to make any inquiry of this kind : it is casting a doubt on us all. Why what do you think we did with the man?" cried Mrs. M'Swiney in an indignant tone.

"Don't try to examine me, my good woman," replied the official, "I don't impute anything to you—"

"Nor to my customers?"

"No, nor to your customers. It is the respect I have for you all that makes me do this. The more straightforward, and open, and above-board, everything is, the better and more honourable for all parties, you, and they, and me. Indeed, this is a much called for proceeding; the High Sheriff dying illegally (I beg your pardon Mr. Fitzwalter)—inconveniently—his creditors demand it. *I* have no personal motive or interest in the matter."

Poor Horace's heart reached zero at this point. He was unprepared for such virtue, and did not know, in the least, how to deal with it, so he made a further effort to stave off the business, and enquired with a very nervous agitated voice, whether no arrangement could be made, which would reconcile the ends of justice, without the distressing formality of an inquest?

"Think of my sister-in-law and her afflictions. I do hope you will contrive to spare us, Mr. Dunne," he said, in a tone as near mendicancy as it was possible for him to assume.

But the incorruptible servant of the crown was inexorable. He and Mrs. M'Swiney went out of the room together, leaving Fitzwalter in a most unenviable state. He knew it was a case for strategy, but he loathed any more of that work, and was thoroughly disgusted at what he had done, and what he felt would have yet to be done.

"I wish we were all as well out of this land of shame as John. He has the best of it. What a life of deception and trickery is before us! I declare, I'm tempted to out with the truth, and get rid of the burden —it is fire and brimstone already. I only wonder that half the world is able to walk about here without displaying the blaze of the lower regions. Combustion— conflagration—must be the end of it: wherever will it begin? At the top of the tree, I hope, whoever is

the victor. The poor are not half so much to blame
as we; we deserve to suffer for our sins."

This soliloquy was scarcely over before a stentorian
voice was heard on the stairs calling—

" Horace Fitzwalter !"

It was the shout peculiar to the " Peeler," and it
was sufficiently familiar to Mr. Fitzwalter to announce
to him that the dreaded ordeal was at hand. He
mechanically obeyed it, rather relieved than otherwise, that the thing to be done, was to be done quickly.
The operation was hateful, baleful, revolting, and
not a little alarming in its consequences, and it took
some effort of nerve to face it. Taking up his hat,
and assuming his utmost courage, our friend de-
scended to the coffee-room, of which he found the
authorities had taken possession.

The inquest had begun, and that *it* smelt of tobacco-
smoke, was the first impression on the reluctant witness, as he entered the apartment, at the door of
which stood two policemen. These were respectful
enough, now that they were face to face with the
gentleman, and touched their hats as he approached.
He was about to ask a question as to the stage the
proceedings had arrived at, and the mode of arrange-

ment, but one of them cut the effort short by opening
the door and announcing—

" Misther Horace, sir," in the tone in which an
indulgent domestic might usher a scapegrace into
" the masther's" presence.

At the head of one of the tables sat the coroner,
and next him there was a young man, with a book in
his hand, who repeated the policeman's familiar words
mechanically :

" Misther Horace," and was about to proceed with
an accustomed formula, when he was abruptly
silenced.

" Hold your tongue," said Mr. Dunne, with a very
peremptory tone.

" I was coroner's clerk, sir, before I came here, sir,
and I know my business, sir."

"Oh, I have no doubt you know the county
Tipperary system, but we are more accurate here,
and you will have to fall into our customs. What
is your name, Mr. Fitzwalter?" said the superior,
in a very bland, reassuring tone, and, as Horace
thought, with the merest possible shade of a wink.
But this he *would not* see. In fact, the sight of
the Book had taken effect on him morally, and he

was going in for truth. The screw was on his conscience, and a blush would have been seen on his face,
if the deadly paleness of a strong resolution would
let it, for he was thoroughly and heartily ashamed
of the whole transaction, from beginning to end.
Prepared to speak, and to act, he answered solemnly—

"Horace Fitzwalter."

"You have no other name?" said the coroner,
enquiringly, as he wrote the reply in a book before
him.

"No."

"I'm glad of that. Two names give two tongues,
they say—equal to making a man a rogue. It is a
proverb in some language or other."

"Sir, I beg that there may be no joking on this
occasion, for I never was more decidedly averse to
humbug than I am at this minute."

"Don't take me up in that way, Mr. Fitzwalter,
I mean you no harm. Come, man, there's nothing
to trouble you in our little inquiry! Is there,
Doctor?" (And the technical administrator of the
law turned to the fireplace where the accommodating
medical attendant was standing.)

Dr. Green had his snuffbox in hand, and advancing

it confidentially to Horace, he began making a little conversation to reassure him.

"Mrs. M'Swiney was here this minute," he said. "'Pon my honour, that woman is a trump! She walked in, and said her say like a lawyer, and there was no more about it."

"How awfully I shall contradict her!" thought Horace; and he looked ruefully at the twelve men who were lounging about the room, every one smoking a long, white, clay pipe, under the soothing influence of which inquest was forgotten.

"Listen to me," said Mr. Dunne:—(" Take the book in your hand.) The evidence you will give in this inquest shall be the truth, the whole truth, and nothing but the truth, so help you God."

These words were sputtered, and muttered, in such a manner as to make them quite unintelligible.

It was impossible for Horace to follow them; but he reverently put the Gospels to his lips, and holding the volume in hand, awaited the momentous questions that he had reason to expect.

" Mrs. M'Swiney has just described to us—and her testimony has been very clearly borne out by those competent and respectable witnesses, the servants of your late brother—the causes and circumstances of his death.   We should require no further evidence, but as you, the next of kin, are eligible to be examined in this matter, we think it well, in order to satisfy the ends of justice, that you should add your sworn evidence to the confirmation of the others ; and these gentlemen will listen attentively, while I inform you what their allegations were, and require you to affirm them on oath.''

" Faix, that's the quarest way,'' broke in one of the jury.

" Silence, you unmannerly fellow,'' said the coroner. " How dare you interrupt me ? ''

" Why, then, haven't I a right ? ''

" No, sir, you have no rights but what I gave you, and I'll take them away again, I tell you ; who are you, pray ?   This gentleman, Horace Fitzwalter, Esq., swears that every word uttered by Mrs. M'Swiney, in your hearing, was the truth, the whole truth, and nothing but the truth ; and this closes the evidence on the death.   The inquest is over.   I dismiss you, gentlemen.''

This was easier said than done apparently, for "the *gentlemen*'' had a general idea that they were summoned for the purpose of " sitting on a body," and of that privilege they were determined not to be cheated. They discussed the matter in little groups, in low grumbling tones. The smouldering embers assumed the aspect of a fitful unextinguished fire, which had still a considerable quantity of combustible material under its power. Short, gleaming blazes shot up in the form of such words as these :—

" Ne'er a one of 'em saw him dead, and who swore he died ? "

" Oughtn't we see the body—lay an eye on it —or touch it ? sure this is no way to sit on it—it should be to the fore, or something belonging to it."

" The docthor told us nothin'."

" An' what he did, we don't believe."

" 'Twas the coroner himself told us all about it."

" Sure, it was—never a word he let wan of 'em say, nor a question did he ask."

" Up and tell him so," said one of the party.

Thereupon an elderly man—removing his pipe from his mouth, taking off his hat, and smoothing his hair down on his brow with his hand, which he passed all over his face, as if to compose his features into a legal condition, with a respectful air, said—

"If it's plazing to your worship, we want to sit upon the body?"

"What for, my man?" said Mr. Dunne, who had risen by this time from his seat, and had joined the doctor on the hearth-rug.

". That's what we come for, your reverence."

"Can we oblige this man, Doctor?"

"Well—" said the gentleman appealed to, "that is as it may be. I don't recommend it, and I won't say what the result of it would be, under the payment of £1 a piece, from each of the jurors to whom I give my opinion. If they will have it on those terms, I shall be very happy to oblige them; but I am not bound to inform every individual one of them how long he would be likely to live after coming in contact with the most hypernatural parallelogrammatical posthumous spectacle that it was ever my duty, in the whole course of my professional career, to encounter."

"Then, you says it would be dangerous, your honour?"

"I *imply* it—I *say* nothing."

At this crisis, one of the jury summoned an amount of courage, that seemed to have forsaken the rest of

the august body, and, with the air of a man determined
to do or die, he began drawing up his coat-sleeves,
and thundered out—

" *I'll* see it, or I'll know why ? "

" Clear the room," said the coroner, with a voice
that summoned to his aid such a body of policemen,
that the twelve anxious inquirers were soon ejected
from the apartment, and Horace found himself face
to face with the coroner and doctor, who were in
broad ecstacies of fun, while the clerk, with a sympathetic leer, was gathering up the documentary evidence of " the Inquest."

CHAPTER II.

THE debts of an Irish gentleman of the old school were never incumbrances to himself, whatever they may have been to his creditors. He inherited some, and he created others.

The first were to his mind the gloomy ghosts of a former *régime*, and he knew he was born to share the family property with them. That they existed, he was perfectly well aware, but where or how, he resolutely ignored. They might do their best, and he would do his best, to get satisfaction out of the unfortunate inheritance; and the struggle generally resulted in both claims remaining unsatisfied.

As to the contracting of similar liabilities on his own account, he had a strong sense of duty about it; which was, that he conceived he owed it to posterity to endow it, as he had been endowed; and so he took a certain pride in adding to the accumulating heap of debts; and at the close of his tenure of the family property, he surrendered his account, with the most impartial disregard of the past, or of the future.

It cannot be said that he benefited himself, for he carried nothing away with him, and it is due to his memory to say, that, to the end of his days, a quiet conscience was reputed to be his constant companion.

An abiding conviction supported him, under all opposing sentiments—viz., that "life interest" was no ownership, and that no private advantage, except the power of credit, was derivable from the privilege of possession for this restricted period. "The *Family* property" was a real idea to his mind, and the rights of heirship had no meaning to him besides the temporary use of all they could make enjoyable out of the estate, of which they had the present control.

A sucession of generations, that could not see why they should pay their predecessors' debts, or for what reason they should not incur the same for themselves, brought up the totals of those notorious items in the Irish domestic economy, to an enormous figure.

Nothing short of a direct and special intervention— a disturbance of the usual course of events—subverting and preventing the continuance of matters in their ordinary routine, could have cut short the process by which this large numerical statement was being rapidly increased. This the famine of 1847 did, and did effectually. It proclaimed the dilemma to the world, and made the law ashamed, under which such misrule could endure. The crown of England became vice-owner of all Ireland for the nonce, and performed, in real life, that which its standard of justice has so long presented *en tableau*. The disputed bone was rescued from the combatants, and the honour of statesmanship vindicated, by the humane and honest institution of the Incumbered Estates Court.

This measure did not approve itself instantaneously to the whole Irish community. Only the sentient, and really suffering portion of it, recognized its value, and those were the creditors. They had had no compensating enjoyment in the recent state of affairs, to dull their apprehension of rectitude, and they immediately applauded the Act, and appealed to it, as their deliverance and protection.

No one found it so difficult to realize the applicability of the new code to his circumstances, as the subject of the incumbrances. He neither could, nor would, see the benefit of it to him; he left this to the opposite party to discover, and to use, the remedy it offered. There was a general rush of the creditor class to the opened way of salvation. It besieged the commissioners, and the amount of petitions to them was such as to fill the public mind with amazement.

The patient endurance of the debtor, under the pressure of his "charges," and the systematic process by which the perpetuation of these charges was secured—their co-existence and cotemporaneousness, with all and every one of the successive holders of the shadows of the estates, while they clung like burrs to the substance, were nothing short of the marvellous, to men who understand "I promise to pay," in the Bank of England sense of the engagement.

It was truly surprising how both parties could have stuck so long to their plans. Mutual interest could alone account for it; and, without doubt, this was the original character of the agreement. But it, like all other mundane arrangements, was subject to change and chance, and these came on it in a moment. Suddenly the horizon of credit was overcast by the clouds of difficulty, and down came pell mell the shower of bankruptcy. From time immemorial the landlords of Ireland had been living well, and paying the interest of their debts off their lands punctually; but when the famine came, the condition in which this was possible was over. By one blow, they were reduced to a state in which they could do neither one nor the other. The peaceful bond that had tied them and the trading section of the community together was broken; and that controversy set in which ended in the entire severance of their connection. The power of sale replaced the awkward necessity for flight, or concealment, which were the ordinary resources of unfortunate owners, whose properties were overcharged.

This relief, however, did not occur until long after Mr. Fitzwalter's pretended demise. The scheme by which this artifice was carried out was but a shallow device. After a year or so, no one believed in his death, and, in time, it was actually known to be a fiction. Credible witnesses were found to prove his being alive; but the facilities for eluding pursuit were so great in those days that he could not be laid hands on.

Mrs. Fitzwalter, Mr. Horace, the Misses Fitz-

walter, and the "young masther," Mr. John, who
was the heir apparent, and in possession, resided in
the old pile of building, that was once the grand
mansion of the Fitzwalter family. For years, during the occupancy of four generations, the house had
been slowly and gradually giving way to the progress of decay, without any resistance being offered
by the usual repairing forces. The lands, likewise,
presented a perfect picture of an incumbered estate.
They and the house represented the facts of the
case. No words could tell more plainly the true
history of their condition and circumstances, than
their appearance indicated. They showed the
mournful state of affairs, that was too common all
over Ireland— the anomaly that made that fertile
country a desert—the presence of the root of bitterness, that, planted in selfishness, was springing up
in misery, and overspreading its fair face with the
evil of pauperization! The lands and house were
evidence, and told all the tale at a glance! On them
it was written, ·in legible characters, that the man
and the soil were being divorced.

The Fitzwalters had been for a long time out-
running their powers. They had spent, until there

was no more to spend. The resource of mortgaging was exhausted. They had done this heavily, elaborately, and intricately. Their affairs were in such an involved condition, that they had long past the comprehension of the family intelligence, and it declined to exercise itself in extricating the subject from its confusion and entanglement. The persons we have enumerated as living on the estate, held themselves secure in their incompetency from all clamorous creditors; and, in virtue of the legal difficulties that beset any meddling with them, they succeeded in obtaining almost a perfect immunity from annoyance.

The mortgagees could do nothing to compel any of the five forthcoming members of the family to answer for the absent principal. They could not accept the death of Mr. Fitzwalter as a fact, and take measures accordingly, without incurring the risk of his return, and defeating all their plans for compromise or settlement. They were in a dilemma, and it was the interest of the *locum tenens* to keep them so; their mistification was his opportunity, and he took advantage of it.

The appearance of Mr. Fitzwalter in his old haunts,

and the disappearance of members of the family from Knocklash House, at different times, were subjects for many romantic tales; and the very fact of a legendary interest growing up round the household protected it from intrusion.

To the tenantry, far and near, the ladies and gentlemen in trouble were martyrs, and their cause was so warmly espoused by them, that nothing but the sight of armed authority made them pay their rents to the receiver, set over the property by the Court of Chancery, in favour of the creditors.

As long as ever the farmers on the Knocklash estate had them to give, the landlord's family felt no want of the common necessaries of life. Substantial kindness was heaped on them; meal, butter, bacon, and potatoes, came in most plentifully, and they were amply provided for in a rough way.

Mrs. Fitzwalter sadly missed the refinements and delicacies of her early days. She fell into a low sort of moaning way, and went about in helpless misery, becoming daily less and less ladylike, and finally deteriorating into a whining old woman, always recounting her former splendours, and repining at her lot, and its woes.

When ten years had passed over her head, no one could have recognised in her the beautiful, elegant creature that had been the admiration of the neighbourhood. It preyed on her mind, that she had united in the mean fraud which was perpetrated on her husband's creditors; and in her imbecility Mrs. Fitzwalter perpetually upbraided her brother-in-law and her children, with having induced her to join them in their deception. Her weak-mindedness rendered her unable to see where her own accountability began, and she continually charged them with being the cause of all the misery she was enduring.

The state of almost fatuity to which she was reduced, was the greatest trial her daughters had to encounter.

They took no blame whatever to themselves on the subject of their father's concealment. Their impressions connected with it were, that the proceeding was one for which no other alternative existed; and they expended all the love of children, and all the intense sympathy of enthusiasm on the fugitive.

An interview with him was purchased with any amount of self-sacrifice, and his occasional visits to them were planned and contrived with an earnest-

ness of love, and an infinity of skill, worthy of a
nobler cause. Towards Uncle Horace a profound
regard was felt by both nieces. He was all in all to
them—replaced father, mother, brother, and all.
Alas! that he should have had to supply the latter
relative's deficiencies!

John Fitzwalter was anything but a comfort to his
sisters. When the pressure of the family calamity
came on him he gave way to every bad passion that
rose up within him, and became abusive to his mother,
uncle, and sisters; and told them, that if once he were
really and truly in possession of the place, they should
quit it; and his conduct and language were so unruly
and menacing, that they were obliged to fall back
more decidedly on the "mystery," than they should
have done, had he been a person of another sort.

It was, in fact, beneficial to them that Mr. Fitzwalter's existence should be supposed, and they
allowed the suspicion to circulate with less show of
contradiction than would have been necessary, if
they had been really anxious to complete their fraud,
and put the young man into possession of the inheritance.

The act of deception was no sooner committed,

than they perceived its error; for immediately on the establishment of his power, John Fitzwalter began to use it for evil. The vicious propensities that had caused him to be expelled from Trinity College, grew with his growth, and strengthened with his strength.

While ever his mother had money, he extorted it from her, and when no more was to be had at home, he besieged all his friends and acquaintances, begging and coaxing it from them, and then spending it on indulgences of the lowest kind. Mrs. M'Swiney was especially troubled by him. He would go and live at her expense, make the freest use of her establishment, and seemed to think it his right and privilege to do so.

She was most kind and uncomplaining, and often got him out of scrapes and difficulties, into which his own wildness, and his bad associates brought him. Not unfrequently she paid his debts, and as often replenished his stock of clothing, and sent him home to his family with gifts, and good advice.

Still, he returned on her hands, got into renewed troubles, and pursued the old mischievous courses, ending, sometimes, with feigned repentance, delusive tears, and ill-founded promises of amendment. He thus betrayed her good nature over and over again into a pernicious exercise of its inexhaustible fund of charity.

Poor Mrs. M'Swiney had cause to regret the dark night's work she did for her grand relations. The connection was, thenceforth, a continual source of pain and vexation to her. John Fitzwalter often kept her in a ferment of anxiety and trouble with his pranks, and Will-o'-the-wisp-like vagaries. He could never be calculated on.

Sometimes when she believed him safe at Knocklash, he would be brought to her, perhaps at night, by a watchman, who found him, beastly drunk in the streets, and his apparel so shabby and dirty, that her very servants objected to his company. Then she would communicate with Mr. Horace, who could only philosophise in return, and suppose that, "when a gentleman is out of his own road, he has to scramble through muddy ditches."

The peasantry, with a fine sense of the incongruity of the "young masther's conduct," condoled very warmly and kindly with "the poor misthriss, and the young cratheres of girls," but it was

very humiliating to the objects of their commisera-
tion. The pride of the ladies was sorely and keenly
hurt by the meanness of their brother, and his complete moral degradation, much more so than by Uncle
Horace's painful struggles to farm their fields, in
order to support the household.

This undertaking of Mr. Horace Fitzwalter's did
equal honour to his mental abilities and kind disposition. The attempt to provide for his own wants was
never contemplated in his early education. He was a
man entirely trained to the theory and practice of idleness! For thirty years of his life he had consistently
followed it as his mode of living; and there was
immense difficulty in his endeavouring to do anything else. This Catherine and Margaret Fitzwalter
fully appreciated, and esteemed his energy accordingly.

He was beginning to take heartily to his work,
and was overcoming the obstacles with which his
habits beset him, when the potato blight occurred.
Poor Uncle Horace! He gave way altogether when
no crops, no money, and no help from neighbours
were to be had.

Oh, the mournful walks through the fields that he

and his nieces used to take at this time. The rotting
crops, the sickening smell of *the disease*, the wailing
cry of the starving and dying beggars that they
heard at every turn they took!

When matters came to this pass out of doors,
the whole party stayed within; and, for some
weeks, the Fitzwalter family endured positive, real
hunger.

Their food was confined to the universal "Ingy
male," and a little salt was all they had to season it.
Their only servant was a nurse, who had volunteered
to share their broken fortunes, and who went, from
time to time, to the little town of Litton to buy
provisions. She carried with her, on each journey,
some article of dress or furniture, by the sale of
which, the means of purchasing even the most
miserable sort of diet were procured!

This state of things could not long hold out. A
very little of it brought Mr. John to his senses.
With a resolute air he walked out one morning, and
was not heard of for some days. A letter was then
received from him, dated "Kildine Barracks," and
it contained the news that he had enlisted in the
—th regiment of foot, and was bound for India.

It was with unfeigned pleasure that Horace Fitzwalter heard this.   He˜ and the girls were inexpressibly relieved by it, and believed that John had
done the very wisest and best act under the circumstances.

"Now, Uncle," said Catherine, " I must be allowed
to do something.   I can teach small children very
well.   Mrs. M'Swiney is looking for a situation for
me, and if I can get £20 a year, you'll see what I
can do with it."

This subject had been often canvassed between
them, but was always cut short by a decided nega-
tive from the distressed uncle.   His opposition, however, got weaker, day by day.

Mrs. Fitzwalter's mental malady was becoming
very trying.   The necessity for placing her in some
suitable asylum, was increasingly apparent; and the
means of doing so, could only be obtained by some
such effort on the part of one of the family, as
Catherine proposed to make.

But what would £20 a-year be towards this object?   It was only half of what would be required,
as Mr. Fitzwalter ascertained; and yet, it was all that

the most sanguine could hope that Miss Fitzwalter's best services would obtain.

There were hundreds offering for every employment open to women. The superabundance of the "reduced-lady" class was the social feature of the day.

Men of broken fortunes thronged into the ranks of the working classes and were able to provide for themselves, in some manner or other, more easily than this poor, helpless section of females.

Governesses were to be had for their food, and gifts of the humblest clothing. Four pounds per annum was their maximum salary, and even the market for this labour was choked.

Servants, that is to say, regularly trained domestic workers, were scarce. Women willing to go to homely, household drudgery, were rare enough to command their wages, for they had a certain demand to supply, and had many resources; while these unhappy "ladies," with their pride and prejudices, were unprepared for teaching, and unwilling to do menial services.

Mrs. M'Swiney could not help poor Catherine

Fitzwalter. No one wanted " a young *lady* to take charge of little children."

"Nursery maids, who could wash the rooms, and get up fine linen," were what most people required. " Surely I can do that; and I will most gladly," wrote the humbled girl to her friend in Kildine; and, pending some arrangements that Mrs. M'Swiney was making, to provide her with such a situation, she and her sister occupied themselves in making some crochet collars, of which the nurse brought them the pattern from Litton, and the information that if they could make them well, they should get four shillings a piece for them.

This needlework employment exactly suited the taste of Catherine and Margaret Fitzwalter, and a little practice brought them on to do it beautifully. They had their mother's old lace for a model, and out of its graceful forms they made exquisite patterns.

The efforts of their skill surprised the dealer in the collars, and for some time he paid the nurse whatever price she asked for their work; but, to their great surprise, as it increased in quantity, it fell in value; and at last, he began to require it at a very low rate.

" Is it your daughter makes this ?" said he, one day.

" What need you care," she replied, " as long as you gets what you wants."

" I'll be bound it's no common woman makes it, for it's beyond what they'd think of," said the trader, " and it is a pity but they'd keep up to the mark, and give us a good supply."

" Oh, don't fear them that works, but they'll keep up," the nurse answered. " It's yourself that falls off. See how you cuts me down of the payment every time, on one excuse or other."

" I'm sorry for it, but I cannot help doing it, my good woman. The shapes and sizes are mostly not right, and anything ever so fine and nice, if it isn't in the fashion, won't sell for me at all. Now, I'm giving you six shillings for that, and may be some day I'll have to sell it for three myself."

After this conversation, the nurse had a shrewd suspicion, that the young ladies were not sending their goods to the best market, and she communicated to them what she thought.

" Send one of these pretty collars to Mrs. M'Swiney, and she'll find out the truth for you, is my advice," said this sage friend; and it was in fol-

lowing it that the Misses Fitzwalter formed their connection with the Kildine Lace School. Mrs.
M'Swiney discovered for them its advantages, and
applicability to their case; and it was at her expense that Catherine Fitzwalter passed a week learning the way to fall into its peculiar system.

On her return to Knocklash, she and her sister
gathered a number of little girls together, and began
to instruct them in the art of making " Irish Point
Lace."

Their productions were most admirable—perfect
studies from the antique laces; and the style became
so fashionable, that the Knocklash School could not
make goods fast enough for the trade, which steadily
increased, and in three years time kept four hundred
hands in constant work !

During this period, the profits of their industry
enabled the Misses Fitzwalter to make their unhappy
mother tolerably comfortable, and their home assumed a more habitable appearance.

The nurse, and a " labouring boy," kept matters,
in-doors and out-doors, in some kind of order; and
some repairs interrupted, in a slight degree, the
decay of the old place.

The few neighbours that remained, remarked the improvement in the establishment; but none were intimate enough with its concerns to know how it was brought about. The silent working of the school, however, told on the district, and its value was well known to the recipients of its benefits.

A factory, with all its advantages, was rising in the midst of the ruined agriculturists! The employers were growing rich, and the employed were well paid, and were being shown the excellent road to independence and wealth. The success that attended the lace work at Knocklash, was altogether owing to the artistic accomplishments of the ladies that undertook the making of it.

They had genius, cultivation, and manipulatory skill; and they united to these intense industry. The Kildine school supplied them with directions as to shapes and styles suitable for the fashionable world, it sold their goods for them, and sent them orders.

This aid relieved them of the trouble of attending to the commercial business, necessarily connected with their employment, and left them at liberty to devote their whole attention to perfecting the manu-

facture they had in hand. Besides, it secured them
—that which they earnestly desired—thorough
privacy in their working life.

The anxiety to preserve this was their sole weakness ; and it was by no means a singular one then in
Ireland. It was the peculiarity of the class to which
the Fitzwalters belonged ; and among the changes
that class has undergone of late years, must be
reckoned as one, and not the least important either,
that this distinguishing trait is obliterated.

Irish ladies have set aside for ever the folly that
tied and bound their faculties, on the subject of
industry, before the extraordinary social occurrences
of the period to which we refer. But, they certainly
had a severe struggle for this freedom ; starvation itself was easier to them, than the *confession* of *need*, to
earn bread.

And even when that Rubicon was crossed, the
word " employment " said, and " remuneration "
hinted at, there still remained to be overcome the
grievous difficulty of separating the idea of " degradation " from " work."

Work intellectual—teaching for instance—might
be tolerable ; but, alas ! for *all* sorts of *real work*, they

were generally totally unfit; and as for work domestic, or work commercial—"business"—they had a profound disrelish for them all.

The latter was their notion of debasement, and utter loss of caste and hope; it was condemnation to low associates—vulgar modes of living—and celibacy!

With these prepossessions, it is no wonder that anything like trading was approached with reluctance; and such impressions, born and bred in people, are not to be abolished at a moment's warning. The Kildine school undertook to meet the difficulties of this class, not by reasoning with the mistaken "ladies," nor by propounding theories as to female employment; but by confining itself to simply encouraging them, with practical demonstrations of the advantages to be derived from the lace business, and by affording them every facility to enter it, with as few trials to their feelings as possible.

No publicity whatever was given to any of its movements, beyond the circulation of information necessary to secure a trade, and make a connection of workers on the one hand, and customers on the other.

N

This plan succeeded in doing more than was expected, for, through its instrumentality, several "ladies," women of great skill in needlework and of artistic cultivation, really did enter on regular "business" occupation, and opened communication for themselves with warehouses, and carried on lucrative commercial employments.

The Misses Fitzwalter were among the first and best of the fruits of this institution. The article they made obtained a high character in the market, and realized good prices for some years.

Their labour force was singularly available. No competition existed for the work of the little hands they trained. They had the field to themselves, and were able to produce excellent goods at a low rate.

This great advantage they turned to a very good account, and it was a great pleasure to see the energy and zeal they displayed in pursuits so different from those to which they had been accustomed. Their constant application to the duties they undertook was testified by the results it attained.

They worked with a will, a power, and an object, and soon felt that there was a dignity attached to honest labour. Industry took root in their minds, and its growth was exhibited in the fact that they learned to respect it. From the time that they began to feel the pecuniary benefits of their exertions, a wonderful change took place in their manner, even with regard to the agency, through which they had accomplished so much.

The Misses Fitzwalter were not ashamed after a while to visit the Kildine school, and to speak openly there of the money they were making in the despised position of "tradeswomen." Their example was one of the best modes of inculcating the principles the school proposed to set forth; and those ladies and others, thus founded an enduring school of morals for their countrywomen, that will long survive the memory of the initiative one, held in the small unpretending house, in a back street of the old county town.

While Catherine and Margaret Fitzwalter were working away at their lace manufacture, Uncle Horace was not idle. He obtained, by great importunity, and much begging and entreating of former friends, a small appointment in a government office in Dublin; to which place he removed, about the same time that the girls began to be interested in their industrial employment.

As soon as he could, he made arrangements to place Mrs. Fitzwalter in an asylum, and he urged his nieces to accept a share of the pittance to which the payment for his sister-in-law reduced his salary, and to come and live with him.

This they resolutely refused to do. They had taken *to work*, and they liked it; and were determined to be independent, and to give the labour they had adopted a fair trial.

In almost utter seclusion, these devoted women worked on. Companionship and sympathy in their struggle, they had none. Their neighbourhood became strangely emptied of all the society that was its boast in their youth.

The famine had crushed into utter ruin all the tottering fortunes left by heedless past generations, and it had removed to distant scenes the owners of domains which they could no longer occupy. Many of the surrounding estates were sold under the "courts," to men of the working farmer, or tradesman class, and these successors of the ruined gentry were not reckoned as possible associates.

The clergy of the district looked on the Misses

Fitzwalter's deeds with surprise, mingled with other feelings.

Religion is not always combined with common-sense, and when it stands thus alone, it is often a serious impediment to good and useful undertakings.

It is *the unpardonable sin* in the opinion of many good people, that children should ever learn anything but that " they have souls, and how to save them;" and these folks conceive that the sole duty that they owe to the poor, consists in cultivating their *religious* sentiments. This is all that many truly Christian persons will undertake to do for them, and they seem to be under the impression that industry comes by nature to the lower classes. There never was a more silly delusion than this, nor a more injurious one as regards the Irish poor, with whom the case is the very reverse. In them the religious element predominates, while the industrial is non-existent. They want no incentive to neglect the one for the other, and but too readily adopt any views which depreciate secular labour, and exalt unduly the temper of mind that disregards temporal considerations. Keenly alive to their spiritual concerns, they pursue them as their first and chief object, as to which all else is unimportant; and this is their noblest characteristic. It at once elevates them from the common level of grovelling, craving beggars, and gives their cry a claim which every Christian heart must admit with warm sympathy.

Religion—a beautiful wild scheme for the subjection of the flesh to the spirit—is natural to the Irish Celt, and Popery develops this peculiarity most exquisitely, by twining it through the infinite ramifications of its superstitions, thereby forming a framework of picturesque piety, which is most sublime and devotional in its aspect. There is something touching and delightful in the fact that mention of the future state, and allusion to our personal interest in it, are always welcome to the Irish poor. To them the unseen is present in the strong grasp of faith, and with them the *one thing needful* outweighs all other considerations. While we yield to no one in anxiety for their deliverance from error, and for their instruction in the plain, simple truths of Holy Scripture, we entirely dissent from the views of those who hold back from schools which are undertaken for the sole purpose of teaching industry. This lawful object is most conveniently done without attempting to convey *religious* information through the same machinery; and there is no doubt that the admixture has been a source of much mischief in Ireland.

When industrial schools were arising there, and looking for pecuniary aid, it was found that the wealthy, benevolent, and *pious* public would not subscribe to them, unless assured that they should be used as vehicles for introducing instruction in certain doctrines. The plain Christian principle of their foundation was not sufficiently recognized, nor the powerful nature of the moral agency they set up fully understood. It was not thought possible to benefit the Irish poor without controverting their Romish dogma, and no one seemed to see that there was a work to be done for their bodies, which has no connection whatever with the ministry directed to the soul and its immortal welfare. Hence almost all industrial schools were sectarian in their character, and any that boldly asserted neutrality were " contraband of war," in a country delivered over to religious belligerents.

This fact was eminently apparent in the opposition

which some lace schools experienced, and that of the Misses Fitzwalter formed no exception.

The rector of their parish earnestly conjured them to have the Bible taught to their pupils, and when they declined to follow his advice, he stigmatized the work as *unchristian*, and preached it down with might and main.

The priest objected to the Roman Catholic children learning to crochet from Protestant ladies, for fear that the stitches might convey heresy; and the partisans of both these gentlemen warmly exerted themselves to prevent the spread of this species of industry in the neighbourhood.

Opposition was met with in nearly every quarter. With some show of reason, the outcry was raised, that such employment rendered women undomestic, gave them too much freedom from pecuniary restraint, and by the independent possession of money, put them into temptation; in fact tended to their moral injury.

"See. how the girls are dressed out," said such objectors, "and what sums of money they have running through their fingers."

It was literally true that they had very large

wages, and that some were disposed to squander their earnings very inconsiderately; but it should be remembered, that this complaint of improvidence was the result of the state of ignorance in which the employment found them, and ought not, in fairness, to have been laid to the charge of the nature of the occupation.

The Misses Fitzwalter steered their way through these adverse currents, and bravely defended their conduct; but their success in argument was not so great as in trade. It was hard to convince the pious of their consistency as professors of religion, while they persisted in carrying out such "godless" doings as having schools that did not convey Scriptural instruction!

But they took no notice of their opponents, and worked along content with the approval of their own consciences, and gratified with the sight of the good that they were doing to their distressed neighbours.

They made no pretence, however, that their undertaking was a purely benevolent one; on the contrary, they made it distinctly evident that they were working for their own benefit, and were endeavouring to make money for themselves; and this avowal

was specially creditable to them, because many, with
equal necessity, scorned such efforts. Some who
were making them carefully concealed their object
under a show of charity, and tried to save their
gentility by resorting to a meanness which made
them the accepters, instead of the donors, of eleemosy-
nary assistance.

The Misses Fitzwalter were very different from such
people—petty little workers, who only strove to
obtain the gratification of small wants in the way of
luxuries in dress and clothing, and trifling indul-
gencies, the remnants of a state of idleness and ease
to which they had never been truly entitled. The
ladies of Knocklash had higher motives and more
elevating purposes. They toiled with an undaunted
resolution.

It was an idea, borne out in every motion of their
fingers. The lace they made revealed it, in the dash-
ing freedom of its graceful figures, their curves and
waving foliage, and the tracery that labyrinthed the
groundwork of its lovely flowers. It was the anxious
aspiration of these hearts to beat free from debt
and dishonour, which were dispiriting their lives, and
depriving them of a possession which they coveted

—not the material inheritance of the landed estate of the proud Fitzwalters—(that they could have relinquished)—but a fair fame cleansed from the soil of deceit and fraud.

CHAPTER III.

EARLY in the spring of 1856, Miss Fitzwalter came to the Kildine school, and brought with her a large stock of lace, which she told the superintendent she must sell at once ; and she requested that the London agent should be directed to dispose of it for cash, at the best price he could get.

She was warned that a very heavy discount would be deducted by any firm who would buy such a quantity; and the difficulty and disadvantage of forcing a sale, was very clearly set before her. But she was resolute in her purpose; there was no turning her from it; she seemed to have some special object in view, that made further argument useless. The goods were at hand—had been brought to the door by a countryman, who had accompanied Miss Fitzwalter; and, according to her direction, the same man carried the box that contained them into the usual sorting and examining office of the school.

The opening of the box, and the inspection of the lace, was being carried on in the ordinary manner; and the invoicing, and other arrangements connected with its reception, were being done, when it was remarked, that the porter did not leave the room, as might have been expected, at the conclusion of his part of the business.

On the contrary, he took a chair. and drew near the fire, and with the ease of a person utterly regardless of surrounding circumstances, he made himself as comfortable as he could, and, with his back to the occupants of the apartment, sat and warmed himself with the greatest composure.

The superintendent, who was present, was not a little surprised at his conduct, and looked at Miss Fitzwalter for an explanation.

Extraordinary embarrassment overspread her countenance, as she said—

"Please let him stay there, Miss O'Brien, he is very ill, and I want to find him a lodging. Can you help me?"

As she spoke she expressed by signs to the super-

intendent, that the presence of other parties in the
room, prevented her from being more explicit. There
was such interest and sympathy felt for the Misses
Fitzwalter by the managers of the establishment,
that Miss O'Brien instinctively felt her aid was
required by the lady, in some urgent manner, so she
immediately made an excuse for sending all the assis-
tants from the room, and then most cordially offered
her services.

There was no half confidence between Miss Fitzwalter and her friends at the Kildine school; she
knew that they were worthy to be trusted, with even
a secret as important as hers was; and she relied
that, in this hour of her extremity, her best help
would come from the same source whence she had
already derived so many benefits.

"Miss O'Brien," she whispered, giving at the
same time a cautious glance round the apartment;
"this is my father. He is sick. I want a home for
him and myself. We must have good airy accommodation, in some respectable house. Do you know
of one?"

"Yes, I think so, but I can make sure, in a few
minutes," replied the superintendent, and she quickly

went upstairs to the department of the school where
the educated portion of the workers were engaged in
composing patterns.

One of these at once agreed to receive the lodgers,
and went home to prepare for them.

When Miss O'Brien returned to the office, the *ci-
devant* countryman had become quite altered in appearance. A large military cloak enveloped his tall,
spare figure, and his hat was exchanged for a gentlemanly beaver; he had put on a pair of gloves, and no
longer seemed to be the rough peasant that had
entered the room a short time ago, bearing a great
load. It was also very evident that he could not have
been long acting as porter, for his looks denied that
he had the power of carrying any great weight, much
less a burden such as he was supposed to have brought.

He was, apparently, very weak, and suffering.
He stood up as the superintendent entered, and tried
to give her the courtly bow of the old school, raising
his hat, and trying to address her in the style of his
former polished manners; but strength failed him,
and he sank down on the chair exhausted by the
effort, and affected to tears both by his weakness and
the novelty of his position.

His daughter used every loving mode of restoring his self-possession, and Miss O'Brien tried to reassure him by her cheerful, friendly greeting, and the kind attentions she showed him.

A car was procured, and the father and daughter went away in it to the apartments provided for them.

For some days Miss O'Brien did not think it right to intrude on their privacy ; but when a note came asking her to go to them, she instantly complied.

The scene that was taking place on her arrival at the lodgings was at once awfully solemn, and intensely interesting, and curious.

The fact was now patent : all the town knew it. Mr. Fitzwalter, who had *not died* at the " Hibernia " some years ago, was now, really and truly, in the act of dying,—*in extremis*, at that moment—moribund, while the law was at length taking cognizance of his life !   Strange anomaly, the proof of existence was being sought in the presence of death !

A number of persons were assembled in the chamber, where lay the unconscious form of the well-remembered *late* John Fitzwalter, Esq.

Miss Fitzwalter had summoned all whom it might

concern to know the truth of this singular case, to witness the fact that her father was alive, and, lo, they came to behold his death !

Dr. Green was not there; Mrs. M'Swiney was not there; the former sub-sheriff was not there. All these three had gone to render their account of their common fraud. Nor were the wife, the brother, nor the son of the departing man around his bed.

Instead of these familiar and long unseen faces, there were those of shrewd, long-headed, sagacious men, learned in legal subtleties, and wise in detecting tricks and disguises. The creditors of the Fitzwalter estate were there, either personally or by attorney, and all were in deep, serious, agitating debate.

The question of identification was incomplete. Not one of them could swear that the emaciated creature, now passing into eternity, was the same man who, a few short years before, had been actively engaged in circulating their cash, and enjoying all the indulgences of wealth and luxury.

The difficulty was increasing when Miss O'Brien arrived. Some of the creditors were very dubious, as to whether this new feature of the " swindle," as they called it, might not be a fresh ruse. Who knew the

young lady herself ? and who could possibly recog-
nise in these death-like lineaments the face of a person who had not been seen for so long a time, and
on whose brow age and vicissitude had wrought such
disturbing effects ?

This was a posing question. No one could solve
it.

Miss Fitzwalter sat at the bedside, and, in mute
distress, offered the testimony of her conduct in addition to the statement she had already made to her
visitors. By a gesture, she motioned Miss O'Brien
to her side, and they sat together, intently and silently,
watching the parting breath.

Meantime, more people arrived, and at every moment some new face entered the room and gazed
earnestly on the dying man. One with an intelligent
glance would occasionally just look, and go out,
apparently satisfied ; and then others, more cautious,
or more curious, would remain, and pry into the features, even raise the head and examine the hair of
the patient.

Some person in the outer room seemed to be taking
down the depositions of each party as he returned
from his inspection ; and a legal, close form of ack-

nowledgment of the fact of Mr. Fitzwalter's identity was being drawn up and duly attested.

As the evening shadows fell, the ladies hoped to see the company depart and leave the debtor to deal with his final account.

During the day Mr. Fitzwalter had given evidence of some remaining vitality. He received, from time to time, spoonfuls of stimulant and nourishment, and, as yet, his system appeared to answer to the restoratives. His relentless creditors were greatly delighted at the prospect of his possible recovery. This may require explanation. In family settlements, in Ireland, as elsewhere, the owner, on his marriage, is made tenant for life; the remainder of the estate is then settled upon the eldest son, subject to a jointure and portions. The longer the tenant for life lives, the better is it for his creditors. This was Mr. Fitzwalter's case. Accordingly, if the creditors could show that any person intercepted any of the rents, in the name either of the eldest son or the jointress, or the daughters, while the tenant for life was still living, the creditors could sue for the sums so received by him. They could also, of course, enjoy the rents and profits of the estate during the continuance of Mr. Fitzwalter's life. It was obviously, therefore, the interest of the creditors to establish the fact of his being still living, and of their consequently having been defrauded of the rents since the time when his supposed death took place.

Darkness settled on the chamber of death. A lamp was lighted, and its dim glimmer revealed the continued presence of the unsatisfied claimants, who went in and out, making sure of that body which should soon be amenable to another *habeas corpus* than theirs.

Miss Fitzwalter was invited to come into the adjoining room, in order to hold a conference with the gentlemen, who had at length arrived at their decision. She arose and went out, leaving Miss O'Brien the sole guard of her dying father.

As soon as she was left alone, Miss O'Brien, with true womanly instincts, began to arrange the disordered apartment, and while she was so occupied was startled by the abrupt entrance of a man in the garb of a common foot-soldier. He came in by the door that opened from the bed-room out on the lobby, and his doing so could not have been seen by those who were in the sitting-room, into which, also, there was a means of communication from Mr. Fitzwalter's room.

He looked hard at Miss O'Brien, and seeing that she was unknown to him, apologized very respectfully,

"I beg your pardon, madam, but I've just come into the town, and every one is talking of Mr. Fitzwalter's being found alive, but dying, and that no one can identify him. I ought to be able to do so. Where is he?"

She pointed to the bed, and threw the full light of the lamp upon it. The new comer groaned, and fell upon his knees at the bedside, drawing the curtain over himself, and in his agony of spirit, desiring to hide his emotion from the eyes of every human being. It was young John Fitzwalter, whose regiment had recently entered a county town not very far from Kildine.

Soon after he had assumed this attitude, some of the same people that had been haunting the room all day came in, and with them Miss Fitzwalter. She approached the dying man, and tenderly addressing him, said,

"Dearest father, I believe that you wish,

in this your last hour, to do the only justice
you* can to those you have injured, and therefore, I agree that they shall take such steps as the
law dictates for their protection. They demand the
custody of your person, but nothing shall separate
you from my care. You will be their prisoner, but
shall remain in my charge. They trust me, and we
shall be undisturbed while we are together now."

A slight movement of the hand showed that Mr.
Fitzwalter had some faint consciousness that he was
being spoken to; but it was not enough to warrant any
further attempt being made to address his intelligence.

With a very respectful air, one of the men, who
had entered the room with Miss Fitzwalter, went up
to the bedside, and placed a paper between the list-
less fingers of the victim. This ceremonial seemed
to be of the utmost importance to the creditors; and
on its being effected, a marked result was immediately
produced.

There was a good deal of commotion in the room,
and some of the party made arrangements to proceed
at once to Knocklash, to take possession of the effects
there, while it was decided that others should stay
and keep guard over the captured debtor.

The transaction was better understood by the object of it, than was thought by the actors, for a motion was visible in the frame, and an agitation distinctly traceable in the features.

The two women present translated the movement into a desire for air, and power to breathe more freely; and accordingly raised their patient up, and put more pillows under his head. He seconded their efforts for his relief, and soon drew a long inspiration:

" I am John Fitzwalter," he articulated, slowly and disjointedly. "I am taken by death. What can I do for you?"

If a voice had come from spirit-land, there could be no greater astonishment in that chamber, than was felt by the hearers; no one was capable of giving a reply.

A thrilling pause succeeded. The flickering life had but emitted a glimmer from the socket, and rapidly faded down again.

Mr. Fitzwalter sank off his pillow, and was falling sideways, when a strong arm was passed under his shoulders, and his head placed on a manly breast. The soldier had come from his concealment, and was now facing the whole range of his father's enemies.

There stood the assembled creditors, and there lay John Fitzwalter, returned from his supposed grave! At one side stood his daughter; and, supporting his almost lifeless form, was the son for whom he had sacrificed so much.

Miss Fitzwalter was transfixed with amazement, but neither she nor her brother thought of each other. Both their minds were absorbed in the passing events —their father's battle with death, and with his creditors. The silence was broken by the young soldier, who declared his determination to take on himself the whole burden of his father's liabilities.

The witnesses were numerous and competent, and his words decided and grave. The state of affairs was changed, and young John Fitzwalter took the place of the old.

The son was served with a writ, instead of the father, and he went that night to a debtor's cell, that his father might die on a freeman's couch. Towards midnight all was over. John Fitzwalter, junior, was gone to prison; John Fitzwalter, senior, had departed to meet his eternal doom. The light of another day ushered in a new phase of life for the owners of Knocklash.

The next business Miss Fitzwalter had to consider was the rescue of her brother from the embarrassments he had so readily undertaken.

She and her sister had been, for some time, paying money into the "Courts," towards the amount accumulating for the payment of the debts on the estate, some of which being of very old date, bound even young John Fitzwalter without any active concurrence on his part.

The deficit left in the rents by the combined effects of famine and emigration was beginning to be filled up by the profit of the lace trade. And almost the entire of these profits were applied by the matchless girls to the liquidation of all the debts honestly due on the estate, irrespectively of any legal objections to those incurred by their father.

Creditors were astonished; lawyers were vanquished; the Incumbered Estate Commissioners were unpetitioned; the Bankruptcy Act was unappealed to; the aid of friends was declined, and all proposals for compromise were refused.

The Knocklash estate was cleared of all its encumbrances, by monies which were derived from three sources—the sale of its timber, the proceeds of its rents, and the profits of the crochet lace!

The amount of the last item was just equal to two-thirds of the second; and this was no small sum, to have been contributed by women, who had earned it by their genius, dexterity, and industry!

The future settlement of these ladies in life was commensurate with their so faithful a discharge of filial and sisterly duties. But though now enjoying all the sweets of hardly-earned opulence, together with the prestige of ancient descent, they find their greatest happiness to consist in the contemplation of the noble and heroic virtues they displayed in the trying years of the famine.

Mary Desmond.

Mary Desmond.

CHAPTER I.

THE winter of 1850 was peculiarly damp, and injurious to the enfeebled frames of the famine-stricken inhabitants of the low lying districts of Carriginis. Fever and ague prevailed, and many lingering and depressing forms of disease abounded. The attendance of children at the industrial schools was not, however, diminished by these afflictive circumstances; on the contrary, strange to say, they seemed largely to increase it.

The apartments were comfortable; dry and clean shelter was offered to those whose cold, miserable homes were decaying around them; the good fires, and, above all, the daily paid earnings of their work, attracted crowds into these institutions.

The classes in them became very full, and the collection of workers formed that winter was the nucleus of the famous Carriginis Lace Schools. Many of the most pitiable objects, that entered the "Relief Room," opened in the town of Carriginis, were afterwards the best hands, and the chief fruits of the cultivation of the lace genius, in that industrial establishment.

Out of the numbers who tried their powers on the sort of work taught there, many were unsuccessful, and did not continue to practise what they learned. But failure was not the rule, it was the exception.

It is a strong assertion, but, nevertheless, a true one, that in every case a certain amount of neat, adroit handicraft was evinced, though, in some instances, it was extremely difficult to utilize it.

Habits of vagrancy and idleness operated against the control of capabilities which were, occasionally, of a high order, and generally very susceptible of improvement. Any girls who would not undertake the process of learning to become *good* crochet-lace makers, usually went off to ephemeral branches of women's ornamental work, such as hair-net making, and fancy woollen knitting; and in the regular lace school were seen no more.

The lace pupils had to undergo severe tests; and if, with patient, painstaking, and diligent industry, they came well through these, there was much to hope. For a victory was won—a victory the magnitude of which can only be estimated by those who are familiar with the characteristics of Irishwomen—their ready quickness of perception, and lively faculties of imagination and imitation, combined with a versatility that carries them brilliantly *into* many an undertaking; but, alas, these qualities seldom last them through the first serious encounter with difficulties; and they are too often foiled, by the early trials that beset a life of labour.

Wherever a steady determination to become a good lacemaker was formed, there a grand moral cause was gained, and a conversion from self-indulgence to self-subjection was obtained: the girl who arrived at that point had overcome the peculiar obstacle which stands in the way of Ireland's progress. It is the nature of the children of her soil, to seek to enjoy that whereon they bestow no labour, and to crave and claim the advantage of wages, for work they do not perform.

Among the earliest of the workers who overcame the tendency of her race to refuse the hardships of a training process, was Mary Desmond. She was a thorough-bred Celt, and developed her compound of bright talents and unwillingness to apply them to any useful purpose, most distinctly. Her face and form were the *beau ideal* of Irish beauty; and she was a well-grown girl of sixteen, when she made her *début* at the lace school. A native grace and elegance were shown in every movement of her nicely proportioned figure; but the expressiveness of her face was most truly exhibited in the light of her dark grey eye, which gleamed intermittingly, according as her feelings went through their emotional cycle.

Mary Desmond would have made a model for an artist. Her very rags were picturesque. It was a matter of surprise, how she collected them to suit her so exactly. They could not have been selected, her poverty forbade that, and how they were assembled in so well contrasted a group of colours and shades, and how they hung upon her, so as to drape her according to the laws of taste and harmony, were mysteries, deepened by the knowledge of the way in which Irish beggars obtain their clothing.

The pieces of garments that composed her raiment must have come to her from the most various sources; a soldier's scarlet coat, denuded of its tails, formed the upper part of her dress, and the continuation was a petticoat, made of an old blue baize bathing dress. Beneath these she had nothing whatever, and beside them only a yellow cotton handkerchief, tied loosely round her neck. Her feet were entirely naked, and they never had experienced the restraint of either shoes or stockings.

Soon after she came to the school, a benevolent lady gave her an old pair of boots, and another bestowed a bonnet on her. These unaccustomed articles she always set aside carefully on wet days, and only on special occasions, and in very bright sunny weather, put them on.

" Erra, why would I be spoiling them?" she used to reply, when it was remarked that they were specially given for protection against cold and rain; " sure my hair is as well able to keep my head warm as a horse's mane, and my feet have soles as good as any leather."•

Her rough locks showed, that they were fitted to her condition, for they seemed to cover her like a thatch, and to be capable of any amount of extension over her neck and shoulders. Whenever she got into a fit of excitement, she used to untie the cord that bound them at the back of her head, and suffer the whole mass of bright, brown, wavy hair, to tumble over her neck and shoulders; people called them her thunder clouds.

The only account that could be got of her was her own very short history of herself, and this had to be elicited by questioning, for she was not communicative on the subject.

"Where did you come from?" she was asked the first day of her appearance.

"No where, ma'am."

"Have you a father or mother?"

"No, ma'am."

"Where do you live?"

"With the Gormans, ma'am."

This was the name of two sisters that had been some time in the school. They were labourers' daughters, and were known to have a good home, and honest, worthy parents. Their story of Mary Desmond was, that she joined them as they sat at work at the road side, and offered to help at a piece of edging : and that, finding she knew the stitch, they let her take on with them. She then proposed to live with them, and earn her "keep" at crochet work. This was kindly agreed to, and the arrangement was found to answer. Such a plan was not uncommon among poor neighbours, and was an evidence of much good feeling; and also a proof that the famous old Irish generosity and hospitality were not extinct, and were not unfrequently more distinctly to be seen in that class, where their presence would be less expected than in ranks very far above it in the social scale.

It is most likely that the Gormans derived no profit from Mary Desmond's work, in any respect save the consciousness that they were relieving "a poor wandthering girl," and "may be saving her from a bad end." This benevolence of the poor to the poor, is very rarely abused among the Irish. The obligation incurred thereby, forms a peculiar responsibility, and protects the conferrers of it from any vicious propensities, that their *protégés* may possess ; and this is so well understood, that people do not fear to receive as an inmate for *charity,* those whom they would not entertain on any other terms.

CHAPTER II.

Only the French can describe the power of such hands as Mary Desmond's. Her performance with the crochet needle, when her skill was at its height, was incredible; it was an art—a sort of legerdemain —known only to herself, something that she worked, as she said, "out of her own head"—a notion stereotyped in thread. Her introduction to the use of the hooked needle, was through the prepara- tory practice of edging making, and, in this stage, the productions of her nimble fingers were admirable, while the complete indocility of her mind was a serious trouble.

Orders for hundreds of dozen-yard-pieces of trim- mings, of a certain pattern, were frequently given by wholesale warehouses, and buyers from them began o visit the Carriginis school every season, and used, themselves, to impress their instructions on the workers, with the stimulus of promises of good pay ; and yet the girls could, with difficulty, be induced to perform what was required from them.

Mary Desmond, like the rest, was almost sure to have agreed to the terms proposed ; and still, when the day came to take in the goods, an extraordinary failure, in the performance of the contract, on the part of the hands, was of constant occurrence, and Mary was more frequently the culprit than any · other pupil in the school. The superintendent was always in a dilemma, caused by this insubordination. Her daily complaint was, the impossibility of executing the regular orders, though a great amount of exquisite work could be procured from the girls.

The feeling of the whole school was expressed in Mary Desmond's reply to an inquiry, instituted to discover the cause of this disobedience ; and it was anything but satisfactory to find that the seat of the mischief was a radical force, one of those strange inclinations of nature, that direct alike the movements of the individual and the species, and are as unaccountable in the plant as in the animal.

" Mary, this is not the pattern you were to have made."

"Sure I know it isn't, ma'am, I don't want to impose on you, nor on the gentleman."

"Well, why did you not make the one you were told?"

"Is it that ugly old thing, ma'am? I never could do such a lot of bothersome work; it would tire the life out of me—all the same, all along, row upon row —I hated to be at it, so I stopped, and then the girls pattherned by me. I'm to blame, indeed, for I put the spirit into them, or they would'nt have dared to do any but the right thing through all."

"Then I wish you would cease inspiriting them to do wrong to me, and injure themselves."

"Oh, ma'am, we wouldn't wrong you for all the world, and we'd be as far from injuring ourselves."

"But you have done both most effectually in this instance, and I will not pay you for labour that is not according to the agreement you made."

"You don't mean, ma'am, that you won't take in these edgings, and give us our money for them?"

"Just that exactly."

"Oh! you never will ruin us that way. What on earth, ma'am, would we do with them? Who'd

take them from us? Sure the cotton is yours, and
the pattern is yours, and no one has a right to 'em
but your own self, and you'll have to get 'em from
us. We must sell 'em to you anyhow."

"But I don't want them. They are not what I
require. Marsland's order was the *Shamrock* edging
at five shillings a dozen. He won't take *Pine* for
Shamrock, I can assure you, nor shall I offer it
to him."

"Then raly, ma'am, he is a great fool, for it's
worth nearly double the money; and it is good value
we're giving him."

"Nonsense, it is you that are fools, to give him
more work than he wants for the money. It is
waste of time and material, for he won't have it.
He and other dealers are particular to have the goods
like the sample. They select for their market; they
know what they can sell; you have no business to
suggest, or to dictate in the matter."

"No doubt, ma'am, we ought to have known better,
but we didn't, you see; so, this once, don't lay the
trouble on us of going home without our week's
money; buy it from us yourself, and some other dealer
will take it from you, and you'll lose nothing by it."

"I knew it would come to this, and that I should have your labour at my own price; but it is not what I desire, and it is not—as you suppose—no loss, but the reverse. Our customer is disappointed, and perhaps injured; he is very much annoyed, and will certainly in future hold our engagements in disrespect. I am made ashamed, when I promise for you, and you fail to fulfil my agreement. We enter on the compact with a fair understanding on both sides, and I must say, it is very humiliating to me when I am obliged to be a defaulter in this way."

"For pity's sake, say no more, ma'am, dear, we are melted to think that you should be put out about it. Take the edging for whatever you please to give for it, and we'll work our fingers to the bone to make good your word to the gentleman."

This was a specious flourish, meant to mollify the superintendent's anger. Mary well knew that there was no time for completing the engagement. It was a matter more easily said than done; and she had no intention whatever of trying to perform her promise.

The superintendent had the pine pattern as "a bargain," and was left to get out of the affair with her correspondent as well as she could.

A bargain, indeed! No greater misconception of the nature of a bargain was ever formed. For whatever price the article was obtained, it could not be "a bargain." It would probably lie a whole year on hand, and when a speculating customer was found to take it, he invariably required it on some such terms as those on which it had been bought, and, finally, had it for a sum as much below its cost as it had been obtained beneath its intrinsic worth from the makers. No amount of reasoning could convey to the girls any idea of the evil influence which the system of selling "bargains," had on the trade. It affected it perniciously from beginning to end. First, it injured the workers themselves, by deranging their perception of the value of their labour, and by destroying, from the very outset, their power of dictating a price for it. Then, instead of the managers being able to pay them, according to the amount of skill and taste displayed in their work, and time devoted to its manufacture, their uncertainty in producing anything "to order," made it necessary for them to purchase from them, on terms protective of themselves, against the refusal of the market to take the goods offered, in place of those which it required.

Often, when they were deluged by the workers with specimens of wild industry, they had just to surrender them to purchasers for whatever they would give for them, and so the progress of the mischief was promoted, which eventually made the whole business irregular, and unsatisfactory to the commercial world.

As the school increased, it became necessary to arrange a system of monitors, and in selecting these due regard had, of course, to be paid to the qualifications needful for such a post. Mary fought hard to be raised to this rank. She urged that her undisputed position as " best hand," entitled her to the elevation.

Her unrivalled skill pointed her out as the most competent to instruct in manipulation, but there was, in the known faults of her character, a serious impediment to her being so promoted.

With the superintendent she frequently argued her case, and dwelt upon it in every form as a " crying shame," and an " injustice."

" Will you raly tell me, ma'am, why you puts

that stupid Ann Thomas over us, and makes the likes of me, that she can't hold a candle to, in regard of work, be under her thumb? Is it because she is a Protestant? That's the way all through the country: they gets the best berths and all the good places, while us, that can beat 'em hollow at anything we wish to do, is kept down."

"Mary, you neither read nor write, and Ann can do both, and keep accounts too; and then, you know, that you cannot be depended on to obey orders, and she has been brought up to do so, and to keep her word."

"Her word! Why then, aren't you very simple ma'am? What word has she, or any other poor creature, but to betther themselves? If she don't chate in male, she will in malt, as you'll discover some day to your cost. I hates those people that are putindin' to be so very honest, and always praching to us to tell the truth, as if every one don't tell lies some time or other."

This uncomfortable misunderstanding as to religious disability, was widely diffused; and it took a long period of consistent management, before the principles on which the business of the school was conducted were vindicated. But, in time, their worth was learned by many; and some were trained into those habits of steadiness and veracity that they formerly despised. It was not easy to inculcate this lesson; it was conveyed mainly through example, for in the Carriginis lace school it was a fundamental rule, that no abstract teaching should be given, and on the subject of duty, perfect silence was obligatory, because the managers, being Protestant ladies, could not, from the nature of the religious differences that existed between them and the Romanist workers, enter on the moral training of those they undertook to help, in the form of regular instruction. However, they did that which was probably, under the circumstances, more effective: they demonstrated practically to the unwilling learners, that there is no better policy than honesty, and that successful industry is inseparable from morality.

It was slow work to impress this on the pupils, for the masses were Mary Desmonds, the units Ann Thomases.

When the art of copying old lace began to be taught in the school, troubles arising from the unconscientious tendencies of the workers accumulated to a distracting pitch; and a plan had to be adopted of dividing the patterns into sections, and getting the different portions of them made by several hands simultaneously. This had the effect of producing the goods rapidly, controlling their price, and of preventing the pirating of the designs, all of which measures were of great importance to the business; and they also acted very efficiently in distributing the employment, and protecting it from the non-execution of orders, which was of such frequent recurrence, before this system of subdivision was devised.

Mary Desmond and her companions became much more manageable under the new *régime;* it afforded good means for classifying the workers and gave each one an opportunity for showing her peculiar capacities.

These were very various. Some of the girls had decided genius for forming the pieces of which the patterns were composed; others had singular taste and expression, in combining and assembling them into suitable groups.

Mary Desmond was of the former class; her intelligence made her the regular model "bi t maker" of the school. When a new design was required, it was she that was usually selected to plan the scrolls, foliage, flowers, &c., and it was most interesting to observe how she seized on modes of expressing the ideas conveyed to her by the rags of old lace that were laid before her.

She had an intuitive perception of what was required to be done, and generally, after a few hours of patient and laborious application, she handed in a "bit," of beautiful proportions and exquisite needle-work, the stitches being chosen with a fine sense of suitability, and the character of the "study" being admirably preserved.

The artistic faculties were largely possessed by Mary, and use strengthened them considerably; so that, after some time, her original compositions were very striking, and the contributions she made to the number and variety of the "bit" stock, out of which the pieces of lace were formed, were very important. But in cultivating her genius, there was ever that immense inconvenience to be encountered, of dealing with her moral condition, in which there was always as much room for improvement, as when she began edging making at the road-side; and her deviations from the path of rectitude were, perhaps, even more apparent, according as her opportunities for exhibiting them increased.

The rule of the Carriginis lace school was, that the superintendent should issue, every day, orders for the making of certain "bits," which formed the component parts of a special pattern, and which was adapted to make collars, sleeves, berthas, flounces, &c., and all other articles of ladies' dress, to which lace is applicable ; and these " bits," and no others, the girls were desired to make. All that they could work of them in the day, were received at a stipulated price, and, if perfect, passed to their credit ; if ill made, they were either rejected as utterly valueless, or received and paid for, according to what they were worth.

The making up of the accounts with each girl, was the most trying duty the superintendent had to perform ; and for it she required the sharpness of a detective, together with a perfect knowledge of her business; and any dulness or weakness displayed in this matter would soon place her at the mercy of the workers. When the settling hour arrived, no worker, not even the acute Mary Desmond, could tell a good

" bit " from a bad one ; and all the little bundles into which every girl had tied her day's work, had to be opened and reviewed. Oh, the differences of opinion then expressed ! Though a tendency to deceit was but too common, on the whole, a good deal of natural uprightness was found amongst the girls. Some were amenable to the first exposure of imposition, and very sensitive to shame ; but others were insensible to any reproof on the subject, and continued to repeat, over and over again, the tricks and artifices, by which they sought to overreach the managers. Penalties inflicted for these transgressions were no checks to them, a few successful attempts amply compensating for any loss incurred by being discovered at other times. Indeed, the triumphs of schemers seemed to engage the sympathies of the whole school, and they banded themselves together in firm opposition to the intelligence of their teachers.

The uneducated workers soon got quite independent of patterns; and after a short insight into the art of lace-making, scorned to be directed in any way. They were supported in this independence by factors, who bought up their uncultivated productions, and who, as long as they were novelties, and showy,

Q

striking looking goods, found them a profitable in-
vestment.

The competition between these men and the ladies
who managed the lace-school, was very active; and
it kept up the value of girls' labour in the district of
Carriginis to an excessive height.

Mary Desmond took advantage of this very
cleverly, and the way in which, by these means, she
and others made money, was most surprising. The
cunning they displayed, and the unprincipled
treachery with which they behaved to every employer,
gave sad evidence of a very low state of morals.

It was no wonder, then, that such people as these
were soon injured by the influx of money into their
hands. The acquisition of it constituted a temptation that they could not withstand. Mary Desmond
became the earner of ten shillings a week, and no
one could have recognized in her, the wild creature
that had come into the school, an outcast and a
stranger. She grew to be, as she promised, a very
handsome woman. She arrested the attention of
even the most cursory observer, and was to many
a subject of intense interest and curiosity.

The family in which she had taken up her abode,

had two daughters employed at lace-making, and she and they were some of the best workers in the school. They led the rest of the hands, and their performances were models of adroitness and skill; they dictated prices, too, and made their influence felt through the whole establishment. The classes who could not compose their own designs, nor get up the goods to order, unless their requirements were supplied by the "bit" makers, were completely under the control of these girls, and most capriciously and wilfully they exercised their power. Adjudication between these contending parties was, indeed, a difficult task!

Notwithstanding the disagreeable characteristics suggested by this kind of conduct, Mary Desmond and her friends the Gormans, were the pleasantest and most presentable specimens of the fruits of the lace manufacture, that were on the school list. They became, in course of time, a trio of interesting, well-to-do young people—gay, thoughtless, and fond of dress and amusement, and as improvident as they were hardworking. Again and again were they each urged to save, and to be economical. "Line upon line, precept upon precept," were addressed to them unavailingly. It was of no use to speak to them on such subjects; they were always turned off with a laugh or a joke, and no admonition had the least effect.

Fine clothes were a great snare to them, but a Temperance Ball was a greater one. When the walls were placarded with notices of one of these customary Sunday entertainments, it was sure to cost these girls at least a fortnight's work—a week before it took place, to prepare their personal decorations, and speculate on probable intrigues, and a week after it was over, to idle and follow up the "fun," that was created on the occasion.

The advocates of total abstinence from intoxicating liquors, by a strange contradiction of their principles, allowed themselves to be led into a very intemperate course, with regard to amusements. Under their auspices proceedings went on, that were far from furthering good and virtuous living, and could scarcely promote that self-denial, which is the basis from which springs the good that teetotalism aims at.

Every faction that gains sway in Ireland does so by pandering to the lowest tastes of its people, and that which is now tincturing its politics most injuriously, used its earliest powers in organizing *fêtes* and amusements, under the name of the "Temperance Movement." The great apostle of the cause had nothing whatever to do with this, nor did it dare to incorporate itself with his noble institution, until his saintly head was enveloped in the mists and shadows that clouded his last days. It began when his personal and vigorous inspection ceased; and the retirement of the great and good old man from his simple-hearted labour, was the signal for a host of double-minded, traitorous men, lay and clerical, to come forward and seize the machine he had contrived as an engine for good, and turn it to the base use of treasonable excitement.

Assemblies, for all purposes of a popular and entertaining kind, were abundantly encouraged by these designers. There were innumerable meetings arranged for tea, music, exhibitions, and excursions, all calculated to catch the fancy of the lately famine-harassed poor, and to beguile from them their newly obtained earnings. It is amazing how soon this highly contrasted state of society set in. The change was electrically sudden.

Lace-making no sooner brought in money, than
"Temperance Institutes" spent it, just as the simoom
makes sport of the luxurious harvest of a tropical
clime.

The active, lively, giddy girls, who were in receipt
of such good wages, that they might have introduced a new era of prosperity for their families, were
the easy victims of this intoxicating system. Aye,
intoxicating! The "Temperance Band" brought in
a new and insidious form, a poison into the hearts
and souls of the poor, untutored multitude, which
worked as rapid a destruction as ever drink did, in
the mind and body of man.

The crochet girls were the peculiar prey of the
diseased action. Joining a "Temperance Room"
sealed their ruin. For, alas! no training in right
ways was found there. It was not the rule within
its walls to "cease to do evil, and learn to do
well." No such thing! In it the influence was all
vicious. There met the young, and the old, the gay,
the vain, the virtuous, and the bad; and these all of
the most ignorant and unrestrained portion of the
population.

No improving element was added in the form kind and elevating teaching. No friendly mind came forward to assist their mental culture, and induce them to try to rise and progress towards a better condition. This it was not the object of their leaders to accomplish. The very opposite was the purpose they had in view. The perpetuation of ignorance, and consequent capability of being made useful for the ends of persons whose schemes were more personally ambitious than patriotic or political, were the true secrets of the interference that promoted the " people's amusements."

The scenes connected with these specious and well-developed plans, for misleading the masses on which they operated, and the public that observed them, were wholly at variance with any scheme for the benefit of a population just issuing from pauperism to prosperity, and passing over the initiative threshold of civilization. With headlong haste the lace-makers indulged their new-born powers, and with ardent zeal their superiors in education rushed to receive them into a delusive arena, called the " Temperance Society." This association had its dis-

tricts well planned out, and each carefully superintended. It had its "rooms," bands, meetings, and
soirées, and all these were pressed on the working
classes by a twofold force—that of the immediate promoters of the organization, and that of the benevolent
public, who were deceived into admiration of its
apparently philanthropic labours.

Very soon after the influence of this society began
to be perceptible in the community, the Roman
Catholic hierarchy set itself against it most com-
mendably, and tried hard to restore order in the
ranks of its recusant flock.　But its efforts were
unavailing.　The sheep were gone astray, and could
not be brought back by any energy it was able to
exert.

"Confraternities," religious exercises, and various
sorts of discipline, were resorted to by the clergy
with very little success.　They met the most uncon-
querable spirit of opposition to their teachings in the
wild rush of excitement and folly, that pervaded the
hosts of their followers, who were still engaged in the
industrial pursuits provided for them in the time of
their adversity.　There was a special aggravation in
the idea, that these well-intentioned instrumentalities

should thus have become the medium of strengthening the hands of the old enemies of order and good faith to the English crown, and should have introduced a condition, rife in mischievous capacities.

CHAPTER III.

THE extraordinary agencies that have been, from time to time, made use of, to further the movements of the young Ireland party, seldom come under the notice of the British public. It is little aware that anything so innocuous as "lace-making," could, by any possibility, be pressed into the service of politics. And yet such was the case.

The peaceful, holy work of the teacher of honest labour to idle hands, was abruptly interrupted, and the converse of the old saying seemed to be proved, for now Satan's power was also connected with busy fingers.

Mary Desmond, the beauty of the lace-school, had about as active and diligent a pair of hands as any woman in the kingdom, and yet she was not exempt from the attacks of the arch-enemy.

When she had reached her twentieth year, and was

in the full bloom of her prime, a circumstance occurred
that greatly tended to encourage her personal vanity.
A lady, one of the patronesses of the school, who was
studying in a school of design, wanted a subject for
a painting, and selected Mary as her model. This
led to frequent visits to the house of the artist, and
much intercourse between the untutored girl and persons of a class of whom she had had no previous
knowledge.

Mary was a close observer of persons and things.
She saw, and heard a great deal in the house of her
patroness, of which she took notice, in a most
especial manner. It was a great field of interest to her.
The lady to whom she sat as a study, was a very
clever caricaturist; and her room contained a great
number of drawings of the sort in which she excelled.
They were illustrative of persons and customs, and
highly expository of Irish affairs, viewed from a
Protestant stand-point.

Mary Desmond took this all in at a glance. She
knew the originals of several of the pictures by sight,
and by character; she understood the situations, and
she at once perceived that it was a discovery worth
making, to have this exhibition granted to her. She

was a true, thorough Romanist. Her priest held, she
thought, her soul in his hand. That subtle essence of
her being, that connected her with an eternity of bliss
or woe, was in his keeping; and, therefore, he was
to her the creature of the highest importance in her
universe!

This object of her supreme veneration was in this
profane room in effigy. A sketch portrayed a priest
notorious as a temperance orator enjoying a steaming glass of spirits and water.

"Oh, holy father!" Mary inwardly groaned, "is
this the way that the Proddys tell lies of you?"

"Mary," said Miss Black, "look at the spot I
told you, and not at Father James."

"I wasn't noticing him, Miss," she replied, with
one of her most bewitching smiles, but in her heart,
she added, "I'll be even with you, some day, for that
picture."

Miss Black's father held a high and lucrative situation in the public service. He had filled it long and
honourably, and was as much esteemed in domestic
and social life, as in civic and official circles. His
family had been creditably reared, and brought up
to occupy a most respectable sphere of life. Two of

his sons were preparing to enter on professional careers; and he had saved a decent provision for his only daughter. Mr. Black was happy and prosperous, and had all the allowable pride of a man who had made for himself the good position that he held.

Such a man must, of necessity, have enemies, and Mr. Black was not without his; they were not many, and they were not troublesome. Sometimes he forgot their existence, and when he did remember them, it was with scornful contempt, for anything they could possibly do to him. In his employment he possessed the confidence of the Government, and also of the public; and private, petty, mean spites he considered beneath his notice. Miss Black was engaged to be married to a good and wealthy man; and this fact, which formed the sum of her happiness, made, too, a large element in her father's.

Altogether, they were a very pleasant family group, and with a mother on whom the calm time of age had crept unconsciously, and who had settled into a state of placid enjoyment at her comfortable fireside, nothing seemed wanting to complete their prospects of social felicity.

Mrs. Black took a great fancy to her daughter's *protegée.* Mary Desmond was made not only a model in the studio, but an inmate in the house ; and was admired, and made so much of, that she was rendered beside herself with vanity. But it was wonderful how well she conducted herself through her honours. Mrs. Black interested herself to discover the antecedents of the girl, and finding that some mystery was connected with them, became increasingly anxious to try and give Mary that feeling of desire to maintain her respectability, which so often forsakes those who have no friends to be hurt or grieved by their fall into evil ways.

The family loaded Mary with favours, presents, good advice, and instruction. They had her taught to read and write, and encouraged her as much as possible to advance in acquiring some little literary knowledge. This she resisted somewhat, and seemed to find literary work exceedingly tiresome ; but, on the whole, their efforts took some effect, and she became finally much improved from the associations with gentlefolks, and got a degree of polish and manner, which, grafted on her natural disposition, increased its powers of attraction amazingly.

Mary Desmond, when Miss Black's picture of her was gracing the walls of the school of art, was a different looking person from the rough, tawdry, awkward girl that had been boisterously lively in the crochet-school. Her voice was toned down, her air softened, and her dress, of course, wholly altered. While the artistic element was still evident in its colours and form, a change had come over the play of her features; Mary's countenance had a subdued pensive expression, that was unknown to it in former days. Her eyes, those full deep orbs, that used to flash and kindle at every emotion, were now quiet, still, and dark. They had a light in them of astonishing brilliancy, but it was hid by a sort of veiling effort, and there was a singular and remarkable power of character betrayed by her every gesture.

Mary Desmond was not quite a servant in Mr. Black's household. Domestic work was entirely out of her line. She sewed, made her beautiful lace, and waited on the ladies, sat with them sometimes, and heard and saw all they said and did.

Mrs. Black could not prevail on Mary to learn any other employment than that of needle-work. Wo-

manly duties, in the way of providing food and attending to other necessities of civilized life, she would
not acquire. It was very amusing to hear her argu-
ing with her mistress on this subject.

"Ah, ma'am, don't be vexing yourself; I'll get
on very well, plaze God. I wish you would not be
saying to me to marry Paddy Gorman : that I won't,
you may be sure. All he ever earns is nine shillings
a week, and I can keep myself better than that with
my own hands."

"Indeed, Mary, I'm afraid you would be a bad
wife for him. He had better take a girl who has a
mind to keep house, and not to go on perpetually at
that rag-making business."

" Well then, ma'am, that'll never be me, for I
won't do a hand's turn but it all my days. I can't
make a bit of fire to boil the kettle, or even peel one
potato to ate my dinner, for fear of spoiling my fingers
and to keep them nate for the fine work."

"Oh, indeed, it is truly an injurious occupation,
and makes every girl that takes to it perfectly useless."

"Now you cant say that, ma'am ; look at all the
lovely things I makes, as good, any day, as Miss

——'s painting. My roses are as like life as hers, and my leaves and shamrocks are as perfect, barring the colour!"

In the midst of this conversation Mr. Black entered the room. "Well, Mary, my girl," said he, "how do you get on?"

"Pretty well, yer honour," she replied, curtseying, as she retired.

On the evening of that day, when the family were sitting down to dinner, the curtains drawn, and the lamps lit, Mary was opening the hall door and looking out, as if anxiously watching for some one whose coming was of intense interest to her.

She looked out steadily into the darkening street. The rain was falling thickly, and the night promised to be very stormy. Mary had in her hand a flat paper parcel, which she carefully kept alike from damp and observation. While she was looking in one direction a gentleman suddenly came up the steps in another, and pushed in the door to enter the house. She turned to see who it was, and in a moment was saluted with a rude kiss.

At first, she was disposed to scream, but quickly checked herself when she found it was no other than

R

Miss Black's intended husband. The action surprised her exceedingly, but the doer of it more so
still. In utter silence she made a dash at him with
every finger nail set like a cat's claw, and tore a
hideous scratch down his face. "Go, give what account you like of that in the parlour," she hissed in
his ear.

"You she-devil!" he said, and turned away into
the street to recover his composure, and, if possible,
his good looks.

"There goes as bad a fellow as walks," she solilo-
quized; "men are all alike, and the grander they
are, the worse they go on. The mean cur, that
would be afraid to do the like to his equal, how dare
he make so free with me? I'll teach him manners
—let him take what he got as a sample—to offer to
do such a thing! and me to be insulted in this way,
that never a man attempted to say a bad word to in
all my life, and that never done a thing that could be
thrown in my face, or bring a blush on my mother,
if she was there opposite me, and we going before
the priest."

Here she was interrupted by the arrival of the
person for whom she was waiting. A man, well

cloaked and disguised, went up the steps; and Mary, with a respectful bend, put the precious paper into his hand.

"Stay there until I return," said the stranger.

"I will, your reverence," was the submissive reply.

The man then went away down the street, and stopped under a gas lamp, opened the parcel, and looked long and fixedly at its contents. He returned to Mary, and motioned her to step out further, and to close the door behind her.

This precautionary measure being adopted, he drew near her and whispered :—"This is all right. I'll keep it."

" Oh, your reverence, don't, for pity's sake. What would become of me if it was found out?"

" Hush! you fool, I'll bear you blameless through anything that happens. Do you not know who I am?" This was said in a very authoritative tone, and seemed intended to overawe her; but she was a girl of some spirit, and she seized the disputed paper. The ecclesiastic held fast by the other end, and they pulled it pretty hardly between them. The strongest had the best of it very soon; but he had also a wholesome fear, of arousing a feeling of resistance that he might hereafter find troublesome to quell.   He thought he knew the girl well, and calculated that she was one of those passionate creatures easily excited to violent proceedings, and who could be made a man's ally, or his foe, in a moment.   He also fancied that the temperance ball-room practice she had had was sufficient to make her turn off lightly, at the sound of a vicious insinuation.   In fact, he saw that she was a woman, warm and impetuous.

"Ah, Mary! you rogue," said he, with a most unsaintly smile, "don't you recollect the old song, ' You know I'm your priest, and your conscience is mine?' "

" I know a great many things you have no business to know," she saucily rejoined:

> " And I'll take no impudence even from a priest."

But she was not a match in strength for this superior of hers, and she was obliged to let him walk off with the parcel, on which she set such store.

He got quickly to his home in the Bawn Friary, and laid his prize on the table, round which sat a jolly circle of gentlemen, in "orders grey." The wrapping was soon undone, and the discovery elicited roars of laughter.

It was Miss Black's caricature of the Priest, and it was laid before one of the originals of her well executed sketch. The first burst of enjoyment of the fun was soon over, and the victim of the artist's skill betrayed considerable annoyance.

"It is very well for you all to laugh," said he; "but to me it is no laughing matter. What a shameful thing to make light of my sacred character."

"Hear him," cried a very red-faced old padre from the chair.

"Yes, indeed, I don't joke. We, none of us, can spare anything off our respectability."

"Oh, come, now, speak for yourself," came from the whole company, amidst bursts of laughter.

"What I say is a fact."

"Holloa, don't put your foot in it, admission is as good as confession," exclaimed the assembly.

"Well, it's of no use talking; I'll see to the bottom of this, and make those that did it smart severely."

"Oh, nonsense," cried the president; "there's no

harm done ; how could you punish the culprit ?—a
pretty little girl, and a heretic too ?   We can't reach
them, unfortunately."

Here the speaker was greeted with such cheers
from the whole party that he was unable to continue,
and being a modest little man, he grew redder than
ever, and sipped up his wine.   The topic of conversation round the table soon changed ; but two heads
laid themselves together apart from the rest, and
talked of vengeance.

" You'll never have the heart to do that," said a
young, gentlemanly, and highly intellectual-looking
young man.   "I don't like to go into intrigues that
implicate us with low people.   They are so treache-
rous.   In my college we were taught to avoid as
much as possible connection with the classes beneath
us.   It was reckoned too great a risk."

" Well, I don't know why you, young men, should
not work upon all your materials as well as we.   In
my young days we found the servants our very best
spies, and many and many a plot they unravelled for
us ; and Protestants are getting worse and worse
every day, more bitter, and more intolerant, and
more scheming.   All this ridicule of me is to depre-

ciate my position, and make me have less weight in
public life, on boards, and on committees, and those
sort of things. Of course, it does not affect my own
flock; but it does the general run of people that I
have to do with. You are not long enough on the
mission to understand those matters, but you will
when you come to have to do with poor-law guardians and other public bodies. These are greatly
influenced by what is said of a man's private life, and
I can tell you that being right well made game of
creates an unfavourable impression that nothing can
efface. There were scandals here about Flagherty,
and they got wind, and he was ruined by them. You
may be sure it is safest always, if you can, to make
away with parties that are in power, if they have any
disrespectful feeling towards you; and now that I
recall Mr. Black's manner to me at the Relief Committee, the other day, I think it was very undervalu-
ing and insulting. No doubt his mind is prejudiced
against me, and that is a great inconvenience."

"Perhaps you are quite wrong. I often meet that
very young lady at Mrs. Maxwell's at dinner, and she
is very friendly—— "

"Oh, now, take care young man. Going to Pro-

testant houses, and dining, and having young ladies
' friendly ' to you won't do.   They are celebrated in
that house for ridiculing priests."

" My dear sir, we won't talk any more in this strain.
I am not at all used to it; at St. Omer's we should
be put to do severe penance for it; but you, Irish
priests, have a license of which we never heard."

" I suppose not, indeed; you have no whisky
there; but come and let us arrange my plan of revenge."

" Revenge, Timotheus cried," shouted a chorus of
voices in tolerable harmony, considering the lateness
of the hour and the depth of their potations, and for
the present all further discussion was at an end.

The senior of the two whose conversation we have
repeated departed, making a strong assertion that he
would have his satisfaction, and that he would insist
on the aid which his brother Gregorian was compelled, by his vows, to give him.   "It is in your
district," he said, "and you must do the work, or
take the consequences."

CHAPTER IV.

MISS BLACK and her intended husband had been acquainted from their childhood, and therefore the terms on which they lived had all the peculiar freedom from restraint that long and intimate association gives.

A few days after the occurrence of the scene on the door-step, between Mary Desmond and her mistress's lover, an account of it was given to Miss Black by the gentleman himself. He told the facts very nearly as they happened, and he did so under the full persuasion that if he withheld the tale, Mary was, from the character she displayed, very unlikely to do so. He calculated that Miss Black already knew the story when he began his narration, and her surprise, at first, seemed to him to be feigned. But this was not the case. Mary had kept her own council in the matter, and had no intention whatever of making it a subject for mischief between them.

She was very little prepared for a strict interrogation about it from Miss Black, and being sadly afraid that the subsequent case, of her interview on the same evening with the priest, would also come out on enquiry, she was very disingenuous when questioned respecting the affair.

"What night was it, Miss, you're talking of at all? There was nothing but fun in anything at all that happened between us; gentlemen does be always going on that way to us poor girls. They says many a thing to the likes of me, that they would not think of saying to a lady; and we have no right to talk about it. I'd be long sorry, miss, to tell you half that is said to me, or let you into it at all. But I am able for them; and, as you see, I spares nobody when they go farther than I choose."

Poor Miss Black felt all this keenly. It was a revelation to her. There was more in the business than she could fathom, and it had an evil influence in it for her. Mary's words complicated the affair, and her manner still more so. Miss Black shuddered at the vicious contact that, for the first time in her life, seemed in close proximity to her. She was led into a mist of doubt where all should have been bright, and fair. William Harris, the man whose perception of all that was pure and excellent in a woman was to Miss Black infallible, had now affected her with ideas that depreciated Mary to her.

As to himself, she loved him so dearly, that many faults would be as powerless as many waters to quench the flame her bosom owned. She liked his frankness; his open, manly way of confiding to her what he freely confessed was an error bound her to him more closely than ever. "It was merely a joke on his part, though a very wrong sort of one," she thought, "and I'll try and make him feel that even the lowest of my sex is to be respected."

Towards Mary, from thenceforward, Miss Black had a changed feeling. She felt repelled, by the hesitation and untruthfulness of her manner, and the insinuations conveyed by her words. She no longer associated her so closely with herself, and withdrew in a very decided manner from the intercourse that had subsisted between them.

Mary was quite alive to this alteration. She knew that confidence between them was over, and the sensation had a bitterness in it, that her temperament could ill bear.

" 'Twas that villain did it," she thought. " He wants to get rid of me out of this house. ' Papist servants don't suit him,' he says. No doubt he wronged us sometime, or why should he be afraid of us ? These half-English-Irish people hate us ; the impudence I hear they puts in the papers in England is, ' No Irish need apply ;' and still they wants us to make us their slaves ! But I'll be no slave ! Ah, 'tis they'll be sorry yet, that they provoked me !"

These feelings were fresh in her heart one day, awakened by some new proof of the loss of her mistress's interest in her, when the drawing-room bell rang. It was Mary's duty to answer it ; and she did so with less than her accustomed alacrity—

" How long you stayed !" said Miss Black, " bring me that sketch of father James that I made long ago, I want to show it to Mr. Harris."

" Where is it, Miss ?" asked Mary, with the most innocent air imaginable.

" Where it always is, hanging in my study. You know it very well ;" and Mary heard Miss Black say to Mr. Harris, as she closed the door, " I think you will say it is the best likeness of him you ever saw."

Mary paused on the stairs, her heart beat, and her head got giddy.

Now had come the crisis. All would be out! What should she do ? Was this a preliminary to the announcement, that her theft was discovered? No, Miss Black's manner forbade that ; but what else was impending ?

With terror in her heart, and a hard struggle with her conscience, Mary nerved herself to the work of deceit. A cold perspiration burst out on her brow ; her cheek was blanched, her lip became livid, and her eye unnaturally dark, bright, and fierce, as she rushed up the stairs. She stood awhile in Miss Black's room,. and even cheated herself into the idea that she was looking for the picture.

" I'll go tell her I can't find it, as soon as I come back to my colour—this face would tell on me—and let her do her best. But what do I care? The priest will make it all right for me. It is as easy for him to pardon ten lies as one—so here goes."

With a rapid step, Mary returned to the drawing-room, and hurriedly said,—

"I can't find it, Miss,"—·

And then darted from the room.   Again the bell was rung, and again the culprit went nervously to her duty.

"Why can't you find it?" inquired Miss Black. "No one ever disturbs that room but you."

"Indeed, Miss, I don't know anything about it. I don't steal pictures; and as to that one—"

"No one ever said you did, Mary," interrupted the lady, "so don't run on in that tone."

"When people are so ready to excuse themselves," Mr. Harris began—

"Don't you dare talk to me," said the excited girl to him, "what right have you to meddle between me and my mistress?"

"I'll take a right now," he said, "and you may prepare to leave on the spot.   My future wife shall not be exposed to the violence of a woman of your temper."

This infuriated Mary, and she dashed wildly out of the house.

With her best speed she ran to her old friends, the Gormans, and dropped down on their floor in a deep swoon.

When she recovered, her anguish of mind was truly terrible; but to no one would she tell the real cause. "Why did they turn you out?" was the eager question from the whole family, whom her abrupt arrival "took all of a heap," as they said.

"They didn't turn me out at all, I runned away from them," Mary rejoined, when, at length, composure returned to her.

"What for, for pity's sake?" asked old Mrs. Gorman; "do you want to go like my two bad daughters, and bring more shame on them that you belongs to? Couldn't you keep a good home, when you had it, you fool, you?"

"No, I couldn't, when they called me Papist and Irish, and made game of me."

"Sure that wasn't calling you out of your name, anyhow; I'm glad it was no worse. You may well swallow that, and more, without being choked. Go back before you sleep, and make it up with the ladies; and sure can't you hate 'em all the same in your heart, all the time, alanna? Do, now, theres a good girl, and dont make an *omadhawn* of yourself."

With these, and similar counsels and advice, Mary

was assailed; but she was also freely and kindly invited to stay, if she was not inclined to follow them.

"You're as welcome as ever to us, my poor girl," said Mrs. Gorman, "and more betoken because you keep yourself proper and respectable, when our own went and done wrong upon us. Oh, Mary, 'tis cruel for girls to go and break a mother's heart, as mine done. But I won't talk of 'em, they're a'most settin' me mad. There was Julia passed awhile agone, walking with a soldier, a smart English corporal, I'm tould he is, and he has no more notion of marrying her than he has of flying, and why should he? Who'd have her now? What dacent, honest man, is she fit for? Oh, my hearty curse down on that crochet, that brought my girls to ruin. Sure, myself thought sarvice was salvation for you; and stick to it, jewel, for God's sake."

"It wasn't the crochet done it. 'Twas the money that they worn't used to, that bothered 'em," said Mary; "and only that I had him *you know*, to take every penny piece from me, as fast as it came into my hands, I'd have been dressing myself up, and going gadding about with the rest. Though I

went to them balls, and was full of my fun, my heart
was heavy enough to keep me down to my work, and
make me mind what I was about. And didn't he
draw every ha'penny farthing from me, and leave
me, many and many a day, that I'd have starved
only for you?"

"Well, and that's a rason why I was glad, when
them ladies took you, and you were where he could'nt
get at you."

"But he did get at me, and still gets the very heart
out of my body, and is for ever frightening me within
an inch of my life."

"Well, acushla, isn't he your father? and hasn't
he every right to all you can do for him? And then
the state he's in—dark, and condemned, and in dread
of his being took up at any moment."

"Oh, he hasn't a bit of fear of being caught.
There's no one so safe as a man that was hung. No
law could do it over again, you know, and his blind-
ness would be enough to melt a stone; but I wish to
goodness that he would go to his people out in Mayo.
Whatever brought him here to Carriginis to bother
me this way. Sure he needn't have misdoubted me.
I'd have shared my airnings with him, all the same."

s

At this point of the conversation the barking of a dog disturbed the speaker.

"Here he is himself, talk of somebody and he'll come! I wonder did he hear me? He have some crooked turns in him, and is very jealous of me telling them to any one; so don't let on we had any discourse about him, Mrs. Gorman?"

"Wisha no, I won't, you crature," the old woman whispered, in the same low tone in which Mary had spoken her last sentence, and went out to unfasten the half door for the new comer.

"Who's that?" was the query of the visitant.

"Me, of course, looking for my child; who else did you expect?"

"Is Mary here? I was down at her misthriss's house, and there was a talk among the servants of the neighbourhood that she was run away, and stole a picture."

"Stole a picture! yerra, good gracious, what put that in their heads? She's safe and sound, but the never a picture, nor a tack of clothes, did she bring out of their house. She came here as empty handed as a new-born babe."

The blind man had, by this time, reached the seat to which Mrs. Gorman led him. His usual guide, a small tan-coloured terrier, had already found out Mary, having been let loose by his master, as soon as Mrs. Gorman undertook his office, when he quickly followed his scent into the corner in which Mary had ensconced herself.

"Ah, ah, Jip, so you got her," said Desmond; "come out here, Mary, and tell us the news."

"There's nothing to tell about it," she sullenly muttered; "I'm here, and I won't go back to Miss Black. I'll go to my work at the school to-morrow, and keep you up the best way I can, and so don't you be hunting me about, and putting me to the trouble of hiding you. I wonder how I bear with you at all, you drain me of all I earn; and now, here I am without a male's mate, but what a neighbour gives me out of charity."

"Mary, agrah, don't talk of that," Mrs. Gorman put in, "you have 'cead mille failthe' here, as long as you like. You are an honest girl, and better to me than my own, so be aisy, and do your best; no more can be got from any one. Barrin' the odd drop of drink your father takes, now and then, he is a

credit to you; and all you does for him, will make a
fine standing in glory for you. Sure he is a curiosity
of grace, brought down off a gallows, and his
eyes thin blowed out in a quarry, where he tried to
get work. I misdoubt there is any other like him in
Ireland. It's proud you ought to be of him, though
I know it's hard to carry on, and him so cruel on
you in some ways, and making your life a milch
cow to him; but sure he can't work himself. Now,
why don't he live on his beggings? They must be
handsome, or it's a quare world! Wheres the one
that wouldn't support him in clover, and make him
their comfort in eternity, if he would only sit quiet
at some chapel door, and howl and moan all day.
But here he must be going about, stravaging, and
strolling; I never saw so much got by that way, as
by sticking to one spot, where people are used to
passin' and gettin' your blessin'; they are so
afeard of your givin' 'em the other thing, that
they'll never dare to forget to bring you your share
of the pence. What do you think of setting him up
with a stool at the chapel, Mary? He'd get the
price of his lodging any day. There was a blind
man down street, that, for a matter of sixteen years,

knelt every evening on his two bended knees, pather-
ing the Lord's Prayer at the people that passed by,
and singing about his ' seven dissolute orphants that
lately buried their mother,' until all the world and
the quality had it by heart, and used to be laughing
about it, and going to hear him, as if he was a play-
acthor; but all the time, my honey, he was filling.
his hat with coppers. 'Deed, an' it was he won the
day, for he died a while ago, and left a power of
money in his bed, and his sons, that kep the public-
house near where he used to kneel, put a tomb over
him, enough to delight his heart. Now, if your
father would settle down in his old age, to a quiet
thrade like that, he might make a fortune for
you."

" Eh, yeh! Mrs. Gorman, my tongue would tire
in a week, of that *cronaun*; many's a ha'penny I give
myself to that fellow to stop his trap, when I used
to be passing by that way, before I knew what blind-
ness and beggary was—glory be to God for the
same! But, sure, I'll go away, 'tw'd be aisy for me,
aisier and betther, no doubt, than being the ruin of
my child this way. I'll go, some day, and end the
time that I ought not to have got in this world, if

the 'old boy' had his own.   Them that gave me the
respite, done it out of mercy, to keep me as long as
they could out of purgatory.   They didn't think it
would come to this pass, when my child would repent
of it, and wish me in it.   She shall have her way,
and I'll take a dip in the say and finish myself, and
I often think, maybe that I'd be in the right of it,
to offer it up as an 'atonement,' and go straight to
heaven.   Only one life can be due to God out of a
man, and it's two I'd be giving him!'"

"Oh, wisha, father," Mary cried, " don't be blas-
pheming that way!   Sure you know I'm willing to
work myself black and blue for you!   Oh, don't
frighten my life out; take my shawl, and get yourself a couple of shillings on it, until I can make some
'bits' and 'buttons,' and go down to the school with
'em, and I'll keep you comfortable all your days.
Oh, for the sake of my mother's sowl, don't be going
on this way, and setting me wild!"   And she burst
into a torrent of tears.

"Come here, my darlint, and don't be breaking
my heart," cried the blind man, "there's a sup in the
black bottle in my pocket, that would do you good,
Mary.   There's an impression on your heart, I'm

thinking, an it wants rising with a dhrop of sperrits."

" No, you may keep your whisky for me, I never took to that yet," replied the girl, drying her eyes and pushing back her massy locks, that were tumbling over her face.

" Well, Mrs. Gorman, dacent woman, don't you be so squeamish, have a small sup for good nature, and against the frost."

" Since you said the ' good nature,' I'll have to take a drain, for fear of bad blood between us," said the old woman, and with no unaccustomed hand, she put the bottle to her lips, and took a part of its contents:

" Och," she ejaculated, returning it to its owner, " that's more than I let down my throat this many a day. I dunna how you gets in such a lot of it, as sets your brain wandhering. The mischief's in it, no doubt; for them that follies on dhrink, never stops or stays at anything. Mary, you knew that these girls of mine wor as good as angels, until they got 'ticed into mornin' houses for dhrams, comin' home from temperance balls! But I must put down the kettle for the man's supper, he'll be in soon. Mary, will you light up the fire, like a darling ! "

Old Gorman had gone out to his labouring work, shortly before Mary had come in, and it was now approaching the time when he might be expected to return. The two women busied themselves with domestic occupation; the blind man lit his pipe and took a seat on a stool near the fire, while his dog, having hunted up an old bone, lay across the door-sill gnawing it. Soon after six o'clock, the master of the house returned, and the party gathered round the hearth to partake of the evening meal. It consisted of tea and dry bread. Sugar, but no milk, was added to the infusion, which was made in a brown tea-pot without a spout, and much marked by its frequent seats on the fire. The company drank out of tin cans or "ponneys," vessels substituted for earthenware, by the very poor in some parts of Ireland.

Desmond seasoned his tea with some of his favourite condiment, and urged his host, very generously, to accept some of the same.

"It makes very good stuff of it," said Gorman; "but I'm not used to so much, so go on with it yourself, and don't mind me. I'd like it of a Saturday

night, when I could rest on Sunday morning, and
wear out the headache ; but the worst of me is, that
I takes it of a Sunday night mostly, and then loses
the Monday morning's work, and often goes a week
on a reel; so don't set me going now. I've a job
that I swore to finish, and it will be worse for me, if
I don't, for it is for the priest, and he'll make me feel
his hand if I don't get it done for him."

" Oh then, Mr. Gorman," said Mary, " go to bed,
and don't be over-persuaded by my father. An' ·
father, go your way, and lave us ; do take to the
road, before the sperrits takes hold on you."

But the old beggar-man was in a jolly humour, and
he would not be dislodged. Mary knew by experience how it would be, and slipped out of the house.
She went down the road, and into a huckster's shop,
and bought a pound of candles, and returned and
quietly passed by the boon companions, who were now
sharing the bottle gloriously. She went into a little
back room, where she had formerly spent many a night
with her friends and fellow-workers, the children of
the old couple who now gave her a refuge; and,
with a weary heart, and slow fingers, recommenced

her old trade of "bit-making." Mrs. Gorman joined her, and drawing the bed-quilt round her, made herself up to keep company with Mary.

"I wonder what 'bits' I'll make at all," said the latter, anxiously. " 'Tis so long since I knew what they were doing at the school. There's 'crowns,' that no one but myself could make, and I'll try them with a dozen of 'em in the morning. They used to be two shillins, so they must be worth something at all events. Can you be making the 'buttons,' the way you used, for the girls, Mrs. Gorman?"

"Wisha, no, Mary, not this night. My heart is too heavy. Do you hear that old fool of a man of mine outside, singing and carousing? Sure it's no harm for your father that's given up to it, and has God's blessing on his sightless state, to do anything he can to enjoy himself; but there's Gorman at it, that has work promised, and will never be able to do it to-morrow. Oh, wirristhru, will he go out, when they drain that bottle, and stay at it till mornin' light, in them murdtherin' public houses?"

"Can't we fasten them in any way?" said Mary, "and coax them to sleep it off."

"There's no managing 'em, when they comes to

this," replied the more experienced woman; and presently the men were staggering about, and helping each other to go and do as Mrs. Gorman's fears suggested. In vain the women protested, prayed, cried, and even used all their strength, in forcibly trying to impede their going out. Blind as Desmond was, he found the way to elude them, and drunkenness gave Gorman all the power to resist his wife, that, in sober moments, he would never have used. He even struck her, when she stood before him; he dashed out into the road, shouting and exulting in his freedom from "women's control."

It was a distressing, a horrible sight! The blind man leading a blinder one into the most awful snare that one human being can set before another. Though Mary and Mrs. Gorman were, in a degree, used to these scenes, they did not the less lament and mourn over them.

With indomitable energy, Mary returned to her work, and closely wrought at it all through the night. No entreaties would cause her to desist. Mrs. Gorman used every endearing epithet, and fond, and motherly argument, to induce her to take a sleep, and go to work fresh in the morning; but without effect. The machine was set going, wound up, and should proceed.

Mary's industry had this peculiar spasmodic action in its nature, and this was a manifestation of it.

" No, Mrs. Gorman, no, it's of no use your talking to me ; and you, without a sup o' milk in your tay ; and I added to your bother ; and your providher on a drinking match ! I will not give in."

Nor did she. When the lace school opened next morning, Mary was at its door, and presented her "crowns," for which she was gratified to find that there was an active demand.

" I thought you were gone to service, Mary," said the superintendent.

" So I was, ma'am, but I left it again ; it does not fit me like."

" Then let me tell you, you are very wrong, but to try to fit it. This trade will not last, and domestic service will, and you are now come to an age when good hard work would serve you and keep you from mischief ; but I suppose you don't like service, and would rather be fiddling with the needle and thread."

" Indeed, that's just it, ma'am, I can't be rubbing, and scrubbing, and polishing—ah, what good is it all ?

And as to cooking, I hate it; it disgusts me to be after food, as ladies wants us to be."

"With such feelings, you'll never be either a cook or a housemaid, Mary; but, I thought it was more as a personal attendant, Miss Black had you."

"And so it was, mum, but I got tired of it; and now while the crochet is going at all, I won't stop from it again. When it fails, why, well and good, but it may last my time—who knows?" And Mary's light-hearted laugh was heard once more by her fellow-workers.

A few days after Mary returned to the lace-school, her late employer, Miss Black, called and enquired for her. The interview was long and exciting. Miss Black's face betrayed extreme emotion when she was departing, and Mary had an air of very unbecoming triumph and spiteful glee.

"I have them all in a fine state," she said; "there's mischief about an old picture that wasn't worth a rush, and they want to make out that a deep laid plot was in it. I don't care what they do, they may make ducks and drakes of it for me; and that fellow that told lies of me about the kiss, I hope he likes the mess that came of his story telling!"

Mary was sharply reproved by the superintendent for making so free with her late employer's name, and for gossipping about the affairs of a family in which she had been so kindly treated.

The matter was, however, soon forgotten, and Mary and her eccentric doings sank into the ordinary routine of work and workers in the busy school.

Meantime she continued to live with the Gormans, and to contribute out of her earnings to their little means; but, as usual, the bulk of her week's pay went to the blind beggar-man. He punctually met her at the door of the school every Saturday, and got the most he could from her by coaxing, threats, and cajolery.

They often walked away together, but it was always her object to avoid taking him to the poor old Gormans' house, where he was sure to introduce drink, and consequent sorrow.

" Why thin, Mary," said he, one day, to her, " it is a meracle you don't get married. The priest himself said so to me,—and all as one, as if 'twas my fault. 'I have nothing to do with it, yer reverence,' says I; ' she is my daughter,'but she don't give in to me, nor be said by me. Strangers has more of her love, and of her money, and sure it's no wonder, I'm only a poor, blind, old fool, fit to sit at the roadside and beg.' ' Don't attempt,' says he, 'to let your child be undutiful. God will not hold you guiltless,' says he : 'you'll be punished if any harm happens her. If she gets into the Gormans' company again,' says he, ' good bye to her.'"

"Don't you trouble your head," replied Mary. "Tell the priest, or any one else that talks to you about me, to mind their own business, and I'll mind mine. And now, good night : it is going to rain, and I must hurry home."

They parted, and Mary took a direction very wide of that which led to the house which she designated by the name of "home." As she passed along the well-lighted streets, she met many girls that she knew, who were walking about for amusement, and not a few of them were intent on no very good pursuits. None of them could attract Mary to join their parties, although many sought to do so, and all had a pleasant word for her.

She went on rapidly towards a building which, though some years had elapsed since its erection, was called the "New Chapel." It was a Roman Catholic place of worship, and though called a "Church" by the educated members of that community, it retains the old name of "Chapel" with the poor, who still adhere to the fashion of saying "going to mass," while the others use the same expressions as Protestants, when alluding to their religious observances. When she arrived at this New Chapel, she walked up and down under the colonnade in front of it for some time, and was evidently waiting for some one.

She had been there for nearly an hour when a priest ascended the steps and, without taking any notice of her, entered the chapel. She followed him, and was close at his heels when he got inside the door. Mary reverently performed the obeisance usually made by Romanists on passing the front of the altar, and rapidly pursued his reverence to the sacristy door. He opened it, and they passed in together, without exchanging a word. The priest was a man of the Italian type, and his ascetic appearance and deeply spiritual expression of countenance had raised him almost to the fame of a saint. Mary stood awed before him. Here was humanity purified from all dross, elevated to something heavenly, and far above any mean, earthly suggestions that might have impeded her, in devoting herself entirely to obedience to his orders. With a foreign accent, and a solemn voice, he adjured her to enter on no service

T

which her conscience did not fully approve: "for there are women," said he, "in this unhappy country who do not believe that the Church is *the* mother who has the first claim, and that the soul is more precious than the body."

"Oh, but they're Haythens or Protestants, yer reverence," said Mary, "but I am, and ever, and always was, a raal, true Catholic."

A smile came over the priest's face, but he did not look much gratified at her declaration. "You are very ignorant," said he, "scarcely fit to be trusted in such a serious business; but I am told that you want to do a good work and earn a heavenly reward, and this is one for which the Mother of Mercy and the Son of God will be your debtors."

Mary dropped on her knees, and clasping her hands assumed an attitude of deep self-abasing worship. The priest looked on in approving silence. She prayed, repeating with earnestness and intense devotion the words of one of the most sacred litanies of the Catholic church, and the ecclesiastic uttered a solemn benediction, to which the fervent and sonorous Latin tongue gave all the effect of a spell to the hearer. She remained on her knees in rapt, adoring veneration, while Father Petruccio folded up some documents into a package and sealed them.

When this was done, he approached Mary. "Now, daughter," he said, "go, and God be with you."

Mary put the parcel into her bosom and tightened the folds of the shawl she usually wore across it. The priest opened a door leading into a lane, at the back of the chapel, and so gave her exit.

The part of the town to which Mary directed her steps was one notoriously the haunt of bad characters. She had a natural reluctance to passing through it, and a refined, timid shrinking from witnessing the scenes that she knew must be common there. But her mission now gave her courage and strength; it was as she thought one of true charity. Her effort was to seek and to save the fallen daughters of Mrs. Gorman, and it led her to encounter contact with vice, from which she would have fled with as much delicacy and horror as the most pure-minded lady. Drunkenness and profanity marked the locality. Outside a public house some sailors were standing, and to one of them Ellen Gorman was replying with an evident appreciation of his joke when Mary stepped up to her.

"Ellen," said she, "I am sorry to bring you bad news."

"I might guess you had something of the sort to bring me," said the other, "or you would not take the trouble to go out of your road with it."

"Your brother Paddy is very bad," said Mary, without noticing this rude remark. "He fell off a scaffold and was nearly killed. He's lying in the Sisters' Hospital, and has had the priest, and your mother is breaking her heart about him."

Ellen, with all the impetuosity of her nature, alive to fun one minute, and plunged in sorrow the next, gave a keen cry—

"Oh, my darlint," she cried, "a boy that I was so fond of, and is there no chance of him at all?"

"None in the world," said Mary; "if you want to see him alive, you had better go now, and the nuns will lave you in; they don't expect that he'll live till mornin'."

"I'll call Norry," said Ellen. "Sure it would break her heart to have him go without a word to her," and putting her head in at the open door of a house close at hand, she called "Norry," in a loud, wild, excited manner, two or three times.

In a second or so this individual came out, and, hearing the tale, joined her sister in the most obstreperous lamentations.

"The best thing for you both to do," said Mary, " is to go to the Hospital, and make peace with your poor brother, or a day will come when you will be sorry for it."

The words had their effect, and Mary saw the sisters take their way over the bridge, directly towards an old house, which some " sisters" occupied as a hospital for the sick poor. She followed them at a little distance, saw that they rang the bell, and were admitted ; she herself passed round the corner of the building and applied for entrance at another of its doors, over which was marked " private."

The door was opened, and on Mary's showing the address on the package given her by the priest, she was speedily ushered into a parlour, and desired to remain there while the porteress went in, to inform the reverend mother that a messenger from Father Petruccio wanted to see her. Mary was some minutes waiting before the reverend mother made her appearance, and when she did so, Mary's sense of religious awe was even more deeply acted on than in the case of the pious father. She made a deep curtsey, and folding her hands on her breast, waited for the address of the lady.

The head of the Benedictine nuns in that convent was a lady of high birth and large fortune. She had founded that establishment of sisters, and had added the hospital accommodation to it. Her stature was commanding, and her air majestic. The graceful queen-like motion with which she entered the room, the benignity and beauty of her face, the sweetness of her smile, and the musical tone of her voice, all combined to affect Mary's exquisitely sensitive temperament. She could have worshipped her.

"I wonder is the Queen of Heaven like that? thought she.

"You are aware," said the reverend mother, "of the nature of the communication you have brought me. Your part of the transaction is done. I have got the girls. Tell their mother that I will use every effort to bring them into the fold of the virgin, and restore them to a holy life."

" May saints and angels crown you," said Mary.

"Daughter," said the nun, " our honours are from the King of kings."

She was about to open the door and send Mary away, but human sentiment of a kind scarcely permitted in such a presence induced the girl to put a question as to what would be done with the culprits that she had betrayed into the hands of the highest tribunal.

The nun, with her solemn manner, waved the point, and, with dramatic emphasis, told her that their interview was over.

" You have confided them to God," said she, " and he renders no account of his workings."

Mary was compelled to be satisfied with this reply and to obey the motion to depart. In a minute more she found herself standing under the starlit sky, no human device between her soul and its Maker.

"I wonder how I shall face Him with that lie on my soul," she involuntarily exclaimed; and walking with even more than her accustomed energy, she was soon at Mrs. Gorman's side, to whom she delivered the message of the reverend mother, while she loudly and bitterly complained of the part she had been induced to take in the affair, and strongly suggested that neither priest nor nun could save her from the sting of conscience, and were as little likely to ensure her the forgiveness of Heaven.

"Ah, you dunna what's laid on me at all, at all," replied the old woman, "I have that to do what will set me day and night, and keep me in torture aiqual to a scald every minute—to bear it, and be silent! Oh, they don't know a mother's heart—how should they?—nor a father's, if they think that Gorman will rest satisfied. It is he'll lade me the life, when he knows that I cemented myself with such a plot."

"Don't tell him my share in it, for pity's sake," cried Mary. "Sure I know he misbelieves in priests and nuns altogether, and says they are no better than the rest of the world; he told me the other day that the picture was the truth, and that Father James drinks like a fish."

"Oh, lave me alone about them all! What came over me at all to be said by these foreign men, that look like ghosts, and that have no more idea of our flesh and blood than if *we* were ghosts; but that lecture to women took the heart out of me clear and clane, and I was only afraid *not* to do it. Now it is done, my mind is distracted. I see no rights in it."

"If we done wrong, Mrs. Gorman, it is those that

made us do it is to blame. Now since the sin is taken off me, I'm as innocent as a new-born babe, and as to you, you had no hand in it, good nor bad."

"No, my dear, no *hand*, sure enough, it is my *heart* is in it, and it is torn to pieces: tell me anything you like now, but don't ask me to be aisy or comfortable for the rest of my days."

"Indeed, I'll spend my life to give you relief, for the hand I had in your trouble.' 'Poor child,' says the Italian father to me, 'why did you tell a lie? Who taught you to venture on it, even for a good cause? But, since you done it,' says he, 'I must take it off you. I thought you were ingenious, and could invent ways, you clever Irish girls; but you are, I see, able only to sin away,' and confess it after.'

'Just so, yer reverence,' I answered, 'we have only one way here with us, and we would be glad to get the other, and it is for that we comes to ye, holy fathers, straight from His Holiness, where every way must be known.' I disremember what he said, but he looked astonished-like, and began mumbling them thin lips of his, and lifting up his beseeching eyes to heaven. I declare, it is enough to make one long to go to heaven, if all the men that get there are like him."

About this time, a new mission of "Fathers" had begun to work among the Romanist female population. Their special object was, the purification and preservation of women's morals; and one of their institutions was, the "Confraternity." Under this head, they united women into "societies" and "orders;" and these were assembled on Sundays, and certain holy days, for instruction. The teaching was of a religious, and highly spiritual nature; and had an excellent design apparent in its system.

The men who undertook this work, were of the strictly ascetic caste, which intensity of devotional fervour and scant knowledge of Scripture produces— modern St. Anthonies, in fact, who would have every woman be a cloistered nun, and every nun an angel. These views, sincerely and zealously followed, were exceedingly effective. The veneration which the ordinary priests had long been losing, was restored to the church by the reaction and return of esteem for purity, that was encouraged by these missionaries, whose own sanctity was undoubted.

The lace-makers, amongst whom they principally

laboured, were not permanently affected by this movement, though they flocked in crowds to the special services, which, in object and nature, strongly resembled those called " revivals " in the Protestant Church. The sad depravity, that had been betrayed by the masses employed in this industry, had profoundly touched the hearts of many truly conscientious Roman Catholic clergymen, and they threw themselves into the work of regeneration, with an ardour which did them credit as men devoted to their ministry. They preached " temperance, righteousness, and judgment to come," according to their interpretation of Apostolic doctrine, and did it heartily. It is but fair to say of them, that they laboured earnestly for good.

With their purpose and design, no one could find fault; as to their mode of carrying it out, however, a wide difference of opinion must ever exist. They held that all was fair in the love of right, and warfare against wrong, which they maintained; and they practically avowed the dogma, "that the end justifies the means."

Hence, Mary Desmond's unhesitating and unquestioning docility, and entire submission in the hands of her spiritual director.　An ascendency to this extent was very easily obtained over the people, with whom the system to which we refer was adopted, and this obedience was so completely and essentially an external operation, that it was easily grafted on any internal deflections from good, and was supposed "to cover a multitude" of them, most conveniently.　The control of the "church" was perfectly established in outward things; but, alas! it was only the rule of the "Church," after all. The Spirit did not descend by it and through it, nor did it convert its subjects apparently into living members of the true Christian body; for the most active and unreserved embracers of this form of religious government were not, thereby, reformed in heart and morals.　Little, or no improvement, was shown in the social condition of the community in which it reigned in its best strength and vigour.

CHAPTER VI.

The abduction of girls like the Gormans with the consent of their parents was not a very uncommon occurrence, at least, with the consent of one of them. The mother was usually a party to the arrangement, moved by her deep religious feeling, which induced her to do violence to the tenderest part of her nature, while the father was, perhaps, barely tolerant, or at best did not resist the proceeding. Gorman was about an average sample of the way in which men bore with this interference of the church with the personal liberty of their children. He complained of it, and somewhat bitterly too, but it was in a subdued tone; "he smothered his grumbling," as the neighbours said. His wife and he had many an unpleasant scene, in which her religion was made the subject of taunts and sneers by him, and his spiritual state was reprobated, prayed for, and bemoaned by her, until his patience

was exhausted, and he was driven much farther than
he meant in expressing disbelief in the church of his
fathers. In the class to which they belonged, public
opinion was divided between recognition of the rights
of the father, and approbation of the duty fulfilled
by the mother. There was much sympathy with
Gorman.

"Poor man, to have his daughters dhragged
away without by yer lave, and no respect whatever
paid him, as if he worn't there at all," said some;
and the same hearts regarded Mrs. Gorman as a
martyr to her faith, esteeming her almost a rival
to Abraham in her self-sacrificing obedience, and
while she drooped day by day, "under the throuble"
that was on her soul, people begged her prayers,
coveted her blessing, and craved for her to put in a
good word for them to the Holy Mother, with whom
they believed she had ingratiated herself by her
act of piety.

She was to be seen every morning of her life
wending her way to the New Chapel, where the
Redemptorist Fathers left the insignia of their office,
in the shape of a collection of instruments to represent those with which our Lord was tortured. Out-

side the chapel door stood the spear, the crown of thorns, and the scourge; and before these, frequently knelt the votaries, whose feelings had been kindled by the orations of the Fathers on "the Passion," and to whom these emblems served as mementoes of their exciting addresses. Mrs. Gorman gave herself up to the contemplation of them, and was on her knees many hours, daily, in all weathers, in her long blue cloak, the hood of which barely permitted her face to be seen; she almost lived in this garment, like a cowled hermit, and gave herself up to what is termed "making her soul," until she almost ignored the presence of her body, and became attenuated and shadowy. She might have been supposed to be immaterial, but for the hollow sound that followed her practice of the Irish Catholic custom of beating on her breast. This pictorial action is supposed to represent that which the publican performed in that prayer, which has since provided all Christian penitents with a form of sound words; but the outward sign that accompanied it seems to be nowhere retained except in the Emerald Isle. None but those who have witnessed the ceremonial of the mass, as performed in Ireland, can have any

idea of the effect of the obligato accompaniment
which this breast-smiting and sotto-voce groaning
gives; but the impressiveness of the scene is lost in
the consciousness of the ephemeral nature of the
feelings that announce themselves with so much
noise and demonstration.

There are few things connected with the Irish
character less easily accounted for, than their submission to religious tyranny and their desire of political
freedom, as evidenced by the conduct of such men
as Gorman. It would have been utterly useless to
explain to him that there was any contradiction between the feelings referred to, much less to have
made him believe that they could not co-exist. He
did not like the interference with his daughter's
liberty; but it was "in the interests of religion,"
and he made no stir about it. His little world
understood his case, and it did not excite itself
to publish as a grievance that which was part of a
yoke borne for a religious motive, as it would have
done any movement on the part of a landlord, or of
the law. It is very well understood among those
people, that the church does not take such a step as
that of incarcerating young women without some

good reason, and it is taken for granted that the act is justifiable, or it would not have been done. The result of the process is seldom made known, so that whether or not it effects the object it proposes, is not ascertainable. This compulsory cloisterage is said to be, on the whole, generally satisfactory ; that is to say, the subjects of it very rarely resist it, after the first outburst of rebellion. Consummate tact is brought to the management of the cases, and nothing is left undone to induce the desired condition of penitence. The removal of two such terrible ringleaders of mischief as the girls Gorman, was a blessing to the district, and if they could by any means be reconciled to living in the asylum provided for them, it was an inestimable advantage to them, even as far as temporal things were concerned—their spiritual benefit, its direct object, is another thing. The convent in which Mary Desmond left them, being devoted to the care of the sick, it was not their ultimate destination. They were, no doubt, speedily conveyed to the care of nuns, devoted to the charge of Magdalens ; and these ladies, being trained to the service, pursue a systematic course of treatment which it is impossible to think can always fail in gaining, at

U

least, outward conformity, and some amount of moral improvement in their inmates. The Romish Church does not contemplate the return of these women to society, and therefore a home for life is offered to them. This is not always accepted, but it is much more usual to do so than may be supposed; hence the institutions in which they are sheltered are mostly crowded. Many leave, after various periods of residence: some who have been very contumacious and troublesome, whom nothing but returning to their evil doings will content, do so with violence, and often become worse than before; they endeavour to bring disgrace upon all connected with them, and occasionally involve in blame even those whose undertaking was well meant, however injudicious its prosecution may have been.

Few, indeed, of this unhappy class of women, either Protestant or Romanist, become really reformed, and the majority of those that come out of the convents, like those who leave our refuges, do not remain in the path of rectitude. There is strong presumptive evidence that life asylums are the strongholds of hope for such transgressors, and, in so much, we must agree that the principle of the Roman Catholic plan is good.

These establishments are generally conducted on the most approved system, are well digested, and applied with great judgment to the case in hand, under all its aspects. Their interiors are inviting to the weary and sin-sick, and nothing connected with them is suffered to be revolting or oppressive. They are very extensive, mostly laundries, and arranged on the most scientific principles.

It is carefully sought to reduce hand labour, and machinery of the best and newest kind is employed in them. Thus, irksome and slavish toil is not a part of their discipline; regularity, accuracy, and obedience are enforced, and all is done under a mild rule, as silent and yet as influential as any authority can be. The supervision of nuns—educated women, often ladies of peculiar culture, and great talents—is close and particular. Every two or three Magdalens have a care-taker, who watches all their acts and words; working, eating, and sleeping, she is at their side, and her judicious guidance and direction are the secret of the whole system. The success attained in the matter of mere industry is great. The washing done in these places is excellent, and they bring the art of getting up linen to per-

fection, so that women who pass any length of
time in them, bring away a knowledge and skill by
which, while they have bodily strength, they may
gain a livelihood. Such laundries charge more highly
than any others, and yet they have the command of
the business, and maintain their position above com·
petition.   The treatment in these houses is kind and
winning, the nuns are zealous and enticing in .their
manner; no effort that can be devised·is spared, every
sense is acted on, and a deeper sincerity of purpose,
and greater care in carrying it out, can scarcely be
imagined.

It would be unfair to withhold this testimony to the
work of nuns in this particular field of labour. They
wield a weighty influence, and they certainly exercise
themselves in using it for good ; but this influence,
of course, depends entirely on faith in certain religious practices which, to us, neither procure nor assure
individual salvation.   The whole scheme is, therefore,
a fabric in whose stability confidence is forbidden,
seeing that it builds on the untenable ground of
human effort, and lays its firmest anchor in the shifting
feelings of the sinner's heart.

We cannot trace the career of the Gormans, nor

is it needful that we should do so. About the time of
which we write, many girls were induced, on various
pleas, to enter Magdalen Asylums. We, ourselves,
have joined in the effort to persuade such, and have
felt a deep anxiety for its success. It was a good
plan for getting them bodily out of harm's way.
We have been permitted to visit the asylums, and
have been profoundly impressed with the power
of the system under which they are worked, and
anxious to import into our Protestant charities of
a similar nature, the rules and regulations which
act so efficiently in them. An impression to the
contrary of this is not uncommon; some people
imagining that the inmates of such institutions
are under a *régime* of terror, and a course of perse-
cution. Nothing can be further from the fact. It
would not be compatible with the sagacity of the
hierarchy of the church of Rome that it should be so,
and it is well to clear away the idea that anything
revolting is connected with the condition into which
it labours to bring its votaries. In fact, herein lies
the insidious nature of its dealings, and the craft and
subtilty of its proselytism.

The subject of young women's abduction by Roman

Catholic agencies, occupies the public mind a good deal, and there is evidently much ignorance as to the true light in which this act is to be regarded. The captives are almost always, no matter how their friends may disguise it, willing or semi-willing. They must have somehow, indirectly or otherwise, consented to the movement : or it may happen that relatives sufficiently interested in their spiritual condition, do it on their own responsibility, and conceal their complicity, for obvious reasons. At all events, the chances are well calculated as to the success of the attempt in relation to the subject of it, and to its effect on her immediate connections. The Church of Rome does not run foolish risks : it has as great an amount of intelligence as any that can be opposed to it, and probably greater cunning, a quality which it avails itself of less scrupulously than those whose faith denies the right of exercising authority over the conscience or free-will of any of its members. Wherever Popery is, it will carry its machinery, and one part of it is this forcible arresting of the career of vice, and the withdrawal of personal liberty, whenever the interests of the individual, or of the church, can be thereby subserved. No tribunal that

we can erect, can adjudicate in the matter, because
no common standard of appeal exists, to which we
can apply for decision as to its propriety. The act
is the dictate of a power that we do not recognize,
and, more than that, which we do not understand, and
what it does is outside of the principles that direct
our conduct; and there must its works remain—an
offence to our sense of freedom, and individual responsibility, a sin against our scriptural rule, a crime at
common law; and yet it is extremely difficult to procure a conviction under any of these headings, the
management of the affair is so skilfully conducted,
and the explanation so clear and satisfactory with
which our direct protestations are invariably met.

Since this is the state of the case, and since we
really cannot put an end, practically, to the recurrence of such proceedings, it is some consolation to
know that it is not productive of the personal misery
popularly ascribed to it. Discomfort and unhappiness
are not the usual effects of being carried off, and it
is susceptible of proof, that when after much excitement and trouble, persons have been recovered, they
have been found to prefer the asylum, and to desire
to return to its shelter. It would not have surprised

us to have learned that even the Gormans were voluntary recluses for the whole of their natural lives, nor to have been told that they had become exemplary inmates of the Magdalens that adopted them; and should they rise to the dignity of lay-sisters in any of the orders of nuns to which they are eligible, it is not impossible that they may present the purest type of female monachism that is to be found in the various communities.

CHAPTER VII.

Soon after the abduction of the Gormans, one evening, as Mary was going across the town, and just as she was emerging from the shadow of the old cathedral of Carriginis, and passing on towards her home, she was joined by a young man, of rather a gentlemanly exterior, who accosted her, with the familiarity of old acquaintanceship.

"I'll see you past the lonely part of the road, Mary," said he, "will you let me walk that far with you?"

"No, nor an inch," said she, "I don't want you, Master Tom. Go home, and behave yourself. It's a shame for you to be talking trash to me this way, of an evening, getting us both a bad name. It may be no harm to you, but it is to me."

"Ah, Mary, I wish you'd listen to me for a minute. I'm not so wicked as you suspect. I

would not bring harm to a hair of your head. Be
my own little girl—honestly, truly, I swear, I mean
you a fair offer. Be my wife; there you have it
now, and I'll do it. Yes, in spite of any father, or
church, or priest. You don't believe me? It can
never be? Why not? If ever man was in earnest,
I am. Don't you see, I would not wrong you, or
mislead you. Have I not been as respectful as if
you were my sister? All these years that I've been
looking at you, did I dare to speak to you, until the
night that I rescued you from the blind man that
was so drunk?"

Mary's face was crimson with intense annoyance
at this reminiscence. She well remembered the circumstance. It was an occasion on which she met
her father coming out of a tap-room, and had expos-
tulated with him on his conduct; he had raised his
stick to beat her, and had clutched her fast, and
would have inflicted severe bodily injury on her, but
for the timely interposition of the speaker.

It must be confessed that the silent admiration
and unobtrusive demeanour of this person, had very
much affected Mary. For some time, Sullivan had
been smitten with her personal beauty; and when

his manners called forth her character and made her show her spirit, in repulsing any advances of his that were derogatory to her dignity as a true woman, his feeling for her deepened into real love.

Evening after evening he had met her, and passed on without venturing to address her, or attempting to make her acquaintance; and the occurrence to which he referred was the first opportunity he had for exchanging a word with her. Since then, they had occasionally spoken to each other, and his manner was always very demonstrative of his admiration, while hers was decidedly repressive of anything like a similar expression.

Never, at any time, did she give him the least encouragement to suppose that she could possibly be brought to treat him in any other way than as a superior, whose notice could only be temporary, and, therefore, must be injurious to her. There was no relenting in her manner, even now, nor in her heart. It was as free as ever from any emotion, save vexation at the remembrance of the encounter with her father, and as devoid of the feelings which Sullivan desired to enkindle in it, as a child's.

But Mary felt kindly and gratefully toward the

young man, and was not rude or abupt in her denial
of his suit. He pressed it with ardour, and, all
the way to Mrs. Gleeson's, argued with her on the
subject of love being a leveller of all ranks, and
such-like sophistries; none of which, in the least,
affected her, or brought her over to his interests.

"The first and last is the same word with me,
Mr. Tom, I don't want to marry you. My feelings
is not like yours. I'm not so fond of you, as you
are of me, ———."

"Then, you are fond of some one else, Mary;
just say that you are, and it will soften the blow to
me. Are you, dearest, or are you only trying my
love, and playing with it?"

Mary was about to reply, when round the corner
of the road came the forerunner of the blind man,
the little tan terrier; and, as usual, his scent was
troublesomely accurate. He pulled and tugged his
master towards Mary; the blackness of night was
no shelter from his sagacity, nor from his master's
sharpness.

"Ah ha, Mary, are you there, my girl? Here,
let me hold you by the hand, for I'm tired a bit with
walking all day. You see, we always find you out.

There is no hiding from us, is there Jip? I feel there's a man in the company, but Jip knows him, he met him before; well that same is no wonder, for all the world knows the blind beggar-man and his dog."

"Go," said Mary, in a pained tone, to her lover, and he, hoping to gain her regard by his prompt obedience, immediately went off, walking away in the direction of the town; the connection between his beautiful Mary and the blind man, who, at one time, was her foe, and another her friend, puzzling him greatly.

"Tell me, as you value my blessing, who that was, Mary, for I know he was a sweetheart by the very step of him," asked old Desmond.

"I'll not tell you a word about him, so don't ask me," answered Mary, very crossly and shortly. "I tell you what it is," said she, "you must quit Carriginis, and that soon and sudden."

"Why for should I be put undther your ordthers," drawled the mendicant, "don't you know I has my work here to do, and a holy and blessed one it is, and salvation is at the end of it?"

"Go do it then, and let me alone. It is a quare service you are in, that don't support you."

" How do you know but it will ?"

" Then, lean on it, and don't come to me for any more money."

The father and daughter parted, and did not meet on the following Saturday evening. It would seem that the blind man was telling truth, when he asserted, that he had found out a means of subsistence, independently of his daughter.

Mary found her circumstances greatly improved by the withdrawal of his claims, and his personal absence was also a great deliverance. She sometimes wondered where he was, but did not seek to discover him, and contented herself by expressing surprise to Mrs. Gorman, that she never happened to meet him, " at mass or anywhere."

Mary's repulse of young Sullivan's suit, was not so effective as she intended. He still prosecuted it, and persevered in putting himself in her way, and doing all that he could to alter her determination. She had not told him that another was before him in her heart ; and he was young, and had all the faith of a true-hearted Irishman in the power of love.

" She can't hold out against me," thought he, " if the coast is clear, and there is no one between us." It was his constant anxiety, then, to solve this doubt, and to press his claim on her attention. Not obtrusively, nor offensively, but steadily and firmly, he adhered to his course; and a day never passed over their heads, but they met, if it were only for a moment, and exchanged a word. Sullivan never, by the slightest act, overstepped the barrier Mary's sensitiveness and reserve placed between them; he endured her coldness and her distance of manner, and lived on in hopes that a ray of the light of love would at last be kindled, by his perseverance, in those eyes which formed for him the only sun whose beams could enlighten his existence.

Interdicted from any other course, by Mary's express commands, as well as completely prevented by her manner, this devoted admirer restrained his conversation within the bounds of ordinary friendly interchange of communication. They often walked together for hours, of an evening, and visited and revisited, in these pedestrian excursions, all the lovely scenes of the valley of the Rock. The understanding between them was, at least, founded on profound mutual respect; and the topics on which they conversed had a bias of a peculiar character,

which contained a strong fascination for them both.
The subject that interested them both so intensely,
and that wrought up their spirits into so extreme a
state of excitement, was that theme so engrossing to
every mind of their race—the idea which absorbs the
whole mental energy of every individual of it, man,
woman, and child—politics!

Mary's acquirement of the power of reading introduced her all the more widely into this arena. She
had quite enough information to enter fully into her
lover's arguments and speculations. The sympathy
between them, about the wrongs of their country,
was intense, and they discussed them until the contemplation became anguish. They both had vivid
imaginations and lively temperaments, strong nerves
and acute sensibilities; and they " agonised at every
pore " over their conception of the state of Ireland.
The weaker of the two, as may be expected, was the
more violent patriot.

Mary's ferocity was worked up to a pitch of readi-
ness for any sort of action, and she infected Sullivan
to such an extent, that he longed for the opportunity
to put her impulses into effect. They had plenty of
inflammatory information supplied to them by the

newspapers and other publications: the pulpit, and all such vehicles of communication with the people, being also freely made use of to circulate inflated statements, and erroneous views of the objects and proceedings of the government.

The "Young Ireland" party was sowing its seed broadcast over the land; and no soil was better prepared for it than those two hearts. Nor were they isolated cases: they represented, unfortunately, a vast multitude, similarly ready for the implantation. The ground was prepared, and in the very condition that suited the growth of that crop, indigenous to the green island—rebellion. In that kingdom nothing else seems to thrive; no matter how statistics inform us of the decrease of other things, this remains troublesomely prevalent, and threatens to become perpetual. It seems impossible to uproot it. Clear away its probable causes, and redress its grievances by concessions—Maynooth grants—Government appointments; cultivate cereals—flax—industry—and all such things; give tenant right and gratify every demand, but all will be fruitless. In vain favours descend from "The Castle," like the dew of Hermon; yea, they may have the full powers of those that fell

x

on Aaron's beard, and cause the "good and pleasant"
spectacle, of brethren apparently living in unity.
But all these fail to secure against the return of the
noxious weed, which, like the upas tree, blights the
beneficent agency, that "good-will" labours to establish.   This root of bitterness springs up again and
again, and leaves no hope that any human interest
shall ever flourish in that land, except such as can
subsist on this description of food.   This is the fact
that drives one to despair of real peace in this unhappy
portion of the British empire.   Generations succeed
each other on its surface, only to exhibit fresh proofs
that they derive their political nourishment from the
seditionary pabulum on which their ancestry also
fed.

"Mary," said Sullivan, one day, when they were
taking one of their long walks, "now that I know
who your father is, and all about his goings on here,
tell me for what he was hung—you may trust me
that far now, I think."

" It isn't for fear you'd inform, or anything of that
sort, that I didn't make it known to you before, but
it is because he is so changed, and got so mean and
nasty since he was blinded and turned beggar, that

myself can't believe it is the same man is there at all
at all, and you'd never be able to believe he was once
dacent."

"Oh, but *I* can, if no one else ever does ; for his
daughter's sake, I shall believe all that ever could be
good about him."

"Well, I'll tell you our whole history ·now, and
judge you, if we haven't cause to bear us up before
God, for anything we'd do to the Sassenachs. When
I was born, my father was a well-to-do farmer, with
his twenty-one acres of ground in the County Mayo.
We had pigs, and fowl, and potatoes ; and sure 'twas
a saying that my mother was 'a woman of three
cows,' for that was her fortune coming to my father.
I dunna how they got on at all, but they run through
a deal. They never had but me. My mother was
a sickly woman, and I was her only child. She was
quite given up to God and the priest, and has a high
place in heaven this minit, her prayers and her
penances were so great, let alone her charity, which
she was always doing,—giving away like a fountain.
My father says she used to leave the house as bare
as a whistle, no matter how the fillin' in was to be
got. Neighbours said, that she had the biggest

hand in the parish, and kep up the priest in shirts, and bacon, and stockings, and eggs, enough to make him as fat as a fool.

"Well, times got bad with them somehow or other, and my father came short of his rent, and the tithes, and then he tuck into his head that he had no right to pay them, and that the landlord was only an invader sent by Cromwell, and that the tithe proctor was the devil's own agent to make people support a sinful religion for the heretics; and so he swore that the man that would force those dues out of him, he'd have his life. My mother seen him cleaning his gun, and keeping it ready loaded, and she, nor no one else, believed he'd use it on anything but a bird or a rabbit. I was a little walking infant, and not up to anything at all, when he done it. He was out of a day, at a funeral, amusing himself, and my poor mother was lying sick in her bed, (God rest her soul!) myself was playing about, as gay as a lark, when a big man came and asked, ' Is Desmond here?' says he. 'No, sir,' says my mother out of her settle, where she was keeping herself warm. 'He's keeping out of my way,' says the man, 'and it is well the cows is not;' and out he went to the shed, and he drives the cows out before him, and down along the road to Mayo. It was the market day, and he up and sold 'em to a butcher, and put the money in his pocket, and went home to his dinner, as if he done no wrong. It was 'the law,' the neighbours said, and they strove to keep my father down, but nothing would hold him.

" ' Go before the magistrates,' says they.

" ' Catch me at such second-hand work,' says he, ' I'll go to my God with the case, and he'll do me justice. There's where every man gets his rights.'

" ' Out he went, my dear, and what would you have of it ? but he shoots the procther that night, as he was riding up to the city to lodge his money in the bank. He never robbed him, but let him lie on his side all of a heap where he fell, and his pockets full of gold ; my father mounted his horse, and rode for his life. But in the town of Slay there was a Protestant man that knew the baste, and set the peelers on the watch. So when news of the murdther was stirred about, they laid hands on my father ; and he did not deny it, but went boldly up, and let 'em do what they liked with him. He was tried, and condemned, and when my mother heard that the judge

put on the black cap, and sentenced him to be hung,
she gave a screech, and fell back in her bed, and
never riz up afther. She was buried the day he was
hung, and he never knew a word of it until long
afther, for them that recovered him didn't tell him
the worst for ever so long. I dunna where he went,
nor how it was managed—some says it was young
docthors, and more that it was bein friends with the
hangman, Galgy by name, that never yet was known
to let any man slip that was real and true to Ireland.
He had a way with him of doing it safely, and get-.
ting them away afther, through means of having the
bodies for a perquisite; an' sure it was himself he
chated, for he could make more money out of a dead
man than a livin,' any day, in his thrade.'

" When I was left thin a poor orphan, praise be
to God! I was taken by one neighbour, and another,
and kep well, and comfortable. All our things
went, of course, to the landlord, and still I had no
want, nor never knew anything about my poor
father, though the very thoughts of him was worshipped by the gossips that stood to me, and they
remembered him morning, noon, and night in their
prayers. Well, I got a crochet needle, and begun

making the edgings, and took into my head to travel where it was giving out as a way of living, and my mind was set upon making for Tauney Convent, when, of a fine day, a blind beggar-man came into Mrs. Hurley's, the woman that had me, and says he, ' God save all here ! '

" ' God save you kindly, sir,' says she.

" ' Where's the little child of the Desmonds,' says he, ' that is about these parts, can you tell me, good woman ? '

" ' In this house this minit, and oppossit you, too ; but she's a grown slip now, and no child,' says she.

" With that, he hullagoned out—you'd hear him a mile off.

" ' Who are you at all ? ' says Mrs. Hurley, says she. ' I'm her father, if I'm a living man,' says he. With that, we all begun screeching, and roaring, and in came neighbours, and joined us, and such a noise as was there, I'll never forget.

" He soon told his story. He took work as a quarryman in Wicklow, and there got blind by a blast of powdher, and then went on the road as a regular beggar, and follyed his dog about the counthry, and that was the short and long of it, my dear. He had heard tell a dale about the lace, and what a power of money girls was getting by it, and he was all for my starting, and getting tached at wanst. So we went, he and I together, out on the world, and I done for him what I could from that day to this."

" And badly he repays your devotion, I must say," replied her auditor. " He does a deal of dirty work, that better men would not meddle with. I wouldn't wonder if his conscience got a twist, when he was scragged that time. 'Stretched' they used to call it in them days; and it seems to have been a real stretch in your father's case. It lengthened his days beyond the ordinary span. How old is he, Mary?"

" Nigh upon seventy-nine, and he so hearty and strong. Can it be the whisky keeps him like this?"

"Many says it is, I can assure you," replied Sullivan, " but if it is, it is a bad spirit it keeps in a man, and he's better dead than giving it his body to work in."

CHAPTER VIII.

Tom Sullivan and his father were both employed in the office of which Mr. Black, Mary's late employer, was the head. Their efficiency and moral worth were very much approved of; in fact, it was the character which the father bore, that procured for the son his appointment, and the arrangement was generally considered a satisfactory one.

Mr. Black had great confidence in the Sullivans, and treated them very liberally. He frequently availed himself of the services of the younger one at his own house, whenever extra work demanded increased activity in the department in which he was engaged. According as Mr. Black aged, this course was often adopted: and during one whole winter, when Mr. Black had very bad health, in order to lighten his labour, and to husband his failing strength, he pursued the system of doing the greater part of his business at home, with Tom Sullivan for an assistant, sending him to and fro to the office with messages and important communications.

This management rather added to Sullivan's duties, but he fulfilled them unremittingly, and was not known to complain in the least of the amount of work imposed on him. His evenings were a good deal encroached on by his additional occupation, and he was prevented from taking as much amusement as he otherwise should have done. But he was amply paid by Mr. Black for the services which he rendered, his earnings being very nearly doubled without commensurate exertion, so that the pecuniary advantages considerably outweighed any temporary inconveniences that he incurred.

Many opportunities were afforded him of being peculiarly useful to Mr. Black, and Sullivan availed himself of them, and was found so generally serviceable and obliging, that a pleasant feeling subsisted between him and his employer.

Miss Black was a person of some interest to Sullivan, as she went in and out of her father's study. He connected her in his mind with his Mary, whose

period of servitude in that house had been to him a
time of intense anxiety and distress. What misery
he had endured as he thought of her attractions, and
imagined the opportunities she had for getting
married to some one in better circumstances than
those to which he aspired.

Anything, indeed, whatever it was, that caused her
to leave off domestic service as an employment, was a
matter of rejoicing to him. He could not bear to think
of her as a servant in anybody's house, and in the
way of the rudenesses from persons above her position, that such a state permits of; his excessive jealousy leading him into an error, as to the risk in these
respects, attendant on the line of life against which
he was so violently prejudiced.

There really is nothing of the kind attached to
the relationship of master and maidservant in Ireland. The respectability of women in this occupation is peculiarly regarded, and specially preserved;
and in no other condition is such protection accorded
to females, as in that of domestic employment.

Had Sullivan known Mary Desmond as well while
she was engaged in it, as he afterwards did, his fears
for her safety would have entirely disappeared. But it

was not until she had quitted the service of Miss Black, that their acquaintanceship progressed beyond the exchange of looks, in chapel and elsewhere. Miss Black little knew that her father's clerk took any notice of her, as she glided about, and, now and then, interfered with the course of business, in order to induce her father to attend to his health. Her sweet, womanly ways were very charming. Mr. Black derived much comfort and pleasure from them; and Mr. Harris, who was a frequent looker on, found them absolutely bewitching. Neither of them ever thought of the clerk, as anything more than a mere writing machine; and, while he sat there driving his quill, as utterly disregarded him, as if he were a clock, or any other such useful, self-acting instrument. .

As to any connection subsisting between him and Mary they knew nothing, and for her they retained no very particular regard. Her violence and irritability left an impression on their memories, that effaced the kindly sentiments which they had felt towards her in the beginning of their acquaintance with her.

"Sullivan," said Mr. Black, one day, " I have a

long job for you, and I wish to arrange with you
for your evening work. I'll pay well, as it is
special business. It may last a long time, so it
will be well worth your while to devote your attention to it."

" I'm sorry that I can't do it, sir; my evenings are
engaged, and I am unable to get free of my occupation."

" Oh, indeed, why I thought it was only an honor-
ary secretaryship that you held in that new society.
Is there a salary then, and a regularly paid agency ? "

" No, sir, there is no salary—it is a gratuitous
affair, but I am as much bound to it as if it was remunerative."

" Nonsense, man; don't be so chivalrous ! You
really can't afford it. You ought to be making
money every hour of the day that you can. It is a
misfortune for Irishmen that they do not know the
true value of time. It is your money; why should
you give it for nothing ? "

" I have my compensation for it in store, sir, and
I am satisfied with it. Perhaps my countrymen,
also, are content in the state that you so much disap-
prove of."

" Oh, may be so. I hope they and you mayn't be disappointed, that's all I have to say."

This conversation occurred as Sullivan was standing up to leave off work one afternoon, and its result discomposed Mr. Black very considerably. He was in a greatly excited state when his daughter entered the room, as she usually did on the departure of the clerk.

" What is the matter, papa?" said she.

" A good deal then," he replied. " I quite counted on Sullivan's getting all those reports and returns done by Easter; and so he could, too, if he would give the time to them; but the idle dog actually refuses to be hired to complete them for me! He declines evening work at any pay, and prefers these meetings, where he spends his time for nothing— giving labour for his soul, I suppose, serving the Church, or the country, or some such folly. I am sick of the bore of dealing with fellows who won't work at anything that is good and useful for themselves, but must spend their energies in doing mischief. I'm convinced that it is politics that is bewildering that fool of a fellow, and keeping him from earning a good living. I wish I could see his

father, and have a talk with him. It may be well to
try and save the young man from the consequences
of the rig that I fear he is running."

" Indeed, I am quite sure," said Miss Black, "that
there is some political agitation going on in connection with that ' Young Men's Improvement Society,'
in which Sullivan is so active a member. Nothing
but some such work would induce him to give up his
pecuniary advantages in this manner. I shall not
wonder if he go away altogether, and leave you to
do this troublesome business with a strange assistant,
without caring how it inconveniences you, or injures
your health. I believe when once Irishmen get the
maggot of patriotism into their heads, they lose all
common-sense, and become mere seditious machines,
without point or object, except the desire to upset
existing institutions, and create confusion and distrust
between the people of this country and the English
government."

" Well, my dear, I hope whatever comes of the
hobby Sullivan is riding at the Temperance Hall
every evening, he'll stick to me till I get my accounts squared with the head office. He, and he alone,
understands my system of registration and abstrac-

tion, and inextricable confusion would result from an uninitiated hand coming in on the business."

"Come to dinner now, papa, and think no more about it," urged the daughter. Mr. Black complied with the first request, but with the second it was out of his power to do so.

The idea that Sullivan might possibly throw up his present employment completely took possession of the sickly old gentleman's brain. Health had, of late, greatly failed Mr. Black, and he was disordered by the want of it both in mind and feelings.

A very heavy amount of overwork had taxed his intellectual powers beyond their capacities, and the reaction was fast setting in on his general system. Sleep frequently forsook his eyes, and nights of wakefulness and excitement were common to his diseased condition. The sympathetic heart, heretofore only recognized in his bosom by its kindly throbs and warm, devotional feelings, now made its palpitations felt, as his greatest physical evil. This dangerous symptom of a fatal ailment, had been latterly very alarmingly developed, and it had awakened the most distressing anxiety on the part of his family and friends.

Every care and every precaution were taken to
keep him free from all that could possibly produce the
least agitation.   The responsibility and deeply trying
duty of attending on her beloved father, devolved
entirely on Miss Black, for her mother had become too
infirm to assist her, and both her brothers were settled
in distant places, engaged in their respective occupations.   They wrote home constantly, and came often
to know how their parents were, but neither of them
could be induced to live in their native city.   The
social condition of Ireland was uncongenial to them,
and they preferred to form the connections of life in
England.

Miss Black had to exercise all the self-denial of
which a woman is capable, in order to perform her
undertaking.   She had to defer her marriage, and
to make the claim of the lover of her youth subordi-
nate to her filial affection.   This severe course
had its effects on her·disposition.   The struggle to
sustain her steps in the path of duty *versus* inclination,
was a serious thing.   It told on her frame, and she
was far from being robust and strong.

Mr. Harris was very discontented with the arrangement, and he clamoured continually against it.   On

Y

the very evening in which Mr. Black had the conversation with Tom Sullivan, just detailed, he attacked his intended father-in-law on the subject.

" I'm sure it is not my wish to stand in the way of my child's happiness," said this gentleman, feebly. " Marry, young folks, and leave me. I am as well able to bear it now as I shall ever be—perhaps better. Every day will see me getting worse and worse, lower and lower. I'm sinking fast—don't wait for my death—let me see you united and comfortably settled. I shall die more easily and cheerfully."

When the old man retired for the night, the lovers sat in deep consultation, and they finally decided that they would marry immediately, and that the family party in Mr. Black's house, should gain a member, instead of losing one.

Mr. Harris agreed to come and live with them, and share with his wife the task of tending her father's last hours. The bargain was sealed, and a scheme for carrying it into effect arranged. The marriage was to be private, and to take place in a few days, so as to bring Mr. Harris into the house at once, and enable him to do for Mr. Black what his own sons were too far off to accomplish.

It was absolutely indispensable, that the burden of his official work should be taken from this aged servant of the public ; and to do this, it was necessary that some person should enter into the whole of his affairs, and gain a clue to their full explanation. There was an exigency coming on, which demanded that there should be no delay in taking this step. The Government had called for voluminous reports and returns, and these, formerly so easily rendered, were now gigantic difficulties to the failing powers of the once clever officer. Sullivan, his right hand, was deserting him, and he was not in health or spirits to seek out a new assistant.

The proposal made by Mr. Harris was the best possible form in which relief could come—a son-in-law, willing and able to disentangle the knots into which his various arrears of accounts had got twisted, appeared providential. The knowledge that such a blessing was in store for him, would have gone far to procure for Mr. Black some hours of rest that night ; but it was unfortunately withheld from him, and his poor throbbing head, distracted by thought, uneasily moved upon his pillow. When morning broke on the household, two of its members met, who, from

very different causes, had not been visited by the
sweet restorer.

Miss Black went to see her father, and, as usual,
take him his breakfast. He betrayed to her watchful
eyes, at a glance, the kind of night he had passed.

" I'm ashamed to say, child, that I fretted like an
old fool all night, and could get no sleep, so I am
fit for nothing to-day; and yet, I must go to work,
aye, and hard work too,—that Sullivan will leave
it all to me, and there is not a man in the town
that I could trust to help me."

" Not even William, papa ?"

" My dear girl, I should not like to bring him
into my office, he has enough to do in his own."

" Not at present, papa, and he desires me to say,
that he will put himself at your command until all
those troublesome affairs are done. He wants to
begin at once, and go into the business. He will
go to work as soon as you like, but he makes a condition." Here Miss Black hid her face in the cover-
let, and was silent for a moment.

" What is the bargain, dearest; how is he to be
paid for harnessing himself to my load, and drawing
it up the hill it is at this minute?—Ah, I see! but

I won't give that—not you, love, oh, no! I can't spare you, though I said I would last night. I am selfish again—I won't let you go. Who would come to me then with breakfast? and who would cheer your mother in the lonely separation that our infirmities are now putting between us? No, no! Think of another mode of payment."

"We have thought of a plan that you will surely like, papa! It is that we should live here, and that I should continue my old duties, and do them along with my new ones."

"Ah, my child, are you able for all? Well, try, I am only too glad not to have to part with you. Have you settled any time or mode?"

"We have—this day week—a private marriage—no wedding, or visiting, or travelling; just go out to church, and then home to work. I know it will please me best, and I am sure William will be happy at it if I am."

"What a sober couple! A quiet move, indeed, in the most joyous affair of life! I'm grieved to cause my child so dull a season for her highest delight."

"Never mind, papa, we shall be the more truly attached since there is to be no show of our love. It will be all for the best. You are content, then ; if so, oblige me by sleeping an hour or two."

"I'll try, but I have a latent uneasiness for fear Sullivan may not come this morning ; and so between his idleness and my own laziness, the day will be lost."

With the ease that the news his daughter brought him gave, Mr. Black's excited nerves were soothed into composure. He soon slept like a baby. Miss Black watched by his side, and was painfully alive to the fact that the clerk did not come .at his accustomed hour. When his ordinary time for arriving was some time passed, she went to see if he was in his place; but there was no sign of him. The library, where he generally wrote, was empty, and all the papers were strewn about, as they had been on the previous evening.

"Has Sullivan been here ?" she asked of the housemaid, who usually admitted him.

"Yes, miss, an hour earlier than usual; but he only poked here and there, and looked for something that he said he forgot last night, and then went out again. I said, 'Will you be soon back? for I'm going up to the bedrooms, and may as well leave the

door ajar for you.' 'No,' says he, 'I'm not coming to work to-day,' and, with that, off he set."

Miss Black discerned that some uncomfortable
doings were going on, and she resolved to try if she
could make a temporary arrangement of the business by telling Sullivan the whole state of the case,
and making it a personal favour if he would come
and finish all the writing and accounts, that he alone
fully understood.

"Do you know where he lives?" she asked of the
servant.

"No, miss. Mary Desmond used to know; myself never inquired. He was ever and always stiff
to us. She thought he was in love with her, and
was so conceited whenever he looked at her; we wor
amused at her blushing. But I don't believe he
ever noticed her at all."

Taking this hint, Miss Black sought Mary at the
lace school, and there again made an attempt to obtain a kind and candid reply to her simple question,
as to the address of Sullivan the clerk.

"I'm sure the sorra one of me can tell you where
he lives," was all the answer she got; and she left
with a painful impression that the ignorance was

feigned, and that the refusal to assist her search formed part of a plot to injure and annoy her family in some way.

Miss Black then proceeded to the Temperance Hall, where she rather suspected that Sullivan had engaged himself in another employment, and she hoped to find him there. She was not mistaken. He was seated at a desk in one of the offices of the hall, and seemed very busy. Miss Black did not catch his eye when she first entered, and, therefore, she had full leisure to scan the place before he gave her any attention.

The interior of the Temperance Hall had a good deal of interest attached to it. It was ostensibly a place built for the accommodation of Roman Catholic societies for the diffusion of knowledge. When it was first opened, it had afforded most efficient aid in promoting various organizations for useful purposes. Benefit societies, industrial associations, and companies, got up among the people for their mutual advantage, such as " loan banks," " *montes de piété*," &c., had all found space for their meetings, and earliest transactions, under its roof.

Some of these were now at work on their own

resources, and no longer required the gratuitous help the relief committee gave them ; and some had fallen to the ground, brought to untimely ends by the sectarian and party spirits that arose in their ranks.

Mr. Black had, at one time, anxiously sought to unite with the people, and tried hard to identify himself with the first efforts of industry that had their beginning in that assembly room ; but he, and other good men and true, were chased away by the demon of discord and disloyalty that was born and bred of the discussions which took place between the members of the committees that had been formed for better work.

Miss Black was keenly sensitive to the atmosphere of antagonism to her section of society in Ireland that was engendered by the principles put forth in the lectures and meetings held in that place ; and she felt the chill of the coolness which was evidently setting in between her father, and his confidential clerk. But she resolved, as it was her wisdom to be conciliatory to Sullivan, to act as if the existence of distrust between them was impossible.

The moment their eyes met, a glance shot from one to the other ; it implied, " I know you, and you

know me." Yet there was no anger in her tone,·
nor the least trace of anxiety, as she said in a calm,
self-possessed, lady-like manner—

"Tom, I'm sorry you have to give up papa's
work so suddenly. Can you spare him a day or two
until he suits himself? And no one knows better
than you that it won't be easy to do that. You will
be difficult to replace. Few realize his ideas of a
good hand. He had you trained to his ways, and
regrets you greatly."

"And I greatly regret him, miss," said Sullivan,
unfeignedly, "but I can't help it."

"Yes, I understand it all very well," she replied,
"there are higher interests than your own at stake."

"No, nothing but my own," he burst in with.
"She is my own—my country is my own—hers are
mine, and I am hers !"

This heroic was interrupted by the opportune entrance of a priest, or the rhapsody might have
led to a very lucid exposition of Mr. Sullivan's
views. The clerical gentleman gave a sharp look of
warning at him, and bowed politely to Miss Black,
who was not a little embarrassed on seeing him.

* He was the original of the sketch that had created such a sensation in her home.

Mary Desmond, Tom Sullivan, and this ecclesiastic, were all suddenly associated in her mind, as connected by an electric chain, whose coils somehow touched her, and those whom she loved. It was a mere passing thought—a phantasmagorical delusion —a scene shifted as soon as introduced—a breath—a fancy—an imagination, and no more.

Was it really no more? Then how did the coincidental ideas arise? were they without foundation?

We know more than she. Miss Black had not our acquaintance with the ties existing between these parties, and yet here she had a glimpse of the truth. It was a penetration, an hallucination, an act of sudden, subtle, sinuous perception which sees and discovers instinctively all that is needful to the well-being to be aware of. An instance of the sensitiveness of human nature, every pore being a vehicle; and of sight being diffused, and not confined to the mere eye-ball, but having a secondary, sympathetic influence in other parts of the system.

Let no one reject the least exertion of this force;

it is supplied for our protection from danger, for our warning in case of enemies; and when it seems to indicate in an unaccountable manner, and undertakes to look, as it were, round a corner, it is but working its own right end. The instinct which is beyond reason is an invaluable gift.

Miss Black had it in some uncommon measure. She now felt that it was difficult work to deal with her father's ex-clerk, and said, very hesitatingly: "Good morning, Sullivan; I hope you will be as satisfactory a servant in your present employment as you were in your former one."

"Thank you, miss," he replied, respectfully enough, and resumed his occupation as she passed out of the office.

The door-step had occupants as she was returning that were not there when she entered. These were the blind beggar-man and his dog. They were well known by sight to Miss Black, as often coming to her house to solicit alms. "God save you, misthriss," said the blind man; "your gownd brushed by me, and I know it is a famale woman that is going out. Have pity on the poor dark creature."

"I've nothing to give at present," was the reply

he received from the passer by, and she was soon
beyond the reach of his mendicant whine, which he
kept up for several minutes, in hopes to extract even
the smallest coin. Its gift would not have failed to
stop his mouth ; and many persons gave it for the
purpose of so doing, when circumstances prevented
their getting out of the reach of his voice. Miss
Black, fortunately for her, had the power of using
the latter method of getting rid of his importunity.

" There's no chance of a ha'penny from her," said
he ; " she's gone too far now. I wonder who she
was at all at all, an' how she got in ; it must have
been when I went for my glass. Will it bring me
anger, I wonder ? Maybe it was Mary was within
courting Sullivan. I hear she do be after him,
though she is so sly to me about it."

While he was soliloquizing, the priest that went
in lately returned.

" You blind thief, why do you let any one in except those that give you the word ? I'll take care
to stop your pay for this sort of work."

" Sure I never done it, yer reverence ; no one
passed here but the brethren, so help me ——— "

" Now stop before you perjure yourself," cried the

clergyman. " You are just puzzled to know who the woman was that passed you. How dare you have let her in against all the orders you receive ? "

" Now, then, yer reverence, what orders ? For no one of ye ever tould me to prevent women, it was always men ye mentioned, and if all the petticoats in town was to be wafting about me I'd never have thought of stopping one of 'em; faith, my belief was that ye wished 'em to be about the place; it keeps off suspicion, like; while famales is in the company no harm is going on, is what people generally thinks."

" Hold your tongue, sir," said the spiritual direc- tor, "and mind my orders in future : don't let in man, *woman*, or *child*, without the pass."

" Oh ! trust me, I never did, nor I never will; she that got in stole in while I was ——" ,

" What, sir; then you were off your post; I believe you can't keep two hours without going for that glass of whisky. It will be the eternal ruin of you, you brute;" and with this kind remark the minister of grace departed.

The blind man sat still on the steps, and his re- flections were not very placid. " I'm a brute, am I ?

maybe so ; other people is worse. I wish Mary was coming along; she has sight, any way, and I'm getting rather afeard that things is looking black and ugly ; there's such brooding and hatching of plots and plans. Some day it will end badly for 'em all; and only my neck got its twist wanst, it might be stretched again. What more can they do to me ? Sometimes I think even the divil himself has no more power over me, and I'm left to live for ever like the wandhering Jew, praise be to God ! "

Just then a hand was laid on his. " Mary," he whispered.

" Yes," said she, in the same tone.` " Are you my own real father ? " said she ; " can I believe it ? will you do a father's part for me this night ? You must ; I'll make you, if a drop of your blood runs in my veins, it will turn and drag you to rescue me ! "

" Eh ! yea ! girl, what's the matter ? Who's going to do anything to you ? "

" Listen, father. As there's a God above us I'll tell all I know to-night, and to-morrow my life won't be worth a straw. I'm in the tortures of hell with my mind : I can't stand it another day, nor I won't. Now, will you save me from them that will

massacre me, and that will find out my informing
the moment the words is out of my mouth."

" Thin why do you do it, if you are so afeard ?
Is any one to pay you for it ? or why are you for
doing it at all ? Can't you keep it ? hould it, I tell
you, the longer you hould it the more the saycret
will be worth. I was near telling it myself a week
ago, when I wanted money ; but now I'm well paid
up. Are you wantin' a trifle ? I could spare it to
you now, Mary. Will you have it agra ? There,
don't shame and disgrace us for ever by turning in-
former."

" Oh, father, father, you don't understand me at
all : mountains of money wouldn't make me happy
now, after what I done—betrayed them that were
kind to me ! Oh, it is I that am sore and sorry :
black misery to them that tempted me ! May they
have the worth of their conduct in fire and blazes.
Oh, let me alone, I can't contain myself, I'm going
wild mad, I tell you. See here, I'll drown myself
the moment I enlighten Miss Black, and make a
confession, and get her forgiveness. It would be
more to me now than the priest's. When I come out
of that house where I am going, I'll want you, and

you must and shall come with me, and stick to me as a father should ! "

" You're taking leave of your senses, child ! I'll mind you, and stick to you ; but it will be to prevent you making a complete fool of yourself. There's Sullivan inside ; and by all accounts he is the comforter and purtector you want, and not your blind father ; go in and talk to him."

" It is from him I want to get ; don't you know ? Didn't you hear that I promised to marry him ; but now I never can do it—no, never. He's safe from me and my troubles. God forbid that I should bring him into my shame."

" Oh, you're taking on a dale too much about shame. Where is it, I'd like to know, but on them that employs the likes of us ? There's the place where the shame will be put, not on us ; and let 'em keep it. They has all the good, let them have some of the bad ; but I'll tell you the truth, I seen no good out of any of their schames. They uses us like an old pot, and kicks us aside when they're done with us ; so I don't blame you to be cracked with anger at 'em ! What do you think Father James called me just now ? a brute, if you plase ; as if flesh and blood

z

could stand that. I was near to kick him, the impudent ruffian, as if I was the dirt of his shoe ! Ah, we know now what priests is made of, we see the other side of them."

"Oh, now father, don't be wicked, there is bad and good among them. They 're men after all, though one would not think it sometimes, they 're so deep and decateful.   But if I'd have minded that good little holy man at the confraternity, I would not have come to this mischief; but I can't stand another moment, come with me, father, dear; I'm your child. Ah, am I not? I have no mother! Where can I turn? Where shall I hide my head. Come, oh come, take me somewhere, anywhere! let me hide my head in any hole, oh, even on your breast.   Have you a heart in your bosom for your child? Did my mother bear me to you? Oh, heavenly Father, look down on me! Oh, Mary, blessed Virgin Mother, am I too bad for you to pity?   Father, get me a sop of straw to lie on, take me home, help me, pity me.   The pains is on me! oh, Saviour!"

By this time the blind man had perceived the state of the case, and had risen, and had put his arm round his daughter. He was truly and naturally affected at last.

"Hold on to me, and let us get into a shelter," said he, as he tremblingly supported her. It was a piteous sight, the wretched woman leaning on the beggar-man, and the dog leading both. They turned into a lane at hand, and went up a creaking stair to the very garret. Desmond opened the door by a secret contrivance, and Mary rushed in, and flung herself on a miserable bed on the floor.

CHAPTER IX.

MISS BLACK went direct home when she left the Temperance Hall, and was just in time to intercept the postman who was leaving her father's letters, and to see which of them was the least likely to injure him, and to retain the others until some day when he should be stronger and better able to attend to them. Several were handed to her, and she took them into the library to examine them at her leisure.

She was looking at rather a strange one as she was walking into the room, and did not observe that Mr. Harris was there before her. Having saluted her with the warm affection of a lover, they sat down side by side on a sofa, and begun the work that they now meant to carry on together—that labour by which they resolved to relieve Mr. Black of most of his cares.

They opened several letters, and one that was addressed to Miss Black herself, caused her a great deal of surprise, and her lover considerable annoyance. It was an anonymous communication. A sample of those so commonly adopted as a means in Ireland to warn and to threaten. This was a warning from "a friend" to Miss Black advising her " to have nothing to do with Harris, who was a doubly-dyed rascal."

"This is more to me than to you, darling," said the gentleman in question, "unless, indeed, you wish to act on it."

" Oh, William, as if I were not used to such things as anonymous letters, and did not know how to treat them!" So saying, she dashed the paper into the fire, and they both stood watching its consumption.

"So much for your enemies," said Miss Black, "look how they vanish, William."

But Mr. Harris did not look, his face was full of a strange confusion. He sat down deadly pale, and with a terrible air of dismay.

" You won't have me now," he said.

"Why not, dearest?" cried the frank, open-hearted girl, "What has happened? Are you ill?

I'm sure you are! Is it fear? To think that a man should mind such rubbish! See, I care nothing about it. I won't even think of it," and she danced joyously about the room.

Her gaiety was not contagious. Harris remained less relieved than he should have been by such an exhibition of her feelings, and was inexpressibly pleased when a servant came for her to go to her father.

On Miss Black's return to the library, she was somewhat disappointed to find that her lover had not been sufficiently patient to wait for her, but had taken his departure.

"That ridiculous letter put him out of temper," she thought, "I'm sorry that he thinks so little of my good sense, as to suppose that I can be affected by such things."

The rest of the letters that had arrived by the recent post, were strewn about, and the volunteer clerk gathered them up and placed them on the "to-be-answered" side of the desk, at which she took her seat. She went through them very systematically, and replied to some immediately, with an announcement of her father's sickness.

One of the letters was a large official document,

and she did not well understand its contents. It was
calling for more "returns," and it was rather
peremptory in its tenor. While she was occupied
in reading it, a gentleman was announced. The card
brought in to her was that of a well-known government inspector, and she rose to meet him as an old
friend.

Mr. Goodfish was not quite so agreeably disposed
as usual. He expressed cold regrets at her father's
state of health; and began at once to enquire for the
clerk and the books.

"The latter are here," she said, "but the clerk is
not. Papa has had young Sullivan in that position,
and you may remember that he was very well acquainted with the business of the office; but this very
morning he threw up the situation, without assigning
any cause.

"Still, there must have been some cause," remarked the inspector; "Had he and Mr. Black any
disagreement?"

"Not a word; on the contrary, my father offered
him more payment out of his own pocket, if he
would stay for a while, and at least finish those
returns that are so pressed for."

"And he would not? How very strange! One can't compel a man to remain in a place, of course, to which he is not bound by any legal tie, but it is not ordinary—very extraordinary, I should say—for a man to walk off in this way and at such a time. Can I not see your father, Miss Black?"

"Oh yes, certainly, as soon as I've prepared him for your visit. His state is very critical; the least emotion may cost him his life, so I must spare him the surprise your visit will occasion."

Miss Black left the room on her errand to her father, and Mr. Goodfish put his feet on the fender, and opening a damp edition of the *Evening Mail*, began to interest himself in the news.

After a time, he found this cease to engross him, and he began to wonder at her delay: "Making himself scarce, too, perhaps, going after his clerk; no wonder if they did fly, if all I'm instructed about them be true! I'm sure he shall have the chance from me. I don't want to hunt him down, poor old fellow! That's a clever daughter, up to anything—the old dodge, 'heart disease,' when wanted for examination—doctor's certificate—when convicted—mad to a dead certainty."

These were the thoughts that ran through the official's head, as he sat and waited for his old acquaintance. But he was not at all prepared for the sight of Mr. Black, when his daughter led him in, pale, and thin, and shaken looking, and requiring the support of even a weak girl's arm. The old style returned to the greeting that the inspector gave the heretofore respected officer. There was no feeling but pity to be evoked by the sight of such a worn, harassed man.

"You will give me time to prepare for your inspection," said the elderly gentleman, "I'm put out by illness and by the absence of my clerk. I'll do what I can to get things into order."

"Oh, of course, of course, I have no desire to be strict, but I have duties to fulfil, and masters to obey, and my acts are of necessity quite uncontrolled by my feelings. Had I not better take the books, and let my secretaries investigate their condition?"

"That is the letter of the law surely, and I will not oppose it. Whatever be the consequences of my neglect, I am willing to abide by them. I confess beforehand, that my whole office work is in disorder. It is a relief to me to resign the thing entirely.

Indeed, it is, perhaps, time that I did so formally. I feel that I no longer am able to fulfil my duties; it is but right to let some one else do them."

"Let me understand you well, Mr. Black, you resign; and I take you at your word. I meant to have suggested it. It is your best course, and will save you a world of trouble. Give me a written letter to that effect, and hand me over the documents of your department: it will be the only way to act, so as to escape all annoyance and inconvenience. I am heartily glad you are doing this on your own account, and that I have not to advise it—I am very sorry for the necessity that has arisen. It is a pity at the close of a long and honourable career—"

"What, sir, do you insinuate that I resign to avoid dismissal; and that anything is laid to my charge that I cannot face and deny?" broke in Mr. Black, rising to a new energy. "I meant no such sneaking proposal; and now I'll never flinch from my post. I'll die at it, and never leave it unless death or dishonour drive me from it. Aye! and with a name unsullied too, and a fame undefiled by any imputation of transgression against the law of honesty and faithfulness!"

The inspector was very much surprised. Miss Black was quite confounded. There was no one now so firmly self-reliant as Mr. Black, the hitherto depressed and desponding invalid.

"Oh, I'm very glad, I'm sure, that you can bear the brunt, as you say, of all that is stated against you."

"Stated against me? How? What? by whom? It is a hard thing to condemn a man, and not to let him know the crimes of which he is accused."

"Leave us, Miss Black," said the inspector, "a few words may settle the matter."

Miss Black was awed into obedience. She left the room, and she also dispatched a messenger to Mr. Harris.

The evening shadows closed into pitch dark night, and still the two men were closeted below, and still Harris responded not to her call. The intolerable suspense of a wretch awaiting a sentence of doom was hers, during the hours she sat, or rather crouched before the drawing-room fire. The servants frequently asked, "Shall dinner be served, ma'am?" and as often had an answer that it should be postponed.

There—as motionless as a statue, her eyes fixed on vacancy, her mind in a commotion as terrible as a midnight tempest on the ocean—was the girl whose heart had but a few short hours before been rejoicing so tenderly in a happy love.

It must be confessed, that it was more of her lover than of her father she was thinking. The anonymous letter returned on her senses with a very different impression *now*. " Was there anything in it ? if so, what ? " Alas, she was bewildered, she knew nothing, and could but weep, and think, and puzzle, and mourn ! It was a miserable closing to her beaming noon. But the sad interval came to an end.

The noise of the hall-door being shut after the departure of the unwelcome guest, disturbed her reverie, and she flew to find her father.

The library was locked on the inside, and she could hear him walking about the room, in terrific agitation. The moans and groans of a man in such agony of mind are not describable. Miss Black could not bear the sound of them—she rapped imperiously, and was at last admitted.

Mr. Black clasped his child in a fond embrace, and they sat down, in trouble too deep for words.

" Where is your—your husband ? " uttered the old man, in a voice broken by sobs.

His hearer did not affect to misunderstand him,

or to notice the substitution of a future for a present designation.

"Oh, William will be here presently," she said; "come and rest."

The aged parent was now her gentle child, and he suffered himself to be conducted to his couch.

All night the daughter sat by his bed, and watched his fitful slumber. His rambling sleep-speech, and his waking words, betrayed the subject on which his mind was dwelling. A considerable sum of money was unacknowledged in his books, and yet was traced to his hands by the unerring records of counter-entry that checked his receipts. The whole thing had the appearance of a deep design. A page was absent from a principal ledger, and a very important transaction book was missing altogether. These had to be found, and that immediately.

Mr. Black seemed to have no doubt but that Sullivan could instantly produce them, and his only annoyance was the bare fact of question or suspicion being for one moment attached to himself.

Early next day Sullivan was sent for, and Mr. and Miss Black were for hours in the library exploring for the missing papers, but all in vain.

Mr. Black then took a cab and went to his public

office in the town, and up to a late hour at night he did not return. Miss Black thought it likely that Sullivan, on being sent for, went there, and joined her father in the search, and so she was not uneasy at his not calling at the house.

No idea that he had never appeared at all crossed her mind, and when, at last, her father's step was heard in the hall, and she ran out to meet him, her greatest surprise was to find him unattended by the clerk, from whom both a vigil, and a kind and careful assistance in reaching home, were not uncommon marks of regard.

" Did Sullivan come home with you, papa ? "

" Did you send him for me, love ? "

" He was not here," replied Miss Black.

" Nor did I see him to-day," said her father.

" Then he has not been found by our messenger."

" He is gone out of the way purposely. Oh, the rascal ! ". cried the poor old man, " to treat me so, to whom he owed so much."

The servant who had gone for the clerk in the morning here added that she had seen old Mr. Sullivan, and that he had offered to convey the summons to his son, but that she had not actually seen the young man. The fact that the elder clerk had not himself come and explained the absence of the younger, was, · in itself, grounds for fresh suspicion. Mr. and Miss Black felt this, and both, in silence, came to the conclusion that something more base than they had yet imagined was beneath all that had, up to the present, appeared.

By this time, the old lady had begun to participate in the family distress, and the evening's post conveyed letters detailing it to the sons of the troubled household.

Harris had not called all day; and this was no small addition to the calamity.

"Oh, misery of miseries," wept Miss Black, that night on her bended knees, "must he be a traitor, too?"

The arrival of her brothers brought affairs to a climax. They soon discovered the whole matter. Sullivan had absconded, and carried off the money, together with the papers connected with the transaction in the office books. There was sufficient circumstantial evidence to prove this. No stain lay on the character of the head of the department. Still he received a great shock from the occurrence, and though he was not deposed from his place, he was obliged to retire from its active duties.

The public got a hold of the matter, with, as usual, the worst side foremost, and reports grossly disparaging to Mr. Black, were rife in the town. If he did not hear these, he calculated on them just as they arose, and their possibility annoyed him so much, that absence from home was considered the best remedy that he could take. So it was arranged that he and his wife and daughter should set out for England. Accordingly, they left for the sister isle; and a deputy entered on the duties of Mr. Black's appointment.

Meantime, Miss Black dealt with her lover more mercifully than he deserved. She wrote him a short, sharp note of separation, which though she would not rescind, nor listen to any remonstrance from him, she did not speak of his unkind conduct to any one, nor the suspicions which it awakened in her bosom. She did not know, indeed, all that rendered him unworthy of her love, but she had a sense—an instinct that he had fallen beneath her level. The expression of his countenance on reading the anonymous missive, would not leave her mind—it was a revelation to her that there was something she could not understand—a guilt somewhere that determined her not to accept his efforts at reconciliation.

Her brothers did not comprehend the case, and were repelled from interference by her independent and characteristic mode of action. They went to their homes, and the daughter, and her father and mother, left for Torquay. Thereupon, in due course of time, "the nine days' wonder" of the investigation in the office came to its natural end.

CHAPTER X

ABOUT the time that the events just described were oc-curring, in the worthy family that had been so kind to Mary Desmond, she was absent from the lace school.

There were several orders to be executed just then, for extra fine work, and among others some from our gracious Queen, who condescended that season to wear a parasol covered with Irish point.

Mary's was the hand for which the superintend-ent designed the most difficult part of the work; and, therefore, she was asked for, day after day, in the class-rooms, but in vain. Her non-appear-ance, when such a remarkable and advantageous piece of employment was going forward, was not a little surprising. Finally it had to be sent to her.

An inquiry was made as to her whereabouts, but no one could tell where she lived. Her work was brought in every morning rather mysteriously, and the orders likewise carried away in the same manner.

A little girl—a creature of about six years old, poor, and nearly naked, came each day, and gave in the "bits," and the message, and ran away before any one could question her. She had what is called by the Irish, "a stop in her talk," and it was hard to understand even the few words that she did say.

One morning she made a laborious speech, and it was translated into a wish that the superintendent should go and see Mary, at a place described in such a manner that it would be almost impossible to make it out—"down a back street into a court, and then across a crooked lane, and through an archway, and up a long alley, and then enter through a door, and go along a passage, up a short stair, and then turn to the left, and down a flight; and then finally ascend five stories, to the top of a high house, where in one of the garrets—the west one—in a corner of it, under the skylight, in the eaves, Mary would be found."

A lady of nerve and sagacity undertook the mission. She came to the indicated spot after much wandering about, and found Mary sitting up in a miserable bed, propped with straw, into a posture in which she could obtain the aid of the small amount of light

yielded by the aperture in the roof, while with her
needle and thread, she was weaving her beautiful
fancies into cotton gems, that were one day to grace
her Majesty's sunshade!

Oh, lights and shadows of human life! Oh, royal
lady on earth's highest throne! Oh, lowliest mother
on the world's face! What brought ye into contact?
Oh, women, both alike in common nature's gifts!
The lace-maker had a baby at her breast, and its
sweet face gave life, even in such misery, a zest that
none but mothers know!

It was some minutes before the visitor was able to
bear the atmosphere of the apartment; it was stifling.
Dirt and poverty make a dangerous combination.

The sight of her guest quite overcame the wretched
inmate of the room. She burst into sad, affecting
wailing, and it was long before any coherent account
could be derived from her; not until the baby's joining
in the crying, did the effort to compose its innocent
feelings restore to the mother her power of expressing herself intelligibly.

Her first distinct announcement was highly illustrative of her womanly instinct:

"This," she cried, pointing to the infant with the

pride of a matron, "is mine! But for its sweet face I would have killed myself long ago."

"You are married then, I suppose," said the lady.

"I am, ma'am," was the answer, but it was accompanied by a wild burst of grief.

"Come, this won't do, Mary. Let me relieve you, what can I do for you?"

"Let me tell you some of my story, ma'am, for God's sake! Oh, listen to me like a Christian woman, and be merciful to me, for the innocent's sake; it done nothing; let it be safe, but do as you please with me. Its father don't know that it's in the world; I never asked him for a penny piece to support it or me; I've worked, and worked, and you never missed my hand a day, and I've never missed your return. Oh, you've kept me up well with the work, and always paid me honestly, and never let me want. I thank you, God knows, from my heart; but I'm broken down, I can't keep it on: there's an impression on me that I'll soon die, and I want to make an atonement before I face my God."

Here the sobbing returned violently, and both speaker and hearer were so moved that a long pause occurred.

"Mary, air, and food, and quiet will restore you; don't despond. Go on; say what I am to do for you."

"Ma'am, if you will hand me over the bundle that is in the corner, I'll do what I can to straighten things first."

This request being complied with, when the parcel was laid on the bed, Mary looked round cautiously and begged her visitor to see if the door was well fastened, "for fear he'd come in."

"Who is *he*?" asked the lady.

"My father, the blind man, ma'am; and I can't let him know anything about this."

When the wrapping was taken off the parcel, a lot of rags tumbled about, and it was disclosed that they were only arranged in order to envelope a package. This Mary placed in the hands of the lady, and did so with an air of extreme mystery and importance.

"Don't open it, I beg, but give it into the hands of Mr. Black."

"I fear that I cannot," said the receiver of this evidently valuable parcel: "Mr. Black and his family are gone away, and may not be back for a long time; but I'll get it conveyed to them safely, don't fear.

You had better tell me what it is, and who it is from."

"Oh, that such trouble should come upon them that were so good to me, through my spite and folly! I ought to tell you, and I will, for I know you will do what is right and good by all that I've injured. Rolled up there in your hand is the book, and the papers, and the money, that Sullivan hid from his master when he was running away. He never took 'em, nor stole 'em, nor made his own of 'em ; but hid 'em, and left 'em with me to keep for three months, and this is the last day of the time ; so now my heart is light, the sin is cleared off, and we are all back in grace and peace! Oh, ma'am, the load they have been to me! my soul was kep in purgatory with 'em. But whatever other wrong I done in this world, I was faithful and honest in this ; I did not betray the trust laid on me. I was not what I ought to be to Sullivan ; but now surely my debt to him is paid. Won't it come all right now, dear madam ? he'll be clear, and I'll be clear, and it will atone for our other sins that we have been just and true in this."

Her auditor was aghast at the discoveries thrust upon her. The money and papers about which all the

trouble and search had been : the disappearance of
the clerk ;—all explained in a few words.   Then the
mixture of vice and ignorance, the confused sense of
honour, and the wonderful tenacity of purpose displayed, were additional and curious exhibitions to the
mind of a woman, who, much as she knew of the
Irish character, had yet never surmised that it was
capable of so great an amount of skilful treachery,
grafted on its kindly sympathies.

When she could comprehend all the inferences that
were to be deduced from the facts revealed, she asked :
" Where is Sullivan now ?   Is he your husband ? "

The last query was the first answered, and with a
glow of enthusiasm lighting up her features the girl
exclaimed, " Oh, no ! not he, not he, praise be to
God ! He ! Oh, dear ! he'd die before he'd lave me
to such misfortunes. No, nor he doesn't know that I
am another man's wife. I hid it to the last ; though,
dear knows, it was near costing me my life ; and,
ma'am, I stood and talked to him the morning of the
day the child was born, and he put the charge on me,
and gave me the parcel, and if I died it would have
gone with me to judgment. There it was with me
ever since I took to bed, and I in dhread and fear of

my life that the blind man or the dog would scent it
out; but God, he took care of it and of me, because
there was worth in it that no one knew of but himself."

"And have you been three months in this room?"

"Yes, ma'am, to the day, and never outside the
door, and I never will, I'm afraid, until I am carried
feet foremost; and I never seen the face of a Christian, but my father and the little girl."

"Do they live in this room?"

"Yes, ma'am; and often has to go to bed hungry
in it, when the old man is on a reel and takes all
that I can rap and run. But I must say he is not so
bad to me, for the child's sake, he don't lave me want
often."

"And you never applied to your husband?"

"No, nor never will, madam."

"Will you tell me who he is?"

"If it wor right I would:—but no, ma'am, let it
be a sacret, and things will turn out best. If I die
it will be no matter, if I live all will be found out."

"Then your husband has behaved badly to you—
forsaken you? Why, if you are a legal wife, refuse
to seek his support and protection?"

Mary's eye flashed with indignation as she answered : "Forsaken ! worse, deceived ! He says it
was no marriage to him, being a Protestant; but I don't
believe it, an' never will ; an oath is an oath, an' he
tuck an oath, an' I tuck oath, an' no religion makes
light of that ; but there's some truth in his wicked
words, and there's some wrong put upon me; but it
is not *my* doings. I was honest and fair, there was no
chating in my mind to him, whatever there was to
poor Sullivan. I wronged that creature, I did, I did,
I confess it—led him along, and all the time there
was another after me ; but I would'nt have heared to
that other, only for them that said to me, ' it would be
the best thing for me to have him, and to bring him
into the true church.' An' sure it is only what I deserve
to be trated in this way—made a fool of ! but I scorn
him and his manners. Oh, when I think of the idiot
I was to believe that the likes of him would marry me !
'Twas pride done it, ma'am ; I did not love nor like
him ; but I thought I converted him, and then he
was a ——; but I dar'nt tell you who nor what
he was—that would be more and more of the
mischief."

"I don't think so," said the lady. "Why should

you spare him? He has not spared you sorrow, and exposure, and want."

"Spare *him!* I don't spare *him.* I spare another, whose heart would be broken at his conduct."

A light flashed on the mind of the listener.

" Did you send an anonymous letter to Miss Black?"

A thick blush overspread Mary's face, and for some minutes she was unable to answer. At length she said—

"I think I know where that came from. It was not done by me. Must I let you know? Oh, you'll surely not betray it? I feel as if it was adding to my sin not to be plain with you; but I can't, indeed, I can't."

" Well, I'll guess; your father did it. You need not tell me any more. No doubt he was well paid to be silent."

" Spare *me,* now, ma'am; spare *me!*" she cried, in agitated entreaty, and she hid her face with her hands, sobbing vehemently. Her request was granted; the lady took her departure; and in many subsequent interviews, the subject was never returned to.

For some time, Mary clung to her idea that a marriage was a marriage—must be a marriage; she tried to persuade herself so, and she tried to make her friend believe that she was still under the delusion that the ceremony performed in her case was binding. There was no suggestion of anything else in all her allusions, until one eventful day, when a letter arrived from America, from Sullivan, and it threw her into an agony of remorse, shame, and regret. She handed it to her kind visitor, in a fit of violent self-reproach, and buried her face in her hands while it was being read. It was a long, loving epistle, and it told her of easy circumstances and a comfortable home awaiting her in America.

"Oh, then, 'tis he'd have taken a life before he left Ireland, if he knew how things was; but I hid them then from myself, as well as from everybody, for I would not believe it."

"But if he knew how things were *now*—would it not be the best could happen you?" ventured her friend.

"Madam," gasped she, "I am not so far gone as that. I have some spirit left! Oh, no! let me live and die in the retrate that is fit for the likes of me."

"If you mean the Magdalen, Mary, I have no objection to offer; but remember that you will have to part with your child."

"Then I'll never do it. I'll stay where I am, and work on."

"But it will kill you, Mary!"

"What matter would that be, ma'am?"

"At all events, I must take you out of this place."

"Oh, that will be the happy day, ma'am, for I'm miserable here. My wretched father don't want me, and I don't want him. There's little nature between us—drink and badness kills all good feelin's. That little stuttering girl is a child of his, that he stole away from her mother, the wicked fool of a woman that married him, and he tries to make himself a greater object by setting it by him as an orphant, to coax more charity by begging; an' sure she's got in the way of it now, and there's no cure for her."

As soon as possible, Mary was conveyed to an airy, clean lodging, and made comfortable. She slowly and gradually improved in health, but her baby fell off and died, soon after its removal into a better and purer atmosphere than that in which it was born.

Strange that it should be so, but all its prospects of thriving vanished after its mother's removal.

Mary mourned her babe, and made herself ill again with weeping over it; but never, in her softest moments, could any entreaty get her to tell the name of the man to whom she had been united by the illegal marriage, nor to discover any of the particulars either of her acquaintanceship with him, his connections, position, nor of the ceremony. These she guarded with jealous care, though frank enough in all other respects. She detailed all her other doings —the story of the picture; the abduction of the Gormans; the employment of her father as a spy; Sullivan's patriotism; the purity of their intercourse —all was simply and plainly told, and the hearer listened to her strange, romantic tale, with a sad consciousness that the wild career had had an appropriate *finale;* but delicacy forbade any allusion to the hideous fact which was the worst and most painful of all that had come to pass.

When Mary's recovery was pretty well established, she sought and found refuge in an asylum for penitent women; and before entering these walls, sanctified to self-abasement, she took an affectionate and grateful farewell of all her kind friends.

The parcel containing the money and missing documents safely reached the hands of Mr. Black, and he was so far restored to health as to be able to come to Carriginis, and hold a conversation with the preserver of them. He and his daughter had a long interview with their former *protégée*, in which she thoroughly satisfied their minds, that the affair of the picture was the root of all the mischief that occurred. The priestly annoyance was a peculiar thing, and revenged itself in a peculiar manner. She was its agent, and so was Sullivan.

An effort was made to expose this to her intelligence, but she pushed it away, though she acknowledged to have chafed and fretted under the rule, and to have rebelled against it, but she would not relinquish it, nor accept that service "whose yoke is easy, and whose burden is light."

"No, sir,—no, miss, I must go into the convent, and end my days in the holiest part of my mother church. I know that there's bad and good everywhere—in her too—among priests and nuns as well as out in the world; but that must be, and I ever and always expects it, because they are only human nature, and but men and women after all. And now that I know that, I'll be on my guard against them; never you fear, and no more plots nor plans will I work in, but labour for my own salvation, and never heed anything else."

Here we must leave Mary Desmond. She is still under the care of the nuns, and Sullivan's name is well known to the public; in fact, it has a world wide celebrity, in connection with the Federal cause in the American war.

Mr. Black is no more, and Miss Black, who is now residing in the south of England, with her widowed mother, has, we trust, in the active and useful life she is leading, ceased to mourn over her painful share in the tale we have told; or, if she still sorrow, it must be mixed with thankfulness that she has escaped a connection with one whose disgraceful participation in one of its events, still gives him an unenviable notoriety in his native town.

Appendix.

APPENDIX.

A.—Page 23.

(Extract from a Letter from Mrs. Roberts to Mrs. Meredith.)

" It will give me great pleasure to give you any information in my power respecting the crochet trade in times past; but I regret to say, it cannot at present be said to exist in these parts. I do not think, for the last eighteen months, it has averaged £2 10s. per month: whereas, in 1852, and to 1859, my payments were £100 to £300 per month. You are aware, I doubt not, the work originated here. I have the original piece, that my deeply-lamented sister-in-law, brought from a friend of hers in Dover, of course, most inferior in design, not unlike crabs and spiders in succession, attached to each other. She, at that time, had a flourishing trade among her poor neighbours in Polka knitting; but just at the moment she was suddenly taken from us, the demand for Polkas ceased: I then taught five poor women to copy the crochet spiders, and then lent them different pieces of old lace,—and of their own ingenuity they brought it to its present perfection. I distributed twenty-eight teachers of it throughout Ireland."

A likeness to the work which bore Mrs. Roberts' name is only faintly traceable in that which the districts produce that received her teachers; for each locality soon formed an independent style and retained it. Mrs. Tottenham made the best specimens of crochet that were manufactured, and her pupils rivalled the antique model laces more closely than any others.

B.—Page 26.

DISTRIBUTION OF NEEDLEWORK MANUFACTURES.

Districts.	Manufactures.	Districts.	Manufactures.
Ardee	Crochet laces	Innistioge	Pillow lace
Armagh	Point laces	Kinsale	Crochet laces
Abbeycourt	Lace-running	Kells	Point lace
Adare	Crochet laces	Kildare	Crochet laces
Anamult	Do.	Kilcullen	Do.
Blackrock	Do.	Killashea	Pillow laces
Ballingarry	Do.	Lisnakea	Do.
Blarney	Do.	Limerick	Lace-running
Bandon	Do.	New Ross	Crochet laces
Borrisleigh	Do.	Oranmore	Pillow laces
Cork	Do.	Roscrea	Crochet laces
Coachford	Do.	Strabane	Plain sewing
Carrigaline	Do.	Sommerville	Pillow laces
Clones	Do.	Tynan	Point lace
Clonmel	Do.	Thurles	Crochet laces
Coleraine	·Plain sewing	Tallow	Pillow laces
Clonakilty	Embroidery	Tullagh	Embroidery
Dublin	Do.	Youghal	Point lace
Garbally	Pillow lace		

D.—Page 78.

The Normal Lace School sent teachers to twenty localities, under the patronage, and generally at the sole expense, of indi-

viduals who became the medium of introducing the work to the
market by their own personal exertions.

Place.	Date.	Patron.	Results.
Stradbally	1852	Mrs. Sidney Crosby	failed.
Tulla	1852	Miss Dwyer	do.
Lismore	1853	P. L. Guardians	succeeded.
Doon	1854	Mrs. Atkinson	failed.
Innistioge	1847	Lady Louisa Tigh	succeeded.
Oranmore	1853	Mrs. Griffin.	do.
Newtown Forbes	1852	Mrs. Digby	failed.
Achill		Mrs. Atley	do.
Garbally	1854	Countess Clancarty	succeeded.
Ardee	1851	Mrs. Ruxton	failed.
Ballindrait	1852	Countess of Erne	do.
Farnham	1852	Lady Farnham	do.
Sommerville	1854	Sir W. Sommerville	succeeded.
Dunboy	1844	Mrs. Puxley	failed.
Headford	1852	Mrs. Hunt	do.
Kilcock	1844	Sir J. R. Euston	do.
Tremore	1852	Mrs. Aylmer	succeeded.
Lisnakea	1852	Countess of Erne	do.
Cork	1853	Countess of Bandon and others	failed.
Killashea	1853	Mrs. Hudson	succeeded.

In some cases it will be seen these efforts were successful,
and that a small amount of lace still continues to be made;
but that in others it entirely failed. Connected with this failure
there is a very remarkable fact to be noticed, and it is that
the lace did not fail to be demanded, but that it failed to be produced. The workers never were content with the remuneration
offered them, though it was generally greater than that which
the lacemakers of Buckinghamshire, and the foreign lace workers

obtained. The hands dropped off from the work, before it dropped off from them. They would not compete with the women who make the same sort of thing in other places, and gave up the attempt in disgust, while females of more plodding and industrious tempers maintain it with persevering patience.

Valencienne, Maltese, and English laces have a certain standard value in the market, and afford only poor pay to the makers of them. This has always been the case, and it is also true that they provide a sort of occupation which is very suitable and agreeable to a great many women in England, and abroad, so available and pleasant, that for many years past rather too much of those laces were being made, and since they accumulated more rapidly than they sold, they, in time, brought down their own value, and this, along with the imitations made in the loom, decreased their commercial worth some time ago. It was not knowledge of these disadvantages that operated on the minds of Irish-women in their rejection of this employment; the truth is, that the nature of the work was adverse to their dispositions. It is mechanical, and uncontrollable by fancy, and has a fixed price which cannot be unsettled by any manœuvring. There are not powers connected with it, whereby a new sudden alteration of pattern may confuse the dealer, and give the maker a temporary advantage.

" I likes the crochet best, ma'am," said a girl, " because there's hope in it. I *may* get ever so much for what I makes, if I happen to hit on a new stitch, and all the time I'm at it, I don't know but I may have a lot of money coming to me, and I'm kep in spirits like, to the last moment ; but that pillow-work—och, 'tis horrid, ma'am ! you're made sinsible from the beginning that you're only to get the trifle of a price, no more, nor no less, and no thoughts will help you, you must go on with the thing to your *ordthers*, which is what *I won't do*, until I can't help it, plase God !"

NOTE E.

There is a stitch peculiar to the Calvados women, called *Rucroe;* it is used to join together the flowers and scrolls of lace which they make on pillows, and is of the same character as crochet " barring."

www.ingramcontent.com/pod-product-compliance
Lightning Source LLC
Chambersburg PA
CBHW021526110726
47902CB00004B/768